Also

What Happens in Texas
A Heap of Texas Trouble
Christmas at Home
Holidays on the Ranch
The Honeymoon Inn
The Shop on Main Street
The Sisters Café
Secrets in the Sand
Red River Deep
Bride for a Day
A Chance Inheritance
The Wedding Gift
On the Way to Us

SISTERS IN PARADISE
Paradise for Christmas
Sisters in Paradise
Coming Home to Paradise

THE PARADISE
Meet Me in the Orchard

LUCKY COWBOYS
Lucky in Love
One Lucky Cowboy
Getting Lucky
Talk Cowboy to Me

HONKY TONK
I Love This Bar
Hell, Yeah
My Give a Damn's Busted
Honky Tonk Christmas

SPIKES & SPURS
Love Drunk Cowboy
Red's Hot Cowboy
Darn Good Cowboy Christmas
One Hot Cowboy Wedding
Mistletoe Cowboy
Just a Cowboy and His Baby
Cowboy Seeks Bride

COWBOYS & BRIDES
Billion Dollar Cowboy
The Cowboy's Christmas Baby
The Cowboy's Mail Order Bride
How to Marry a Cowboy

BURNT BOOT, TEXAS
Cowboy Boots for Christmas
The Trouble with Texas Cowboys
One Texas Cowboy Too Many
A Cowboy Christmas Miracle

Dear Readers,

Tripp and Willa Rose welcome you back to Spanish Fort and the Paradise. Of course, Aunt Bernie is up to her old matchmaking business, but since Willa Rose is on the fence about staying in the area, she definitely does not want Tripp to get tangled up with her. However, Christmas is a season of miracles, and there are some things that even Aunt Bernie can't control.

Like Willa Rose, I dearly love antiques. Be it a fancy settee or a teapot, I imagine them telling me a wonderful story about what they have seen or heard in their lifetimes. And like Tripp, I also love the smell of leather. It always reminds me of western wear stores. I love to step inside one of those places and let my imagination run wild about cowboys. I was one happy author when Tripp decided to build a leather shop in a historic old barn in Spanish Fort, and Willa Rose had plans to use the old store building for an antique shop.

Now that I've finished writing the story, I miss all the characters and the ever-growing family at the Paradise. But as the old television commercial said: WAIT…there's more! Don't go away for very long because Knox is already sitting on my shoulder and telling me his story.

    I hope you all enjoy going back to Spanish Fort, Texas, and to the Paradise as much as I did, and that after you finish the last words in this book, you are ready to read Knox's story.

Until next time,
Carolyn Brown

A Little Christmas Matchmaking

CAROLYN BROWN

sourcebooks
casablanca

Copyright © 2025 by Carolyn Brown
Cover and internal design © 2025 by Sourcebooks
Cover design by Elizabeth Turner Stokes
Cover images © K.Decor/Shutterstock, Evgeniya Litovchenko/
Shutterstock, CK Foto/Shutterstock, Wirestock

Sourcebooks and the colophon are registered trademarks of Sourcebooks.

All rights reserved. No part of this book may be reproduced in any form or by any electronic or mechanical means including information storage and retrieval systems—except in the case of brief quotations embodied in critical articles or reviews—without permission in writing from its publisher, Sourcebooks.

No part of this book may be used or reproduced in any manner for the purpose of training artificial intelligence technologies or systems.

The characters and events portrayed in this book are fictitious or are used fictitiously. Any similarity to real persons, living or dead, is purely coincidental and not intended by the author.

All brand names and product names used in this book are trademarks, registered trademarks, or trade names of their respective holders. Sourcebooks is not associated with any product or vendor in this book.

Published by Sourcebooks Casablanca, an imprint of Sourcebooks
1935 Brookdale RD, Naperville, IL 60563-2773
(630) 961-3900
sourcebooks.com

Cataloging-in-Publication Data is on file with the Library of Congress.

Printed and bound in the United States of America.
KP 10 9 8 7 6 5 4 3 2 1

*This is for my brother, Douglas Gray,
for always believing in me*

Chapter 1

"Did you do that? If you did, it's not funny." Tripp Callahan pointed to a sprig of mistletoe hanging from the porch post.

His twin brother, Knox, threw up both palms. "I did not, but I'll give you three guesses who probably did and the first two don't count."

"I only need one," Tripp grumbled, "and that's Aunt Bernie. I've managed to sidestep every attempt she's made at setting me up on blind dates. She's hung that up there to prove to me that she's not giving up."

"Aunt Bernie intends to see that you are married and settled down right here in Spanish Fort. You can run, but you cannot hide," Knox singsonged.

"Don't I know it!" Tripp reached up, pulled the mistletoe down, and dropped it on the porch. "And Brother, I'm running out of excuses about all the blind dates she tries to fix me up with. Besides, when would I have time for a wife, much less a yard full of children?"

"She wants all three of us putting down permanent roots here so the family won't be broken up," Knox said, "and she is a persistent old gal. Our seven sisters are living proof of that. She takes credit for having all of them married and settled down. Besides, the holiday season kicks off in just a few days, and a miracle could happen."

Tripp wouldn't wish anything bad on Aunt Bernie, but neither she nor those seven sisters were really his blood kin—or Knox's either, for that matter. So why did she have the right to meddle in his love life?

"I'm not going anywhere, so she can back off. She'll have to be satisfied with the fact that I can't get any more settled in Spanish Fort than owning a business. I haven't even had time to go to the barber in two months. Instead of a woman, what I really need is someone to help me in the shop so that I'm not working sixteen hours a day. Do you think Aunt Bernie can put aside her matchmaking business and work some magic in that area?"

Knox looked down at the pitiful little bunch of mistletoe lying at his feet. "Brother, you never know just how much magic that little mistletoe can work, so don't knock it until you've given it some time. Who knows? Maybe it will even find a buyer for your plane you're still holding on to in Bandera."

"I'm not sure I want to sell it. Dad and I had a lot of good conversations flying around the state in that little six-seater plane. Besides, mistletoe only works in romance, so I'm not interested." Tripp kicked the sprig off the porch. "Quit talking and get the door open. That north wind cuts right through my coat to my bones."

"What do you expect? It's Texas in the winter. One day

we're wearing coats and shivering. The next we are swimming in the Red River," Knox smarted off.

"Technically, it's fall." Once they were inside, Tripp removed his denim coat and threw it over one of the two leather recliners at either end of a long sofa. He tucked his gloves into his hip pocket and warmed his hands in front of the fireplace blaze. "It's not really winter until four days before Christmas, and Thanksgiving isn't even until next Thursday."

Knox hung his sherpa-lined leather jacket on a coatrack hook. "All work and no play has made my brother an old grouch."

"Sixteen hours a day doesn't leave much room for play. Too bad you didn't learn this trade instead of carpentry so you could help me." Tripp headed across the open-space room that included the living room, kitchen, and dining area. "I'm going to make some coffee."

"That sounds good. But Bro, every now and then you need something more than steaming black coffee to keep your blood flowing. Something like a beautiful redheaded woman to wake up to after a steaming night of good old hotter'n hell sex," Knox said.

"I haven't heard any noises coming from your place, or a red-haired woman doing the walk of shame in the morning either. I'm up before the crack of dawn, so I wouldknow," Tripp told him.

"I like tall blonds or brunettes," Knox fired back. " You're the one who has always liked the gingers who are short and sassy. Maybe I'll tell Aunt Bernie to narrow down the list she's making for you."

"Remember what Mama used to tell us about familiarity breeding contempt? The way you are talking tells me that we've been spending too much time together these past weeks," Tripp said.

Knox got two mugs from the cabinet and filled them with freshly brewed coffee. "Ain't possible. We've been together since before birth. I argue with you to keep your blood pressure up."

"Are you saying that I'm boring?"

"I'm saying that you need some spice in your life."

The doorbell rang and Knox chuckled. "That might be the mistletoe working its magic even from out in the yard. Maybe Aunt Bernie has found a blue-eyed redhead who will make you fall in love with her at first sight."

"Or maybe it's just Aunt Bernie, and she wants a place to warm up before she and that yappy little mutt of hers head back to the Paradise after Pepper's daily walk."

Parker poked his head inside. "Anyone at home?"

"Come on in," Tripp yelled. "Want a cup of coffee?"

"Can you make that two?" Parker asked as he and an elderly man came into the house.

Parker was the husband of the youngest of the seven Paradise sisters, the preacher of the only church in Spanish Fort, and damn good at building anything with wood. He barely came up to Tripp's shoulder, but he could almost outwork Knox in the carpentry business—and that was saying a lot.

"I want y'all to meet a friend of mine, Hank Thomas, from down in Poetry, Texas. Hank, this is Knox Callahan and his twin brother, Tripp. Knox is the carpenter I help out sometimes, and Tripp is the one I was telling you about who needs help in his leather store."

"Pleased to meet y'all," Hank said with a shiver and removed his cowboy hat.

Tripp took a couple of steps forward and shook hands with Hank. The guy stood eye to eye with him and had lots of salt in his dark hair and crow's-feet wrinkles around his eyes. He could be anywhere from sixty to eighty years old. He had a firm handshake, and his brown eyes seemed to have a little sadness in them.

Knox stood up and stuck out a hand. "Glad to meet you too."

"Y'all take off your coats and have a seat. Coffee is coming right up. Cream or sugar?" Tripp asked.

"Just black for me." Hank removed his coat and draped it over a recliner before he sat down.

"What brings you up this way, Mr. Thomas?" Knox asked.

"Just Hank." He chuckled and eased down on the sofa. "I was in Nocona and realized that I could drive up here and see Parker. Long story short is that I lost my wife last year on New Year's Eve and…" He paused. "My daughter, Willa Rose, says I use any excuse I can find to escape from the house. She's right most of the time. Today, I decided to drive up here to put some flowers on my grandparents' graves down in Nocona."

Tripp poured two more mugs full of coffee, carried them to the living area, and handed one each to Hank and Parker. "So, you're just stopping by then?"

Hank took a sip and smiled. "Yes, and this smells like good coffee, not that thin stuff you get in restaurants."

"Thanks for this," Parker said. "This hot mug feels good in my cold hands. I left my gloves on my desk at the church. We have talked Hank and Willa Rose into staying with me and Endora tonight and attending church with us tomorrow. But that's not why we are here. Hank is a leatherworker, and he might be interested in working for you."

Tripp almost choked on a sip of coffee. He had been advertising for help in his leather shop for more than a month, and not one person had even called. For more than a minute, he was speechless. Surely, that damn mistletoe didn't have anything to do with this.

Knox chuckled and Tripp shot a dirty look his way.

"Have you worked with leather? What have you done? Saddles, boots?" Tripp stumbled over the words.

"All of the above," Hank answered. "Plus belts, purses, custom women's jewelry, and whatever else you can think of."

Tripp intended to rush outside and bring that sprig of mistletoe in the house. He might even give it a prominent place on his nightstand, so it would be the last thing he looked at every night.

"Would you be willing to move to Spanish Fort?" Knox asked.

"Yes, I would, and the sooner the better," Hank answered.

Tripp envisioned making a special shadow box for the mistletoe and hanging it above the fireplace in his new place next door to the barn. "There is a small efficiency apartment that comes with the job. I lived in it while we were building my house. It's right through that door, so you wouldn't even have to get out in the weather to come to work."

"Even better. I won't have the space to accumulate so much stuff. I've always said that when I die, I want everything I own to fit in a shoebox. That way Willa Rose won't have to deal with so much. My wife and daughter hit every garage sale, junk store, or auction within a hundred-mile radius. Vada, that was my wife, left my poor daughter a two-story house full of stuff, mostly antiques, that she'd have to deal with some day," Hank said.

"How long were you married?" Tripp asked.

"Forty years, two days, and seven hours. I'm seventy years old, retired from truck driving, bored to tears, and needing a change."

Tripp did the math in his head. With a name like Willa Rose and a seventy-year-old father, she might be in her late thirties. Another bonus. Too old for Aunt Bernie to try to fix him up with.

"Hank's dad owned a little custom boot and saddle shop in Poetry years ago, so he grew up in the business," Parker said.

"I've been looking for something to keep me busy, and I think this place and a job—full time or even part time—would fit the bill," Hank added.

"How will your daughter feel about moving to a town this small, or even more so, how will you feel about leaving her?" Tripp asked.

"Poetry isn't any bigger than this place, and Willa Rose is a grown woman. I'll miss her something fierce, but it's up to her whether she comes with me or stays in Poetry. If you hire me, I can go to work the Monday after Thanksgiving."

"You can make a move that fast?" Knox asked.

"I can."

"You are hired," Tripp said.

"That's great." Hank grinned. "Can I see your shop? Parker has been telling me all about it."

Tripp stood up and reached for his coat. "Yes, sir. The parking lot and my front yard join up with each other, so we'll just walk over there."

A gust of bitter cold wind swept into the cabin when he opened the door and stood to the side. Knox elbowed his brother on the arm as he passed by and pointed toward the sprig of mistletoe tumbling away from the house. "Never underestimate the power of that stuff."

Tripp chased the stem down and tossed it inside the house before he closed the door. "I don't like clutter in my yard."

"Yeah, right." Knox chuckled. "You don't want to tempt the powers that be or make Aunt Bernie mad. She might fix you up with someone as sassy as Audrey."

"Who are Aunt Bernie and Audrey?" Hank asked.

"Bernie is our family's personal matchmaker," Knox

answered. "Her newest claim to fame is that she worked her magic on all seven of our sisters *and* on Brodie, our older brother, and he will be getting married in two weeks. Audrey is his fiancée. Tripp is next on her list."

"Be careful if you decide to move here, Hank," Tripp warned. "She will be trying to set you up with one of the widow women here in Spanish Fort."

"Not me," Hank declared. "I had the love of my life, and I'm not interested in a second round. And Willa Rose won't be either. She and her boyfriend of several years broke up about a year ago, and she's not over it yet. But that's her story to tell, not mine."

Fantastic news, Tripp thought and led the way across his yard and the gravel parking lot to the shop.

Why does she get two, and I can't even have one? Willa Rose thought when she looked at Endora's huge, pregnant belly.

It's not written down anywhere that life is fair, the niggling voice inside her head reminded her.

Endora's voice brought Willa Rose out of her thoughts.

"I'm supposed to be at the Paradise—that's the family home—in about half an hour to talk about the church Christmas program. I thought we might take a tour of the town before I take you to meet some of the family."

"I would love that," Willa Rose said even though she didn't want to talk about Christmas programs. Two years ago, she had helped her mother with the event at her church in Poetry. Last year her mother was bedfast and couldn't even go. The happy memory from one year did little to override the sad one.

Endora pulled on her coat, but it wouldn't zip around her middle. "Would you please drive? I'm so short that by the time I get my feet on the pedals these babies are pressed into the steering wheel."

"Be glad to, and we can take my SUV," Willa Rose answered. The next time her father wanted to take a little day or even weekend trip, he was going by himself. All Willa Rose wanted was to get back home to Poetry. This would be the first Thanksgiving without her mother, and she had a lot to do to make it exactly like their traditional big day.

Endora handed Willa Rose her coat and then opened the door. "The weatherman says we're in for a hard winter. For once, he might be right."

I don't care what kind of winter is coming around the corner. I just want to go home.

Willa Rose felt guilty about even being rude in her thinking. Endora was doing her best to be a good hostess. "If this wind is any indication of what's to come, I'd say he knows what he's talking about. Tell me more about this leather shop."

"Parker remembered Hank mentioning that he was practically raised in a leather shop when he was down in that area for a revival before I met him. He figured Hank might like to take a look at what Tripp has built. I think Parker had Sunday dinner with your folks."

That's when Mama was alive, and she really wanted me to like Parker. God! Can't you just see me as a preacher's wife?

Endora crossed the yard, used her hands to brace her stomach from the bottom, and eased into the passenger seat of the SUV. "These twins are identical like me and my sister, Luna. We already have four sets in the family, and my babies will make five."

"Four?" Willa Rose gasped.

"Yep, Mama had two sets, and then we got another one when my sister, Rae, married Gunner, and we added his girls to the family. Last Christmas we found out about Brodie and his brothers, so we inherited a fourth."

"How do you ever keep up with a family this big?" Willa Rose tried to be attentive since she had to spend the night at the parsonage and go to church the next morning—thanks to Hank, who had promised her that they would be staying in a historical hotel but didn't make reservations.

"I'm the baby of the whole bunch, so I grew up with the sisters. The brothers came later and there are only three of them. Do you have siblings?" Endora asked.

"Just one sister," Willa Rose answered.

I'd just as soon never lay eyes on Erica again.

"That is so sad. Family is everything," Endora said. "You and Hank should stay for Sunday dinner with all of us at the Paradise. I'll introduce you to the sisters and brothers that aren't at the Paradise this evening."

"So, the brothers are older than you?" Willa Rose could

hardly believe that one woman birthed ten kids and had time to write all those wonderful romance books.

Holy crap on a cracker! Didn't the famous author Mary Jane Simmons know anything about birth control?

"Tripp and Knox are about a year older than me, and Brodie is three years older," she answered. "There's Parker's truck, and the lights are on in the leather shop. I thought that we would probably find them in there."

I'll have trouble talking Daddy into leaving for sure. Why didn't Mama insist he keep Grandpa's tools so he could set up on his own, and why did there have to be a leather shop in this place?

"Three boys and seven girls. That means your mother gave birth to ten kids," Willa Rose said.

"Mama didn't birth the boys." Endora chuckled. "Last Christmas Brodie knocked on the door and said he was my adopted father's son. Daddy never even knew that Brodie's mother was pregnant or that he had a son. After Brodie was born, his mama and daddy adopted twins, Knox and Tripp. They are not identical. So, we immediately added three grown brothers to the family."

"Y'all should have one of those reality television shows."

"That's an idea," Endora said, "but we've got too much going on in the family to put up with cameras all the time."

Willa Rose parked her vehicle close to the door. "If my dad is in there, he'll have to be dragged out. The smell of leather is like catnip to him."

"Tripp has been looking for someone to help him."

Endora slung the passenger side door open. "Maybe Hank would be a good fit. He said that he would like to relocate somewhere outside of Poetry."

"No!" Willa Rose declared. "Daddy will never leave Poetry."

When we get home, I will clean out the garage and help him make his own leather shop. Poetry is as big as this place. If there's enough business here, then there should be plenty in our part of Texas.

"Let's go on inside. I'll introduce two of my new brothers to you—Knox and Tripp. You can meet the oldest one, Brodie, tomorrow either at church or at Sunday dinner."

Willa Rose dragged her heavy heart out of the vehicle and walked around to find Endora already taking steps toward the building that looked like a big barn.

"This is a leather shop?"

"Yes it is." Endora bent forward and braced herself against the wind. "Mama did a lot of research about this place when she was writing the historical books about what happened to the original ladies who lived in the Paradise. She couldn't find when it was originally built, but it's over a hundred years old. Tripp bought it and the whole community pitched in and helped him remodel it into a leather shop. Kind of fitting, isn't it?"

"It does make for an interesting place to put in a western type of shop," Willa Rose agreed.

"Let's get on inside out of the cold," Endora said as she stepped up onto the porch.

"Be careful," Willa Rose said. "You look like you could have those babies right here."

"They can't come before Thanksgiving. The middle of December is what we're shooting for. We have moved the church Christmas program up a week from the usual in hopes that these little girls won't make their appearance until after that. Our family tradition is that we all gather up at the Paradise and decorate the whole place on Friday after Turkey Day. Then the next day, Parker and I will trim our first Christmas tree together on Sunday afternoon. He has bought two of those ornaments that have 'Baby's First Christmas' on them."

*I've fallen right into the middle of that old television show—*The Waltons—*with reruns that play on television late at night.* Willa Rose bit back a groan.

"We always do our decorating on the weekend after Thanksgiving too." She tucked strands of her long, dark hair behind her ears, and came close to cussing the wind that had made a tangled mess of her hair.

Warmth and the smell of leather rushed out of the building when Endora opened the door.

"This reminds me of my grandfather's shop, only his was a tiny little building on the edge of Terrell," Willa Rose said.

Hank looked up and smiled like he used to do—before Willa Rose's mama died. He laid the strand of leather that he was busy weaving into the edge of a belt off to the side and she knew in that moment that he had already made plans to move to Spanish Fort.

No! No! No! she wanted to scream out loud.

"Hey, Willa Rose, guess what?"

I know what you are about to say from the expression on your face.

"I have just taken a job, and I'm moving to Spanish Fort. Tripp even threw in a little apartment right over there as part of the deal"—he nodded toward the right—"so I've even got a place to live. Parker says you are welcome to live in the old parsonage if you want to come with me. He showed it to me on the way here. It's about half a block from the church so you wouldn't have to drive to go to services in pretty weather."

"No, you are not, and no I am not," she declared.

Hank's expression changed to one that she remembered from childhood—the one who said, *I'm not changing my mind.*

"These guys have invited me to move in early and have Thanksgiving dinner with the family at the Paradise. So, I will be leaving Poetry on Wednesday. It's either come with me or stay at home. You can make your own choice, but I will be living in that apartment and starting work on the Monday after Thanksgiving."

"But, Daddy, that would mean we would be leaving right at the holiday season, and you know this was always Mama's favorite time of the year. I've already gotten the tree out of the garage. Let's just wait until after Christmas."

"I'm taking the job, and I'm moving," he said, leaving no room for argument. "The only question is are you moving with me or staying in Poetry?"

"We'll talk about that on the way home."

Changing your mind will be easy once we're out of this place and you get the smell of leather and saddle soap out of your nostrils.

"Where are my manners?" Endora's tone sounded bewildered.

You do not air family arguments or dirty laundry in public. Vada's voice popped into Willa Rose's head.

Endora went on, "The blond-haired brother with the ponytail is Knox, and the one over there at the table with your father is Tripp. He's the one who owns this business. Knox is a carpenter and is responsible for turning this barn into a leather shop and apartment."

Willa Rose appreciated Endora's effort to make the best of an awkward situation, but all the horses in Texas would not make her move to this part of the state.

"I'm glad to meet y'all," she said with a forced smile.

Knox was cute with that blond ponytail, but Willa Rose could tell by the twinkle in his eyes that he would be a handful. Tripp studied her like she was a bug under a microscope. He was one of those tall, dark, brooding types. Neither one appealed to her. The only thing she wanted out of either of them was never to see them again.

"Pleased to meet you," Tripp said. "Come on in and make yourself at home. Would you like something to drink? Maybe a cup of hot chocolate to take the chill off, or a soda, or a beer?"

I just want to get out of town and never look back.

"Nothing for me," she answered and whipped around when she heard her father humming quietly as he worked. That and whistling when he was busy had always comforted her, and she hadn't even realized that both had dried up the second that her mother drew her last breath.

I can't leave Poetry. I can't walk away from the house where I was born and raised, and what about all of Mama's antiques? No, that's not right. If I wanted to, I could leave my friends, my home since I was born, and the house I inherited from my grandparents. But I won't.

"You've always wanted to put in an antique store. Use everything in the house to get started," Hank said.

Endora touched her on the shoulder, and she jerked her head around.

"I didn't mean to startle you," Endora said. "That's a tough decision to be sprung on you so fast, but I just wanted to say that we don't have an antique store in this county. We have some of those places in Nocona where folks can rent a booth, but people in this part of the state have to drive a ways to get the good stuff. Knox owns the old store building. You can see it from here, and I can drive you by it on the way to the Paradise. He might rent it to you since it's sitting empty."

"No one would drive up to this place to buy antiques," Willa Rose said.

"That's probably what folks told Jake when he started a winery, or the feedback Shane got when he and Luna built the convenience and fishing store, but they are doing very well." Endora's eyes flashed aggravation more than her tone. "You might be surprised if you give it a shot."

Well, well, well! The pregnant lady wasn't all sugarplums and Christmas candy, so this isn't The Waltons *after all.*

"You won't know if you don't try," Knox agreed. "You can use the old store, free of charge, if you are really interested. It's just a big, empty building right now with a tiny bathroom in the back closet, and a little extra room off to one side. The place wouldn't pass inspection codes to turn it into a restaurant like Tertia and Noah wanted to do. I understand it was a general store back when the cattle run came through here after the Civil War and Spanish Fort was a big place. It's even got some of the original shelving around three sides, so you'd be ready to go."

"What do you say to that?" Hank asked.

She didn't care what the building was used for. She wasn't leaving Poetry, and neither was her father. "My head is spinning. Let me think about it for a couple of days."

"Fair enough," Hank said. "I'm going to stay here for a while. See you back at the parsonage."

"We need to be going anyway," Endora said. "We're going to the Paradise for an hour or two."

"Nice meeting y'all." Willa Rose remembered her manners and waved over her shoulder as she followed Endora outside.

"Are you really considering moving, or are you going to try to talk Hank out of the idea?" Endora asked as soon as they were in the car.

"Daddy is happy when he's working on leather," Willa Rose whispered. "After the past months, it's good to see him with joy in his face, but there's no way we are leaving Mama's memories. He'll come around to see that this was just another of his escape trips by the time we spend a night or two at home."

"Just how big is Poetry?" Endora asked. "If he is dead serious and you feel like you have to come with him, will the move be a culture shock?"

"Not at all. Poetry used to be a small town, but Dallas commuters have found it and it's grown a lot. I worked over at the Long Elementary School in Terrell until the pandemic hit. I lived a couple of doors down from Mama and Daddy in a small house, and I taught from home while everything was shut down. During that time, Mama got sick and needed me, so I quit my job last summer to help take care of her. But"—she flashed her best smile—"Daddy loved Mama too much to ever leave her. He still visits the cemetery every day."

"I can't imagine losing my mama," Endora said.

"I hope you don't have to experience that pain for a long time. Have you always lived here?"

"Not always. Luna and I were raised here, but we left after we graduated high school. We returned a couple of years ago," Endora told her. "Now I write children's books as well as serve as the preacher's wife in the church, and I love it. I taught school for a while, but I don't miss teaching one bit. My mama told all seven of us to do what we love. From what I heard, you love antiques."

"I do, and I loved teaching, but I've been away from it for a year and a half," Willa Rose answered. "Do you ever look back with regrets?"

"Not one time," Endora said. "Turn right at the next place. The Paradise is at the end of the lane."

"Why do you call it that?"

"That was the original name, and it's stuck for way more than a hundred years. In the beginning it was an old brothel," Endora answered.

Sweet Lord! Don't turn over in your grave, Mama.

Chapter 2

NINETY PERCENT OF THE church congregation seemed to be at the Paradise for Sunday dinner that day. Willa Rose would never be able to put all the names with the faces. She needed to figure out how to use that association game, but the sisters' names were all so unusual it was impossible. If she couldn't talk her father out of moving, then she would come to visit him regularly, which would mean socializing with the family.

"They are either kin to each other or extended family," she muttered to her reflection in the upstairs bathroom mirror. "And there's another generation coming on fast since all seven sisters have gotten married in the past couple of years, and the oldest brother, Brodie, has his wedding coming up soon. I can remember Rae and Endora because they were at the house yesterday, but that's about as far as it goes right now."

You always wanted brothers and sisters. Her mother's voice popped into her head again.

She cautiously glanced over her shoulder, fully expecting to see Vada Thomas standing behind her, but she was alone in the huge bathroom. Her mother had been there. She had heard her voice loud and clear.

Why don't you give the antique shop a try—at least for six months? That was something the two of us talked about for years, her mother asked.

"But Mama, *you* are in Poetry, not in this place," she argued. "And all my friends are there, and our church family."

I am wherever you are, my child. Distance has no bearing on anything anymore. I will always be with you right in your heart.

"Friends? Who am I kidding? I lost touch with most of them when Mama got sick," Willa Rose muttered. And the folks she had known in church her whole life would be changing soon since the preacher who had been there for more than twenty years had taken a job at a bigger church in San Antonio. A new, younger one was taking over in two weeks.

"Who are you talking to?" Rae's seven-year-old twin daughters rushed into the bathroom without knocking.

"The woman in the mirror."

"That's silly." Heather giggled.

"Don't you ever talk to yourself when you are brushing your teeth or fixing your hair?"

"Nope, I talk to Daisy them times."

"Mama sent us to find you. Dinner is almost on the table, and we're hungry, so if you are finished talking to whoever is in the mirror"—Daisy giggled—"then please go to the dining room so we can eat."

"Thank you, ladies, for looking for me."

"We ain't ladies." Daisy giggled again—or was it Heather that time? "Aunt Bernie is the queen, and we are princesses!"

The girls raced out of the bathroom and slid down the banister.

Willa Rose's mind went back to when she was a child growing up in the only two-story house in Poetry and doing the very same thing. She could hear her sister's high, squeaky voice telling on her, and their mother fussing at both of them—Erica for tattling and Willa Rose for doing something dangerous.

Her thoughts were so real that she didn't realize anyone was around until she looked down and saw Rae looking up at her from the bottom of the staircase.

"I see the girls found you. We were afraid you'd headed back south."

"Not without Daddy," Willa Rose said. "I'm sorry if I kept everyone waiting for dinner. Thanks for sending Daisy and Heather to find me. Those two are identical except for what they're wearing."

"You'll get to where you can tell them apart before long. It took me a while, but if you look closely Heather has a freckle below her left ear. Endora said that you probably aren't moving with your dad?"

"I haven't made up my mind, but probably not. *If* I do decide to make the move with him, Daddy has to promise not to sell our house for a year—just in case either of us changes our mind. *If* I come with him, maybe we can rent it to the new preacher and his family, but I haven't even discussed this idea with him yet."

"All of us in the family are hoping that Hank comes up

to this part of the state to help Tripp. He's working himself to death," Rae said.

"Every time Daddy turns around, something reminds him of Mama, and he's been trying to escape the grief that it brings. When he accepts that she is gone, he will want to go back home to Poetry where his roots are. That's just my opinion, but I know him pretty well."

"Well, if you decide to move with him, I guarantee that we'll do our best to make you feel at home."

"Thank you for that," Willa Rose said.

But I won't be coming back here ever again, and neither will Daddy after I get him fixed up with a leather shop at home.

"I understand that you only have one sister, but do you have cousins or an extended family in Poetry?" Rae asked and headed toward the way to the dining room.

"Nope," Willa Rose answered. "It's just me and Daddy."

"I can't imagine life without a big family, as you can well see by all this." Rae motioned toward the dining room where several folding tables made a U. "When we have big crowds, we often do buffet, but Mama likes to serve things up family-style on Sunday."

"But there's got to be twenty or more," Willa Rose gasped.

"You judged about right, and there would be a lot more, but Tertia and Noah have to be at their restaurant until midafternoon. If y'all could stick around for the evening service at the church, you could meet them too."

No, thank you! I'm getting hives just looking at all these people.

"We had better get on the road right after we eat, but the aroma of fresh baked bread sure smells good."

"I understand completely," Rae said. "I teach at the Prairie Valley school. A couple of times a week the cooks make bread, and the scent of it baking fills the whole building. It's a wonder any of us can even remember our names on those days."

Mary Jane, the mother of the seven sisters, tapped on a glass to get everyone's attention. "I think we are all here, so y'all claim a chair. We'd like to welcome Hank and Willa Rose to our family dinner. Soon as everyone is seated, Joe Clay will say grace."

Rae sat down in a nearby chair and patted the back of the one beside her. "You can sit by me. The twins always opt to sit on each side of Aunt Bernie." She lowered her voice. "Beware of that old gal. We all love her, but she is the self-proclaimed matchmaker of Montague County. You are a fresh face, and she would love to add a notch to her reputation by sending you down the aisle in a pretty white dress."

"Noted." Willa Rose felt Tripp Callahan's presence even before he pulled out the chair right beside her and sat down, but like she had just told Rae, she did not have time for romance. She was only twenty-eight and had plenty of years left to delve into relationships, even if the last one had left her both angry and heartbroken. Right now, she had other more important things to take care of.

Tripp recognized the sparkle in Aunt Bernie's eyes when he looked down the table and caught her staring at Willa Rose. But when she shifted her gaze to him, she frowned, narrowed her eyes, and shook her head. Could her expressions mean that she was willing to play matchmaker with Willa Rose, but not with him?

Hot dang!

The mistletoe was working. He might have the whole sprig bronzed and display it on the mantel above the fireplace.

If he misread Aunt Bernie's facial expressions, or if she was trying to use reverse psychology on him like she did with Tertia and Noah, then she could use some eye drops and wash that twinkle right out because he was way too busy for relationships—not even with the cute brunette sitting beside him. A miracle had happened when Hank had showed up in Spanish Fort, and that was enough holiday magic for him.

Willa Rose's hand brushed against his when she passed the basket of hot rolls. He argued with himself that what he felt was not a spark, but merely static electricity. Aunt Bernie must have put the romantic notion in his mind by hanging mistletoe on his porch, but even if there was a mild attraction, he would simply practice mind over matter.

I will decide who I fall in love with, he thought. *Aunt Bernie can keep her ideas to herself and stay out of my heart and life.*

Willa Rose passed the big wooden bowl of salad to him, and this time the electricity was even more pronounced than before. He glanced across the table and Aunt Bernie frowned. Could she really have powers that could let her see the sparks that he felt?

"So, you are the middle son?" Willa Rose asked. "It's hard to believe that you and Knox are twins."

"We get that all the time, but technically, I'm the youngest. Knox was born five minutes before me," he said.

"You are what?" Aunt Bernie's gravelly voice went up a notch.

Tripp had been trying to get a rise out of Bernie for months, and he had finally succeeded. "Didn't Knox ever tell y'all that he was born before me?"

"I was not!" Knox exclaimed. "According to the birth certificates, I came a few minutes after Tripp. He just doesn't want to be the middle child."

"Why?" Rae asked. "Tertia is technically the middle child among us, and she never minded."

"Yes, she did," Bo argued. "Ursula and Ophelia bossed all the rest of us around and never let us forget that they were the oldest. They told Tertia she was the middle child and closer to us sets of twins in age, so they had to help Mama raise all five of us."

Ursula held up a palm. "Hey, now, I didn't boss. I advised and guided."

Tripp jerked his head around when Willa Rose chuckled. "What's so funny?"

"You all," she answered. "We didn't have this kind of banter around the dinner table."

"Bless your heart, and I mean that in a good way," Endora said from across the table.

Tripp was glad the conversation had shifted over to something other than him and Knox. But when he glanced over at Aunt Bernie, she shook her head again.

And she doesn't even know this woman, he thought. *She could have a boyfriend in Poetry who will follow her up here. If that is so, I hope that Hank has already trained him in leather work. The way the business is going, I would hire a third hand tomorrow.*

"How long have you lived in Spanish Fort?" Willa Rose asked.

Her question stopped Tripp's woolgathering, and he turned to look at her. Dammit! Why did he have to be a sucker for brown eyes? "It will be a year at Christmas. We came here for Brodie to meet his father, Joe Clay, and wound up staying."

"Have you had a leather shop that long?"

"No," Tripp answered. "It took a while to get the old barn remodeled. I opened up for business last summer. I lived in the little apartment until Knox finished building my house. I only moved into it a few weeks ago."

"Brodie has a farm, right?" she asked. "I'm having trouble keeping y'all straight."

Tripp chuckled and nodded. "I still get confused sometimes, but I'll answer any questions you might have."

"Which one is Ursula?" Willa Rose lowered her voice. "I've read Mary Jane Simmons's books for years, and I had a fan moment yesterday when I actually met her. Endora said that Ursula writes, too, and I've already ordered one of her books, but I'd like to put a face with the name."

"The one sitting by Mary Jane is Ursula. Remy, her husband, is right beside her and holding their son, Clayton. He was a year old back in the fall. The family had a big party for him. This will be our first Thanksgiving here at the Paradise, but let me tell you, their celebrations are pretty awesome. You'll have a great time," Tripp explained between bites.

"But Daddy and I are not family, and I'll come with him to help him get moved"—she lowered her voice—"but I won't be moving away from Poetry."

"If you change your mind, watch out for Aunt Bernie."

"I've already been warned," she whispered. "Do you really think she'll try to set me up with someone? She doesn't even know me."

"That's never stopped her before," Tripp said out the side of his mouth.

Chapter 3

"I will not go!" Willa Rose declared.

She had failed to talk her father out of moving to Spanish Fort. He was already packed and ready to go, and tonight he was hosting one last Monday-night card game with his buddies—the ones that were left of them. When she left the house, they were telling Hank that retirement wasn't all it was cracked up to be and how much they wished they had an opportunity like the one that had landed in Hank's lap.

"Who am I trying to convince?" she whispered.

Dead leaves crunched under her boots on the two-block walk to the cemetery. She hunched her shoulders and sent out a puff of steam every time she exhaled. She was on a mission, and nothing would keep her from tattling to her mother. She trudged on past several tombstones marking past generations of the Thomas family.

When she reached her mother's gray granite tombstone, she sat down on the cold ground in front of it. "Mama, I don't know what to do. I don't want Daddy to be up there by himself. What if he had a heart attack? It would take at least three hours for me to get to him. But, on the other hand, I don't want to go and leave you."

A bright-red cardinal landed on a low limb of a big oak tree and began to sing. Her mama had often told her when they were visiting the cemetery that such a bird meant someone who had passed on was thinking about her. In a few minutes the bird finished singing and flew off to the north.

"I'm not going, no matter what sign you are sending me," Willa Rose said.

Her mother's last words came back to haunt her. *When I am gone, don't make a shrine to me. Move on and live your life.*

"I can do that," Willa Rose muttered, "right here in Poetry."

She closed her eyes and waited for her mother's voice to pop into her head. But nothing happened. She squeezed her eyelids even tighter. Still nothing. She heard a bird chirping and opened her eyes wide, expecting to see another cardinal, but it was a house sparrow that had lit on a nearby tombstone. Evidently, Vada Walsh Thomas was not going to give Willa Rose a bit of help.

Before they left the house on her first day of kindergarten, her mother had stooped down so she was on Willa Rose's level and told her that she was strong, she was independent, and she was not to cry when Vada left her at the school. The last thing her mother told her before she slipped into a coma was that Willa Rose was strong and independent, and she was not to cry.

"You are to relive all the good times and enjoy the memories we have made," her mama said and then she closed her eyes. Ten hours later she was gone.

"I didn't cry then, but I would now if I left. My mind is made up, and I got that from you. You never sat on a fence about anything, including how you wanted your funeral to be done."

She stood up, laid her hand on the tombstone, and walked away, but she hadn't accomplished a thing by going to visit her mama that evening. Her heart was still heavy, and there was no peace in her soul. Until she found something faintly resembling a calm spirit, she was not going back to her father's house or to her own. Not even if she froze to death sitting in the pavilion right outside the cemetery.

She shivered and pulled her stocking hat down tighter over her ears. The cold concrete seeped up through the fabric in her jeans and reminded her that this was winter, not spring. She stood up, walked across the road, and crossed several yards on the way to one of the few two-story houses in Poetry. When she opened the wrought-iron gate to her parents' property, she nodded.

"Okay, if I go with Daddy and put an antique shop in that old building..." She paused and waited, but nothing happened. "Let's try it this way. I'll go with Daddy and give it a try for a year. That will be long enough to get him settled or decide to come back home. It will also give the new preacher and his family who is interested in renting Mama's house time to build or find another place to live."

She could hear the men inside her father's house laughing and talking when she sat down on the porch swing. A whole flock of cardinals settled on the bare limbs of the mimosa tree.

"Okay, okay, I'll go with him," she huffed.

Surprisingly, calm filled her heart.

She awoke on Wednesday morning and could hardly believe that they had gotten so much accomplished in such a short time. But all Hank had to do was make one phone call and his trucker friends had rallied and moved heaven and earth to get things loaded out of Willa Rose's small two-bedroom house. Everything had been packed and Cooter, a big burly guy who still drove an eighteen-wheeler, had volunteered to drive up to Spanish Fort, unload her stuff, and then go on to Oklahoma City to pick up his next load.

"This is all happening so soon, Daddy. Are we doing the right thing?" she asked as she handed her keys off to a neighbor.

"Yes, it is coming about really soon, and yes, we are doing the right thing. I saw your mama in a dream last night for the first time since she passed. She had long dark hair again, and she looked like she did before she got sick. She gave me a kiss on the cheek and told me that she could truly rest in peace, and then she was gone. Don't you think that means she approves?"

"Probably so, but that doesn't mean I have to like leaving her like this."

Hank patted her on the back. "I know, Baby Girl, but even though it hurt, remember what she told you about not making anything into a shrine for her. She would be so proud for you to follow her dream and start up an antique shop, and honey, if we keep your mama in our hearts, she's never really gone from us."

"You are right, but it's still easier said than done," Willa Rose said with a sigh. "I'm not sure that I won't cry like a baby when I sell the first item, or that I'm going to like living in Spanish Fort."

"When someone carries out a teapot, or even a big piece of furniture, you should think about the day that you and Vada found that piece, and how much fun you had coming home and telling me all about it," Hank suggested, "and the sweet memory will help you not to be sad."

Willa Rose nodded in agreement and hoped that her father was right. "Okay, then, we're burnin' daylight. Let's get on the road to the new adventure."

"That sounded just like your mama," Hank said.

Willa Rose looped her arm in his and together they walked out of the house. "That's the best compliment I've had in weeks, so thank you."

She held back the tears until she was behind the steering wheel and bringing up the rear of the caravan. Cooter drove the eighteen-wheeler about half-full with her furniture and what she needed to live in the old parsonage. Hank's fifteen-year-old pickup truck, that was more like his friend than a vehicle, was behind the big truck, and she brought up the rear in her SUV. More of Hank's friends would arrive the day after Thanksgiving to pack up the two-story house and bring it all to the general store in Spanish Fort.

"Even though I believe every word Daddy said, I still feel like I'm abandoning you, Mama," she whispered as she left Poetry behind in her rearview mirror. "We should have thought about delaying this kind of radical move until the end of the year at the very least. This is our first holiday season without you, and it should be in *our* home, with your things all around us."

Her mother's voice did not pop into her head. But all Willa Rose had to do was glance over at the passenger's seat to know that Vada would say: "This is like ripping the Band-Aid off a cut. Do it fast and don't even stop to think. It will smart for a few seconds, but then the hurt goes away, and everything heals up."

"Buy it, and let's go," Vada often said when Willa Rose was agonizing over whether to buy an antique piece or not.

"I hear you, Mama, but I still don't like it."

For some strange reason, a vision of Aunt Bernie popped into her head. "If that old red-haired woman thinks for one minute that she is going to play matchmaker with me, she's dead wrong."

"Hey, it's time!" Knox yelled through the open door. "Mary Jane just sent a text and said the caravan has passed by the Paradise, so it should be at the old parsonage by the time we get there. Remy and Joe Clay are on the way to help unload. Parker and Endora are already there."

Tripp fastened a custom-made leather buckle to the belt he had just finished lacing and laid it to the side. "I'll grab my coat and be right with you."

"So, how does it feel to be able to close up shop in the middle of the afternoon rather than working until midnight?" Knox asked as Tripp got into the passenger seat.

"I couldn't have done it if Hank wasn't coming to work for me on Monday morning," Tripp answered. "Who would have thought that a simple visit up here to see Parker could net me an employee?"

Knox started up the engine, backed out onto the road, and headed west. "Or that Hank would have a daughter who will bring another business to Spanish Fort? The idea of putting an antique shop into the old store never entered my mind. That will help bring folks to this area, and they might even stop at Luna and Shane's convenience store for gas or to get something cold to drink."

"Or at Tertia and Noah's café for lunch, or Ophelia and Jake's to check out their wine selection," Tripp added. "Maybe someday, we'll even have a hotel here, and this place will become a tourist attraction."

"That's dreaming big, but then who would have thought we'd drive up here and find an organic farm for sale?" Knox parked behind a whole row of vehicles. "Look at that. Brodie and Audrey are here too. If we just sit here a few minutes, they'll have everything unloaded."

Tripp opened the passenger door. "Your conscience wouldn't let you do that. Mama's probably sitting on your shoulder right now fussing at you for even thinking such a thing."

"Yep, she is, and Mary Jane is on the other one," Knox admitted. "Let's get to it, and then we can help Hank get settled into the apartment."

"Aunt Bernie is coming around the end of the house," Tripp groaned. "She must have parked out back. Did I tell you that she tried to fix me up with a woman who bought a belt for her father's birthday? And that if I read her right last Sunday, she doesn't want me to like Willa Rose?"

"That woman scares me," Knox said with a mock shiver.

"I thought nothing in this world could terrify you except snakes."

"I've added redheaded women to the list. If you haven't noticed what color Aunt Bernie's hair is, then open your eyes," Knox whispered.

"I knew that you were afraid of snakes, but redheaded women?" Knox asked.

"They terrify me," Knox admitted. "You can bet the farm that they've got secret powers. Believe me, if a gorgeous redhead shows up in Spanish Fort, I will move out to the Panhandle."

"And I'll be right behind you," Tripp said.

"Well, Brother, now that you have hired some help and can't use the excuse that you have to work sixteen hours a day, what are you going to say when she tries again?" Knox asked.

"I'll figure out something," Tripp answered.

"You better have an answer ready. Remember how many times she sent poor old Brodie on blind dates. He was about to run out of excuses by the time he and Audrey finally admitted that they had feelings for each other."

Tripp stopped in his tracks and cocked his head to one side. "Yep, and then Aunt Bernie took the credit when Brodie and Audrey got together last summer. You could help me out and ask her to set you up on a blind date. Who knows? From that twinkle in her eyes when she stared at Willa Rose, she might have you in mind, not me."

"Oh, no!" Knox shook his head. "Not even for a million bucks. When she finally gets you married off, I'm going to find a fake girlfriend. Maybe one who lives in Oklahoma or out in West Texas. Every now and then, I'll go visit some of my old friends down around Austin or Dallas and tell her that I'm going to see the love of my life. That should move her on to greener pastures."

"I swear she has magical powers. She will see right through a lie," Tripp warned him. "You and Brodie have both always liked brunettes. And Willa Rose is easy on the eyes, so what's the issue if Aunt Bernie tries to fix you up with her?"

"No sparks. No vibes. Not even a hint of electricity between us, so my answer is simply not interested," Knox said.

Tripp thought of the chemistry he had felt at the Sunday dinner table. "You've never seen a pretty brunette who you wouldn't at least flirt with a little bit. What's the problem?"

"Why should I waste time and money on dates with a woman who won't stay in Spanish Fort? I'll wait until the next gorgeous brunette comes along. I'm thinking of that song from a few years ago about turnip greens."

"So, you're going to sit out by the road, sell produce and hope a pretty lady comes along and asks for directions?" Tripp asked.

"It worked in Billy Currington's song, so who says it won't work for me?" Knox countered.

"I'll believe you when you start planting a garden," Tripp said with a rare smile.

Chapter 4

THE SUN HAD DROPPED behind the trees out in the backyard that evening when Willa Rose finally eased down on the sofa in her new house. Endora had brought over cookies and brownies. Audrey had put milk and lunch meat in the fridge and a loaf of bread and bag of chips on the cabinet. With all the help from the Paradise family, everything was unpacked except for the boxes marked PERSONAL in her bedroom. Even the bed was made and ready for her to crawl into later that evening.

"I've never known support like this. Not even my church family would have chipped in and gotten so much done in such a short time," she murmured.

A hard rap on the door brought her to her feet with a groan.

"Daddy, you don't have to knock," she scolded when she opened the door.

"That knock was done with the toe of my boot. I needed you to open the door so I could carry supper in." He glanced down at the box in his hands. "Tertia sent a lasagna, a loaf of fresh bread, and a pecan pie over so we wouldn't have to cook tonight. Tripp is bringing the rest of it in for us.

I thought we could share it for supper. I'm starving, and I imagine you are too. I invited Tripp and Bernie to join us for supper. She brought me the food, so it only seemed right to ask her. She's parking her truck out front, and Tripp is carrying in the rest of the food." He set the box on the kitchen table and looked around. "This is amazing. Who would have thought we'd have such a welcome? You'll have to come see my little apartment. It's just perfect."

Tripp opened the back door of his truck, picked up the second box, and turned to find Aunt Bernie right behind him.

"We need to talk before we go in there." Her tone reminded him of the days when she was so against Brodie and Audrey's relationship—something between scolding and downright anger.

"What's going on?" Tripp asked, suddenly feeling a little of Knox's fear of redheaded women—no matter what age they were.

"Willa Rose is not for you, and this is not reverse psychology. I'm as serious as a judge having a heart attack. That woman is only going to be here until summer. I can see it in her eyes, and she might even convince Hank to go back to that Poetry town with her. Neither you nor Knox are to flirt with her," she warned.

"Why?" Tripp asked.

"Because I swear to God on Parker's Bible that I refuse to

see you marry someone and leave these parts. It would break Mary Jane and Joe Clay's hearts. I will give up my front seat in heaven for a back seat on a hot barbed-wire fence in hell before I allow such a thing." She shook her finger at him. "We will go in here and eat with these folks, and we will be sociable. I want Hank to stay, but there will be no flirting."

"Yes, ma'am, and thank you," Tripp said. "I have too much on my plate right now to even think about a relationship."

"Now that you have some help in the store and we've got that settled, it won't hurt for you to get your toes in the dating pool. You've been here almost a year and haven't been out nearly enough. So you are out of practice, but I've got several women who would be perfect for you—maybe not marriage material, but some that would do for a fun date or two."

"But not until after the holidays. Even with Hank's help, I'm too busy and, for that matter, too tired to date," he said.

"We'll see about that." She knocked on the door.

Tripp didn't know if he'd been saved or condemned. One thing for sure, Bernie would still be trying to match folks together when she got to heaven, so if anyone in the whole county even thought that death could help them escape, they had better back up and think again.

"Meals on Wheels has arrived," he said when Hank opened the door and motioned them inside.

"Looks more like Meals in Box to me." Hank chuckled.

"Come on into the kitchen," Willa Rose called out. "I've just finished setting the table. Does everyone want sweet tea?"

"Yes," Hank and Bernie said at the same time.

"Same here," Tripp answered.

Most women, including his mother, would have been totally flustered at having people show up the first night in their new place, but Willa Rose appeared to be calm and collected. Bernie could be wrong about her not staying in Spanish Fort, and if she did, maybe the old gal would turn her attention to plying her matchmaking skills on Willa Rose instead of focusing on him.

Dinner conversation had never been Tripp's strong suit, but then most of the time he had lots of people around him. Or at the very least, Knox and Brodie were close by to take up the slack. He was a fish out of water with only four people around the table that evening. Thank goodness Bernie was there to ask questions, even if she did shoot more than one dose of evil eye across the table when no one was looking. Tripp tuned out the small talk for a while, but when Bernie kicked him under the table, he gathered in his wandering thoughts and listened.

"Was your wife from Poetry?" she asked Hank.

"No," he said with a chuckle. "She was a waitress at my favorite café near Chaparral, New Mexico, just north of El Paso. She had a cute little brunette-haired daughter, Erica, who was about five years old. Vada wasn't one bit interested in leaving that area, so it took me a year to convince her to marry me and move to Poetry."

"Did she like it there?" Bernie asked.

"Oh, yeah. She fell in love with the town and the people right fast. What about you, Bernie? Have you always lived here?"

"I grew up around these parts, left right after high school, and just moved back a couple of years ago," she answered. "So, tell me more about yourself, Willa Rose. I understand that you were a schoolteacher."

"That's right, but I quit my job a year and a half ago. Mama needed full-time care." From the set of her mouth and the quick eye roll, it was evident that she didn't want to talk about herself.

"It was an adjustment for me to leave my job and move to these parts," Tripp said, hoping to come to Willa Rose's rescue. "I worked in my dad's oil business, wore suits and ties, and pored over accounting books most days."

"I figured you had worked in leather your whole life," Hank said.

"I tinkered with it and wanted to put in my own shop in Dallas, but…" He shrugged. "My mother had other ideas for me, and I didn't want to disappoint her. Then she and my father both passed away, and we three brothers sold the business. Brodie wanted to make a trip up here to see his biological father, Joe Clay, and we found the organic farm. That was his dream. Mine was a leather shop, and Knox has been a carpenter for years."

He stopped and waited in awkward silence for another question and hoped it wouldn't be something he had to answer. He had just said more words than he usually did in a week—unless it was about his leather work. He could talk about that subject about for hours.

"I'm glad you wound up here," Hank said with a smile.

"If you hadn't, then I wouldn't have a job. Now, changing the subject. We saw a carnival in Nocona when we drove through it. Isn't it late in the year for that?"

"The town sponsors a big parade on the Saturday before Thanksgiving to usher in the holidays. At the end of the whole thing, Santa comes in on a fire engine and there's the whole picture taking with the kids and handing out sacks of fruit and candy. And there's a carnival. It will stay until the day after Thanksgiving. Then it will break down and travel to Oklahoma where it stays until spring," Bernie explained.

"Remember how much you loved carnivals when you were a little girl, Willa Rose?" Hank asked. "I don't know which you liked best: the cotton candy or the Ferris wheel."

When Willa Rose smiled, her eyes lit up. "I loved both, but I was a little brat. Erica hated heights and she didn't like to get her fingers sticky. So, I would eat cotton candy while I rode just to torment her. Mama would tell her how brave I was, and how she needed to face her fears. When we got back home, she would get her revenge in all kinds of ways."

"I never knew that," Hank said.

Willa Rose reached over and patted him on the cheek. "Erica got the blame for a lot of things because she did them right out in the open or else I tattled, but I instigated some of them behind everyone's backs. We were normal sisters."

Tripp chuckled. "I got to admit to the same thing with Brodie and Knox. They were always so fearless that I was jealous of them. I caused some fights in my youth too. I bet if you asked any of the sisters, they would tell you the same story."

"I can certainly relate," Bernie said with a nod. "My twin sister and I never really got along, although we mended fences before she died." She pushed back her chair and stood up. "It's getting late, and my dog Pepper is probably whining to get outside, so let's get these dishes done."

"No way," Hank said with a firm shake of his head. "You brought supper, so it's only right that Willa Rose and I take care of cleanup."

Tripp was of two minds about the evening. One side was glad that it was over. The other could have stuck around, although he wasn't sure why he felt that way. "Thank you for inviting me. We'll see you tomorrow at noon for Thanksgiving dinner, right?"

"Wouldn't miss it." Hank walked them to the door. "That Sunday dinner was awesome, and I don't just mean the food."

"They tell me that tomorrow is even better," Tripp said.

The moment he and Bernie were off the porch, she huffed. "I was hoping to get Willa Rose to talk more about herself so I can fix her up and get her out of here. She's bad news, Tripp."

"Bad, good, or in between, you don't have a thing to worry about," Tripp assured her.

Chapter 5

Tripp's last Thanksgiving dinner had been a takeout family meal from a local restaurant. Brodie had set it all up on a table beside his mother's hospital bed, but not even the hospice nurse could talk her into taking a few bites. When he looked around at the table at the whole Paradise family, including Aunt Bernie, and now Hank and Willa Rose, he wished that his mother was there to share in the whole noisy day.

After the meal, when everyone who loved football retired to the living room, he quietly snuck out to the porch swing in the enclosed back sunroom. The hum of conversations and the giggles from Rae's daughters followed him, but at least he could hear himself think.

He set the swing in motion with the heel of his boot and was trying to sort out all the feelings he had when Willa Rose was around.

Speak of the devil, and he will appear, he thought when Willa Rose sat down on the other end of the swing.

"Hey, what are you hiding from?" she asked.

"Everything? How about you?"

"The same," she answered.

"Well, hello!" Bernie said with a beer in her hand as she and Pepper came through the door and she sat down between them. "If I'd known you were out here, I would have brought y'all a beer. Person needs something to settle their stomach after a big dinner like that."

"Thank you, but I'm not a beer drinker," Willa Rose said.

"Vodka then?" Bernie asked.

"Whiskey. Preferably Jameson, but I like Jim Beam too," she answered.

Tripp could almost hear the wheels in Bernie's head humming faster than the noise from in the house as she filed away mental notes. The virtual profile Bernie would work up would say that Willa Rose would like to leave Spanish Fort and that she preferred whiskey over beer.

"I do like a little nip of Jameson in my morning coffee," Bernie said as she undid the clasp on Pepper's leash and poured the last of her beer into a small bowl at the end of the swing. "He gets downright cranky if…" She stopped talking and pointed. "That damn pig of Brodie's has rooted under the fence again. She comes to visit Pepper every chance she gets. Now I'll have to take her outside and put both her and Pepper in the barn until Brodie or Audrey can take her back home. Y'all might as well come on with me. I might need some help corralling the thing. For a short-legged, potbellied pig, she can outrun a lightning streak."

"Why do you put them in the barn?" Willa Rose asked.

"Because once Pepper sees Pansy, he howls if he can't be with her, and Pansy squeals like someone is chasing her with a butcher knife," Bernie answered. "So, when Pansy runs away and shows up here, they have a playdate in the barn."

She snapped the leash back onto the Chihuahua, started outside, and turned back with a frown. "Well, come on. I told you that I might need help."

Tripp and Willa Rose stood up at the same time and followed her outside. Pepper and Pansy bumped noses and then the little round critter fell in behind Pepper like they were playing follow-the-leader. Tripp didn't think Bernie would need help with anything, but when they reached the barn door, she motioned with a flick of her wrist.

"You can open it for me, Tripp," she said.

What have you got up your sleeve or, worse yet, hiding under that red hair, besides a set of horns? Tripp wondered, but he threw the door open and gasped right along with Willa Rose.

"What is all this?" he asked.

"Most of it is Christmas decorations. Pansy and Pepper love playing chase in and around everything," Bernie explained and released Pepper.

"Is it for the whole town or something?" Willa Rose asked.

"Nope, just for the Paradise, and we'll all be on hand first thing tomorrow morning to help haul it out of here and situate it all around the Paradise," Bernie answered. "That includes you, Tripp, and Hank. Since you have help now, you can spare a day."

"What about Willa Rose?" Tripp asked.

"Her antiques are arriving tomorrow," Bernie reminded him. "But when she gets finished, we would appreciate the help. Sometimes I think Mary Jane wanted all those sons-in-law so they could help with the decorating."

"Now she's getting Audrey for her first daughter-in-law, right?" Willa Rose asked.

"Yep," Bernie answered. "There they go! I hear Pansy squealing over there"—she pointed to her right—"about where the sleigh is."

The yippy little bark off to the left told Tripp that Pepper had heard her and was on the hunt. Tripp hopped up on the sleigh's buckboard, and Bernie wasted no time in sliding in beside him. She patted the area right beside her and motioned for Willa Rose to join them.

"Might as well get on up here where we might catch a glimpse of them once in a while," Bernie said. "They'll get tired pretty soon, and Pansy will flop down on that fat little belly of hers. That's when Tripp will catch her and take her back to Brodie and Audrey's farm."

"Why me?" Tripp understood now what helping Bernie entailed.

"Because Audrey and Brodie have a bet going about who will win the football game. Ain't no way I'm draggin' either of them away from the television on a day like this. I want to see all the hoopla when Brodie's team wins. It should be quite the show."

"What makes you think Brodie's team will win?" Willa Rose asked.

"I was a bartender for more than fifty years, and believe me, I've heard or watched enough football to know which team will win." Bernie laughed.

"When Pansy gets tired, y'all could go with me out to the farm," Tripp suggested. "Willa Rose hasn't been out there yet, and maybe Pansy will handle easier if Pepper rides along with us."

"Oh, no!" Bernie protested. "Willa Rose and I are headed back into the house. Endora and Rae found out through Hank that she helped with both the school and the church Christmas programs down in Poetry. They both want to talk to her about lending a hand for Christmas programs at the Prairie Valley school and the church. I wouldn't be surprised if Rae doesn't try to convince her to join her in teaching the little kids' Sunday school class too."

When the virtual light bulb went off, Tripp had to fight the urge to slap his forehead. Bernie had fussed and worked what she called reverse psychology in the past, but mostly she just griped and cussed about one of the sisters *not* dating some guy. This time, though, she meant business in a very serious way. She was not taking any chances on Willa Rose and Tripp even riding out to the farm together.

"Looks like the playdate is over," Tripp said and pointed to a clear area where Pansy had flopped down on her stomach.

"Does Brodie raise potbellied pigs?" Willa Rose asked.

"Nope," Tripp answered. "He didn't even want this one, but a tornado back in the spring must have dropped her close to the farm, and we wound up with her. She's just a pet and a huge nuisance. Always digging out from under her pen no matter how secure we think it is."

"And when she does, she heads for the Paradise." Bernie chuckled. "I think she gets lonely for company. You go grab her, Tripp, and I'll take care of Pepper. When you get done at the farm, come on back for a leftover supper."

"Yes, ma'am," Tripp said with a nod.

Bernie whistled loudly and Pepper ran out from behind a cutout of a snowman. He panted as if he'd just finished a marathon in the Sahara Desert. Bernie scooped him up in her arms and motioned for Willa Rose to follow her. Tripp eased one hand under Pansy, and the other one over her, but before he could get a grip, she slipped out of his arms and ran across the barn and hid behind the sleigh's runner.

"You can catch her," Bernie yelled. "I've got faith in you, and you should tell them to do a better job of shoring up that pen this time."

Tripp dropped down on all fours and was reaching under the sleigh when the barn door slammed shut, and Pansy took off again. Instead of chasing her, he crawled back up on the sleigh and waited for her to run all her energy out and flop down to rest again. He wouldn't be surprised if Bernie hadn't slipped away before dinner and turned Pansy loose just to have an excuse to send him away for a while that afternoon.

"Nope, can't be," he muttered. "She couldn't have known that Willa Rose and I would both want to get away from all the noise at the same time."

That there were so many decorations in the barn had

surprised him, even though he and his brothers had arrived during the holidays the year before. He had forgotten about the Paradise being decorated more than any Dallas mansion he had ever seen. Or that after New Year's Day he and his two brothers had helped the family put away all the cutouts, the sled, and boxes and boxes of other things. Now, starting tomorrow, it all would come right back out of the big barn again.

Pansy finally got tired of chasing under and around everything looking for Pepper and dropped down on her belly one more time. Tripp eased off the seat and this time he got a firm hold on the critter. He carried her out to his truck and didn't let her go until he was behind the wheel. He closed the door and shoved her over the console onto the passenger seat.

"I should tie a rope around your fat little belly and make you run behind the truck all the way back to the farm," he grumbled. "If I had to tell something I was thankful for again today, you would be at the bottom of my list."

The skies had begun to turn gray when he parked in front of the place where Brodie's house used to be before the tornado blew it away. He reached over and got a firm grip on Pansy before he even opened the door. He carried her out to her pen, and sure enough, there was a big hole under the fencing where she had rooted out.

He set her down and she ran into her igloo. He found a couple of chunks of concrete leftover from when they cleaned up the tornados mess and shoved them into the holes. "That should hold until Brodie can figure out something else. After the holidays, I'm going to suggest we dig an eighteen-inch trench all the way round this pen and fill it with concrete. That might slow you down."

Pansy answered with a squeal but didn't come out of her safe house.

"Don't you sass me. I heard the carnival in town had a petting zoo with goats, sheep, and even a potbellied pig. If you dig out again, I will make sure that you leave with them," he threatened.

Willa Rose snuck away to the sunporch again that afternoon. She pulled a fluffy throw up to her neck and looked out over the land at the bare trees and cattle on the ranch next door. She had no intention of staying in this part of Texas, no matter how beautiful and quiet the scene before her. One year from now, hopefully before that, she and her father would be back in Poetry where they belonged. This was like a little extended vacation. If her store did well, she might consider turning the big two-story house where she grew up into an antique store.

"Aunt Bernie said she saw you come out here," Rae said as she came through the door with Endora right behind her.

"We've both been trying to corner you all day to talk to you," Endora said.

Willa Rose pushed the throw away from her neck but left it lying on her lap. "Bernie said that you want me to help you with the young kids' Sunday school class. And Endora, you want me to be kind of your understudy with the church Christmas program?"

"That's right," Endora answered. "These babies might not wait until the middle of December, and I need a backup."

"Why not one of your sisters?" Willa Rose asked.

"They will be helping, but I need a planner—kind of like a wedding planner, only you won't be rushing around for a wedding. Your job will be to get the kids or the old people waiting backstage to go on at the right time," Endora answered. "I have a notebook from last year, so it shouldn't be a problem, and I hear you are really good at organizing."

"Hank says you taught second grade and helped your mother with a Sunday school class, so please," Rae begged. "I'm all out of ideas to keep them occupied when they aren't onstage for their part of the program. If you weren't putting in an antique shop, I would try to recruit you to either substitute teach or else put in your application for the fourth-grade position that's coming open at my school."

It will just be a one-time deal for the program and a few weeks of helping Rae in the classroom and some Sundays at church. It will give me something to do other than sort through antiques and get the store ready for the grand opening in February.

"Okay, I'll be glad to step in and help y'all," she answered.

"Thank you! Thank you!" Rae said.

"Yes, thank you so much," Endora added. "We'll be helping get the Paradise all decorated for the holidays, but early next week, we'll sit down with my notebook and go over it."

Before anyone could say another word, Heather and Daisy rushed out of the kitchen into the sunroom. "Mama, I need to show Willa Rose—I just love that name—the pictures of us at the carnival."

"I'm going to have all baby girls, and I'm going to name the first one Willa Rose," Daisy declared. "Heather can have all baby boys."

"Hey, I want some girls, too," Heather pouted.

"Let's hope neither of you have to worry about baby names for a long time," Rae said.

"And that you change your mind a dozen times before you have a child," Willa Rose said. "I always wished I had a more modern name like my sister, Erica, did."

Both girls seemed to ignore her advice, and Heather laid a book in Willa Rose's lap. "Aunt Bo had this book made for us in Nocona. The carnival people had a pig like Pansy, a bunch of goats, and sheep. And we've got all the pictures that were taken that day."

"We thought they would have pony rides, but they didn't," Heather said, "but they've got a camel, and we got to ride him. Daisy was scared, so we rode him together. Look at this picture. His name is Clyde."

Endora giggled. "I wonder if they named him after that old song by Ray Stevens about Clyde the camel?"

Daisy turned the page. "And here's one of us with the pig like Pansy. His name is Porky."

"I wish we had a camel and a pig," Heather sighed.

"Oh, no!" Rae put an end to that idea. "You'd want to

bring them into the house on cold nights, and that is not happening."

"We could build a barn and have stalls for the animals and have all kinds of critters," Daisy said. "If Daddy says yes, then I want a camel of my very own for Christmas."

"Santa doesn't have room on his sleigh for a real camel, but I bet you might find a stuffed one under the tree," Rae said.

I want a set of hyperactive twins for Christmas, Willa Rose thought. *They wouldn't take up nearly as much room in Santa's sleigh as a camel.*

"Look!" Heather pointed out the window. "Uncle Tripp is back. Come on, Daisy, we got to go show him our new book. I bet Uncle Brodie will let us keep a camel on his farm if Daddy says no."

They rushed out just as quickly as they had appeared and left the door open. Rae closed it, sat back down, and nodded at Endora. "You've got that to look forward to, little sister. I have a whole new appreciation for Mama these days. She raised two sets born so close together that we might as well have been quadruplets."

"I can't wait," Endora replied. "But right now, I'm going back inside. Parker and I are leaving as soon as I help Mama put out the leftovers for supper. The weatherman says the temperature is going to drop even more and we might even get some early snow or ice."

"What about all the decorating Bernie told me about?" Willa Rose asked.

"Honey, we're like the mailman. We deliver in rain, snow, or sleet," Rae told her. "The Paradise has a reputation for getting decorated no matter what the weather is and having our annual Christmas open-house party as well. By Sunday this place will look better than the North Pole. We're glad you are here to celebrate with us. But a little word of warning: Aunt Bernie does not want you and Tripp to get together."

"Or you and Knox," Endora added.

Willa Rose frowned. "No worries there, but why?"

"She swears that you won't like Spanish Fort and will move either back to Poetry or to another place before you even have a grand opening for your store. She's even playing bookie with bets from some of the folks in town as to when you'll leave," Endora said.

"Oh, really, think one of y'all could place a bet for me?" Willa Rose chuckled.

Chapter 6

"What are you doing in here?" Knox asked Tripp.

"Having breakfast?" Tripp answered and slid into the booth across from him at the local café. "With another half day anyway of decorating at the Paradise, I figured I'd better have a good, hot breakfast."

"Me too, and biscuits and gravy sounded good."

"Mornin', Brothers," Tertia greeted them as she came up to their table. "What brings y'all out this early?"

"Good mornin' to you," Knox said. "We need hot food to get us through the final Paradise decorations."

"Startin' with coffee?" Tertia asked.

"Yep, and I may quit the construction business and put in a café," Knox answered.

Tertia slipped her order pad out of her apron pocket. "Why's that?"

"You and Nash are inside out of the snow."

She patted him on the shoulder and grinned. "You are beginning to understand. What else can I get you this morning?"

"I'll take the special on the blackboard," Tripp said.

"Me too, but add an extra biscuit and gravy," Knox told her.

"Will do," Tertia said with a nod. "I didn't get to spend a lot of time with Willa Rose and Hank yesterday, but they seem like good people."

Tertia was the third of the seven sisters, and she owned the café with her husband, Noah. From what Tripp had been told, they had been one of Bernie's reverse-psychology couples.

"Yep, they do," Tripp said.

"Well, I'm off to wait on those ladies." Tertia nodded toward three older ladies brushing snow off their shoulders as they entered the café. "But I'll get that coffee and your breakfast out soon."

The women removed their coats, hung them on the hooks at the end of the booth, and sat down at a table close to Tripp and Bernie.

"Good mornin', Tertia," one of them said.

"A snowy mornin' to y'all," Tertia said. "What can I get you ladies this morning? I'm surprised to see y'all out in this weather."

"We don't miss our Saturday morning unless the roads are closed, and even then we all live close enough to the café that if we get stuck, someone will come along and drag our vehicles back home," Gloria said.

"We'll just have coffee," Millie answered. "Bring cream and sugar. Gloria and Ellie are pansies and can't drink it without putting a bunch of crap in it."

"Oh, hush," Ellie answered. "Neither of you can hold

your whiskey worth a damn, so if I need to doctor up my coffee, then I'll do it."

"First order of gossip," Gloria said when Tertia had walked away. "I hear that Bernie is trying to get the woman who is putting an antique shop here in town matched up with someone who will get her out of town."

"I've got five dollars in the pot. I figure she'll be gone by Valentine's Day," the one with stovepipe-black hair said. "And Gloria, darlin', I see silver roots. You need to get to the beauty shop soon."

"Got an appointment on Tuesday," Gloria said. "I've got a twenty on her being gone by Easter. If I win the pot, I'm going to spend a weekend at the spa in Wichita Falls. How about you, Millie? What are you going to do with the money if you win?"

"I've got my eye on an opal necklace," she answered. "My date on the calendar is April Fool's Day. And I'm betting double because I bet that her daddy will leave with her on that day."

"Holy hell!" Tripp whispered. "Are they talking about Willa Rose and Hank?"

"Yep, and evidently Bernie is the bookie," Knox replied out the side of his mouth. "Do you remember even seeing those three at church?"

Tripp shook his head. "Now I really understand that Bernie is serious about me not dating Willa Rose."

"Looks like it," Knox answered. "I wonder why?"

"She told me that Willa Rose would never stay here,

that her roots were in Poetry, and she refuses to let me leave with her," Tripp answered. "But from what those women are saying, she doesn't care where Willa Rose goes, as long as she leaves this area."

"Would you go with a woman if you loved her?" Knox asked.

"Nope, I've got what I want, and I'm happy."

Knox frowned. "All's fair in love and war, or so they say."

"Brodie did the war thing with Audrey. I'm not sure I'm up for all that scrappin' and fightin' just to get to a happy-ever-after," Tripp said.

Knox laughed out loud. "But just think of the wild makeup sex after the arguing."

Tertia returned with their coffee. "What's so funny?"

"We were just talking about"—Knox lowered his voice to a whisper—"how Brodie and Audrey went through the fightin' business to get to happiness."

"Want to make a side bet?" Tertia whispered. "I have ten dollars that says Tripp can convince her to stay."

"I'll take that ten," Knox said. "I don't think Jesus could convince her to stay here. She's only putting in a store to appease Hank."

"Tripp, you can be our bookie," she said and then delivered the ladies' coffee to them.

"I thought she was a matchmaker. Lord knows, she's always bragging about how that she fixed up all seven of the Paradise sisters," Ellie said the minute that Tertia was out of hearing distance.

"She don't want her around the two remaining Callahan men. Have y'all met either of them yet?" Gloria whispered.

"No, but I hear they're both pretty sexy." Gloria giggled. "We really should attend church here in town or go into the leather shop to see for ourselves."

"I heard that Bernie's having a devil of a time keeping them apart, and that Willa Rose has a terrible reputation wherever she comes from," Ellie said, "and that she's out to land a rich husband. We all know that all those boys are rich."

"I hadn't heard that," Gloria said, "but they must have money to be able to come into town and buy a farm and the old barn."

"And the youngest one bought the old store," Millie added.

"But Bernie says the Callahan brothers are good people, and she doesn't want them to get involved with anyone who will leave Spanish Fort."

Tripp frowned and took a sip of his coffee. "Is that fire engines that I hear?"

"Either that or an ambulance," Knox answered.

"Oh, sweet Lord!" Millie gasped. "I just got a text from my daughter who lives in Nocona. She said that the church here in town is on fire. We really should have gone at least one Sunday so we could get a look at those Callahan men."

"Well, I'm glad that we have always gone to one in Nocona. I hope all these people don't transfer their membership down there," Gloria said. "Right here at Christmas we don't need them butting in on our plans."

Tripp and Knox both were on their feet in seconds and headed out the door.

"I just got a call from Mama," Tertia yelled as they left the café. "Keep us posted. We'll shut down this place if you need us."

"Will do," Knox shouted over his shoulder.

"This goes to prove that we need a volunteer fire department in Spanish Fort," Knox said as he got into his vehicle.

"Brodie was in that business, but I bet there would be plenty of guys..." Tripp didn't even finish the sentence, but climbed in behind the wheel of his truck and followed Knox out of the parking lot. Neither of them slowed down for the ninety-degree turn to the left but slid around it with the expertise of a NASCAR driver.

Tripp's heart was beating so hard that he couldn't breathe when he saw the Nocona firemen already on the scene and a blaze shooting out of the church's double front doors. He braked so hard that pieces of the gravel parking lot flew every which way. He hurried over to stand beside Parker, Endora, and a big, burly man stretching hose from the truck to the church.

"What can we do to help?" Tripp asked.

The man with Capshaw on his turnout coat turned around and faced Tripp and Parker. "Can you find out if there was there anyone in the church?"

"Just me, and I called 911 as soon as I smelled smoke coming from the foyer," Parker answered. "Thank goodness the wind is coming from the north and blowing the smoke away from the old parsonage and the new one. We've got lots of family here. Just tell us if there's any way…"

"I'm not sure we've got enough water in the truck to put this blaze out." The man gave a hand signal, pulled back a lever, and water shot out of the end of the hose.

The blaze seemed to eat up the water and beg for more.

"There's a well out back," Parker answered. "And the Red River is only a few hundred yards to the north. Will either of those work?"

"Hopefully," Capshaw answered. "I hope we've got enough hose to reach the river."

Tears flowed down Endora's cheeks and dripped onto her shirt. "What are we going to do? The Christmas program is ruined, and oh, Parker, where will we have services tomorrow?"

Parker drew her close to his side and kissed her on the cheek. "God will provide. He always has. Joe Clay's barn is empty. We could set up the folding chairs and have it there. No one says there has to be a steeple on the building for the spirit to be there."

"I'm sorry." Joe Clay draped an arm around his youngest daughter. "The ice storm that's coming this way has already closed bridges across the Red River and part of the highways."

Tripp wondered what that had to do with having services in the barn, but then Joe Clay went on to say, "I invited all the carnival folks to bring their trucks and equipment to the Paradise. They have trailers for the people to stay in, but their animals need a warm place. They can't get home to

Ringling, Oklahoma, where they winter, so I told them they could stay at our place and put the animals in the barn."

"We don't have to worry about services tomorrow anyway," Parker assured Endora. "I'd decided to put the word out that we wouldn't have Sunday school or church since the roads are getting so bad."

Mary Jane moved over between Joe Clay and Endora and wrapped her daughter up in a hug. "We've got two weeks before the Christmas program, so stop worrying. Your dad and I will see to it that everything is taken care of. You just concentrate on…"

Willa Rose walked up in front of Endora. "I've got the notebook, and we can do a couple of rehearsals in the old store. I got word this morning that the antiques won't be delivered until the roads clear up. I'll get busy cleaning the place up and make sure that it's warm."

"Thank you to all y'all." Endora sniffled and then squared her shoulders. "Not only will God provide, but my family will do the same. We're in good hands."

"Smoke coming out the roof," a firefighter yelled. "That means we'll need more water. I'll start stretching a hose and pump down to the river. That red water will make an ugly mess, but maybe we can save part of the building with it."

"I was a volunteer firefighter," Brodie raised his voice. "I can stretch hose."

"Then get to it, and Wilton, you carry the hose and help him with the pump," Capshaw yelled above the noise of the flames.

"Yes, sir, Captain," a tall, lanky guy hollered and draped a flat hose over his shoulder.

"Dayton, you get ready on the other end to start shooting water soon as that hose fills up."

"Yes, sir."

Sleet and freezing rain fell from gray skies, and the people who had gathered around started leaving the scene.

"Come on, Endora, we're going to the Paradise," Mary Jane said. "You are freezing, and that's not good for the babies."

"I can't leave Parker," she groaned.

"Yes, you can," he said. "You can't do anything here, but I might be able to help them determine what caused this if I stay."

"Willa Rose can go with y'all, and we could talk about the Christmas program," Hank suggested. "I just wish there was more we could do right now."

"Okay, then," Endora agreed.

Parker kissed her on the forehead and mouthed a thank-you to Mary Jane. When she, Endora, and Willa Rose were in her SUV and away from the church, Parker turned to Tripp and Knox. "We have got to start planning a volunteer fire department here in Spanish Fort. It took almost half an hour for the truck to come from Nocona. If we would've had something closer, we might have saved more of the church."

"We're in and so is Brodie," Knox replied with a nod. "He can even head up whatever it takes to get the idea off the ground since he did some of that work in the southern part of the state."

Willa Rose followed Mary Jane and Endora's lead and hung her coat on a hook inside the front door of the Paradise. She didn't have a thing to do that Saturday morning since the weather had stalled out the delivery of her antiques. She could have easily been cleaning the old store, but her father had volunteered her to babysit Endora, and she had no choice in the matter.

"Did you bring the book?" Endora asked.

"Nope, but I've got an idea of how you've done things in the past. It's not a lot different than the setup my mother had for our program in Poetry. The smallest kids first so they can leave the stage and sit with their parents. Then the older children and all the way up to the senior citizens who usually deliver some fun songs."

Endora sank down on the sofa and Mary Jane scooted a hassock over for her to prop her feet on. "That's the order. Do you have any ideas to spice it up?"

"Well…" Willa Rose paused and smiled.

"Sit down. I'll get some hot chocolate while y'all talk shop," Mary Jane said as she headed out of the living room.

"Well, what?" Endora asked.

"The weatherman said that this storm has stalled out over this area, from here all the way across north Texas past Sherman. If the carnival people are still here when we have the program, we could have the whole thing in the barn and use the real animals. Daisy and Heather said there's even a live camel," Willa Rose answered. "We could do the program in degrees. Instead of having the children of all the ages and then the older folks, we could put up several curtains. Little kids, and then draw that curtain back. Older kids and do the same, until we get to the end with a live nativity scene and the folks in that part singing, 'What Child Is This.' Maybe Luna's baby boy could be the one in the manger?"

"That's fantastic," Endora said and then swiped away a tear trying to escape down her cheeks. "We wouldn't have had room to do something like that in the church, but we will in the barn."

"Then why are you crying?" Willa Rose asked.

Endora's chin quivered. "Pregnancy brain. I'm so glad that you decided to move here."

"Hello!" Bernie yelled as she came inside the house. "It's colder than a well digger's belt buckle in Siberia out there. Gloria Perez just texted me and said"—she stopped midsentence when she saw Willa Rose—"that the church is on fire. I told her that was a hoax, that nothing could be on fire in this kind of weather."

"It was not a hoax. The foyer is blazing, and we don't know how far into the sanctuary the fire has gone," Endora said between sobs.

Bernie set Pepper on the floor and plopped down on the other end of the sofa. "Holy smoke, and I don't mean that as a pun."

"We're already talking about having the Christmas program in the barn, and maybe church services when the carnival is gone," Endora said.

"At least the barn is cleared out since we finished decorating late last evening. Good thing we did because this storm is supposed to set records across the state," Bernie said. "What about a carnival?"

Mary Jane came out with a tray filled with mugs of hot chocolate and cookies.

Bernie pointed a finger at Mary Jane. "Why didn't you call me and tell me that our church was on fire?"

"You don't have any business driving on the slick roads," Mary Jane shot back at her, "and you couldn't have done a single thing. The Nocona Fire Department is there, working to get it under control. We won't be able to have services in the church until it's rebuilt, but these girls are figuring out how to have the…" She eased down in a recliner. "I guess we should call it the 'community Christmas program' this year. Anyway, they've got some ideas, I'm sure."

Willa Rose handed Endora a tissue. "Yes, we do. Parker can't have church in the barn, since the carnival people are on the way, but…" She went on to tell them how things could work for the program.

"I like it," Bernie said. "But would someone please tell me what's this about a carnival?"

"The bridges are closed into Oklahoma, so Joe Clay invited the carnival folks to stay on the Paradise grounds until the roads are opened up again. They should be arriving anytime," Mary Jane said and then patted Endora on the shoulder. "I told you that things would work out. No matter how long it takes, we'll rebuild the church. We might have lost the post office, and the old school, but the church has been the heart of this town for more than a century."

"Thank you, Mama, and you." Endora focused on Willa Rose.

"You are so welcome."

The sound of tires crunching on a sleet-and-snow-covered yard sounded through the closed doors. Then the front door flew open, and it seemed to Willa Rose like the population of the whole town flooded into the house.

Parker didn't even remove his coat but rushed over to Endora and sat down beside her.

"Is it out?" she whispered.

"It is," he assured her, "but it will be a while before we can have services again."

"How bad?" Mary Jane asked.

"The ceiling in the sanctuary is partially destroyed," he answered.

"The foyer and bathrooms will have to be rebuilt," Joe Clay said. "But the room at the back of the building where y'all store the Christmas props is good. We really are lucky that the wind was blowing away from the houses on this side of town."

Bernie raised a hand. "Do y'all think it's time to put up a new building?"

"It'll take some time and good weather, but we'll salvage what's there," Knox promised.

Brodie made his way into the room and said, "The Chief found a couple of dead and burned animal carcasses in the attic. He wasn't sure if they were rats or squirrels, but there was evidence that they had chewed through some of that ancient wiring."

"We'll redo all the electrical stuff while we're remodeling," Knox said. "And changing the subject there, but while I've got all you guys here, we need to set up a time to talk about a volunteer fire department here in town."

"I agree," Noah said.

"I'm in," Hank told them. "I might not be able to do a lot, but I'll do what I can."

Willa Rose felt as if she was not only losing a battle, but the war. They had only been in Spanish Fort since Wednesday, and her father was already digging his heels into the community.

Chapter 7

Willa Rose wished that at least one person she had met would have been hateful, or at least standoffish, but oh, no, they had to all be nice folks. Mary Jane and the sisters that were in the kitchen had even invited her to help fix lunch for all the family who had shown up at the house.

"Endora, you sit down in a chair, and we'll visit while we get out the sandwich makings. There's a slow cooker full of soup because I thought it would be good on a cold day like this, so we should have enough to feed everyone. Willa Rose, you get out the lettuce and tomatoes from the fridge and get them ready. Rae, you can make a fresh gallon of sweet tea," Mary Jane ordered everyone around.

Willa Rose knew the difference in the sound of an eighteen-wheeler turning into their driveway at home, so when Tertia asked if Nocona had sent a snowplow up their way, she shook her head. "No, ma'am, that's not a plow. It's more than one big truck, and it sounds like they're coming right up to the Paradise."

"The carnival is here!" Joe Clay called out.

"Are we going to get rides?" Heather asked.

"No, those are all packed away, but you could probably

spend some time in the barn with the animals," Joe Clay answered.

"But only if either me or one of your uncles or aunts go with you," Rae told them.

Bernie made her way to the window and pulled up the blinds. "I love carnival people. They used to stop at my old bar when they were on their way home to Ratliff City. Such good, down-to-earth folks. I hope this ice and sleet lasts for days."

"Did they bring the camel?" Daisy asked.

Heather grabbed Daisy's hand and together they ran across the room to stand on either side of Bernie. "Can we ride him if they did?"

"Honey, I'm sure he's tired of being ridden and would like to just rest for a few days," Rae answered, "but we can go out there every day after school. Maybe they'll even let us help with the feeding."

"O…kay," Heather sighed.

Willa Rose remembered using that same tone on her mother when she had to settle for a compromise to what she really wanted to do. That would have been twenty years ago, about the same time that her sister, Erica, graduated from high school and left for college.

"I'll grab a bowl of soup later," Joe Clay said as he put on his coat and headed out the back door. "I'm going out to make the visitors welcome."

"And I've got a sandwich waiting for me at the old store, which is going to be Vada's Antiques when this weather clears up. So, I'm going back there to work on my sketches for where I'm putting things when the trucks arrive," Willa Rose said. There was just so much family she could handle for one day. "Endora, I'll drop in soon and we'll talk more about the Christmas plans."

"Anytime," Endora answered.

Willa Rose grabbed her coat, scarf, and gloves on the way through the living room and hurried outside before anyone else caught her. She shivered as she hurried across the frozen, crispy yard. Planning the holiday play and helping Rae figure out something new for her kids was causing her to already settle into the community more than she had ever intended to do.

She opened her SUV door and did a slippery dance on the ice. If she hadn't had a firm grip on the handle, she would have landed square on her ass and wouldn't have stopped sliding until she hit the porch steps. Finally, she got some traction and slung herself into the vehicle, just in time to hear Tripp laughing from the front porch. She didn't even stop to confront him but drove straight to the old store and carefully made her way up the ice-covered steps.

Fuming, she stomped into the warm room, shoved her gloves into her coat pocket, and tossed her scarf over an old ladder-back chair that looked too rickety to sit on. She sat down on the floor close to the open-face heater with her sketch pad and pencil. "It wasn't funny. I could have broken my leg or, worse yet, my arm, and then how would I arrange everything in this store? Maybe that and the fact that the trucks can't bring my stuff to me is a sign that I need to go home and start an antique shop right there in Poetry."

"Hey." Tripp stuck his head in the door.

"What are you doing here?" she snapped.

He came into the big, empty room and closed the door behind him. "I came to apologize for laughing at you."

"Apology accepted. I'm busy," she said.

He sat down beside her and looked at the sketch she had started. "Thank you, and I can see that, but you don't have to be so prickly. Tell me, are you planning to cut and run by summer?"

"If you don't leave me alone, I may be out of here as soon as this ice melts," she answered.

"What's so bad about me?" Tripp asked.

"Why do you want to know if I'm not planning on making this my permanent home?"

"I asked first," he said.

Infuriating man! Willa Rose thought.

"Nothing is bad about you. Now your turn."

"There's a bet going on about whether you stay or go," Tripp answered. "I figure if I know the exact time, I could win the pot."

"I've only been here three days!" She could hear the chill in her own voice.

Tripp nodded. "I know Hank isn't putting his house up for sale for a year, and that you have a smaller place in Poetry."

"That's right, and it's nobody's business but mine what I

do in the future, and I am not going to tell you anything…" She clamped her mouth shut for at least two minutes.

"Well?" Tripp finally said. "Are you going to answer me or ignore me until I go away?"

"Neither one, because I have no idea when I might leave, or *if* I will," she finally said.

"Fair enough," Tripp told her. "But if you would give me a heads-up when you do figure it out, I could still win that pot."

She slapped him on the forearm. "I believe that is called 'insider trading.'"

Tripp chuckled. "Only if I get caught. Tell me, though, what did you do for fun in Poetry? I looked it up and it's not even as big as Spanish Fort."

"I lived there, but I went to school in Terrell, and there's plenty to do there," she argued.

"Were you one of those wild girls or a nerd?" Tripp asked.

"That, sir, is none of your business."

"Ever go skinny-dippin' or snipe huntin'?"

She bristled. "That is none of your business either. And I think you are baiting me into a fight."

Tripp couldn't argue that point. He had already gotten enough of a rise out of her to see that a temper was boiling beneath those pretty brown eyes. "Is it working?" he asked.

"Yes, and I don't like it, so stop," she told him.

He saluted her as smartly as he had seen Brodie do when he was in the military. "Yes, ma'am."

"I never date military men, truck drivers, or firefighters," she said.

"Did I ask you for a date?"

"No, but I'm just putting that out there," she answered.

"I was not in the military. I have never been a firefighter. Brodie was both. I've never driven a truck and don't even have a commercial driver's license. And, honey, I wouldn't date you either."

"Why?" she asked.

"I don't date anyone who is prettier than me," he teased.

"Well, you should go out with mud ugly women, then," she countered.

"On that note, I'm going home. You have a good day with your sketching, but the storm is going to get worse through the next few days. Call me if you can't get out to go to Sunday dinner tomorrow."

"I would never," she told him.

"Let me finish, Willa Rose," he said. "Call me and I'll send Hank after you. Church services had already been called off for tomorrow, but we always eat at the Paradise. If you don't show up, someone will come huntin' for you. I wouldn't ever want to come in with you in tow, since I only go out with ugly women."

She jerked her head up and glared at him. He moved over slightly and cupped her face in his big hands. The anger left her eyes, and they went all dreamy.

"Don't you dare," she challenged.

"You should never dare a bred and born Texan," he said.

His mouth closed on hers and her palms went under his unbuttoned jacket to his chest, sending waves of heat all through his body. When he released her, they were both panting.

"That was a big…" she gasped.

"What?" he asked.

"It was amazing, and I loved it, but…"

"But what?" He grinned. "Was it worth sticking around for another one? That's the only way we'll ever have a second. Because I'm here for good, putting down roots, and I don't have time for a fleeting romance."

"Not even if the kiss about melted all the ice from here to the river?" she asked.

"Not even," he answered and turned to walk away.

She grabbed him by the arm, and suddenly her arms were up around his neck, her fingers splayed out in his thick hair, and her eyes were closed. She tiptoed up to meet his lips, and he almost pushed her away, but he had to see if that first kiss was as hot as it made him feel.

That time when she took a step back, she said, "Yep, it wasn't just beginner's luck. It was as good as the first one. I'll see you at dinner tomorrow. And Tripp, I still won't tell you if or when I plan to leave."

He waved over his shoulder on his way outside where he took a running leap off the porch and slid like a professional ice skater all the way to his truck. That was the result of skating in his socks on his mama's hardwood floors when he was a kid. The leather truck seats were cold, but he was still warm from the steamy kisses. When he pushed the button to start the engine, the radio came on full blast. He sang right along with Josh Turner singing "Your Man."

When he saw Knox's vehicle in his front yard, he groaned, "This is not what I wanted to come home to."

He hopped out of his truck, got a running start, and slid right up to the bottom porch step. But he missed the newel post when he grabbed for it and fell forward. His feet were still on the ground, toes against the bottom step, and face planted firmly on the cold porch when his hands finally wrapped around the post.

The door flew open, and Knox stepped out. "Drunk or just clumsy?"

"Neither one," Tripp answered as he took his brother's offered hand.

Knox's feet slipped on the icy porch, and he went down right beside his brother. Tripp managed to find enough footing to sit up, but Knox's eyes focused on the sky for several seconds.

"Are you drunk or clumsy?" Tripp asked without cracking a grin.

"Probably the latter with a little stupid thrown in for coming out here in my socks," Knox panted as he sat up. "Maybe we should both crawl into the house and come back out with some salt for the porch and steps. You go first. I'm still trying to get my breath."

Tripp moaned when he got up on all fours and silently fussed at himself for being so cocky earlier. "We ain't kids anymore, sliding on hardwood floors."

"Is that what you were trying to do?" Knox grabbed a railing and tried to stand but it didn't work, so he followed his brother into the house on his hands and knees.

"Yep, but I didn't do a good job." Tripp almost added, *like the first time*, but changed his mind at the last minute. If anyone knew that he had kissed Willa Rose or that she had kissed him, the teasing would never stop.

Knox took off his wet socks and stood up. "I need a cup of hot chocolate to warm me up. How about you?"

"Yes, a big mugful," Tripp said.

I'd rather have a longer make-out session with Willa Rose to heat me up.

When Tripp finally got to his feet, he went straight for his bedroom to change into a pair of flannel pajama pants and a warm sweatshirt. He heard Knox's deep voice scolding someone when he headed back to the living area and found his brother shaking a finger at Bernie when he peeked around the corner into the kitchen.

"Tripp and I both took a tumble on the ice, and you surely should not be driving on these slick roads."

"I'm not clumsy," Bernie argued, "and I've taken care of myself for more than five decades, so don't fuss at me. I came to talk to Tripp. Where is he?"

Tripp stepped out from the shadows. "I'm right here. What's on your mind, Aunt Bernie?"

"I took Pepper out to the barn to meet the animals. From what the weatherman says, the carnival folks might be here a while, so I expect the critters will be nice to Pepper after they get to know him. They were a little standoffish to him today," she answered and sat down at the table. "Fix me a cup of that chocolate. Next time I buy a truck, it's going to have a heated steering wheel."

"Give her mine," Tripp told Knox, "and I'll make myself another one. Did you come out on the ice to tell me that Pepper got his feelings hurt?"

"Of course not," Bernie barked and took a sip of the hot chocolate that Knox had set before her. "While I was out there, I met and visited with the owner of the carnival. His name is Zeb. Right nice man. Mary Jane has invited the whole crew to join us for Sunday dinner tomorrow and told them to feel free to use the bathroom out in the barn since we don't have one of them portable toilets like the cities provide when they set up the carnival. Some of them have tiny little bathrooms in their RVs, but some of them live in makeshift quarters behind their vendor's stands, so I wouldn't be a bit surprised if they even set up cots in the barn for those."

I don't need to know about the carnival folks since God created dirt, Tripp thought as he made another mugful of hot chocolate in the microwave.

"I'm not surprised that Mary Jane and Joe Clay are being so kind," Knox said. "They sure took us in without hesitation or questions."

Bernie took another sip of her chocolate. "I'm starting to thaw out. So, I met Zeb, and he is retiring. When they get home to Ringling, Oklahoma, his son, Finn, will inherit the business."

"O…kay," Tripp drew out the word.

Bernie frowned and set her mouth in a firm line. "Don't you take that tone with me. I saw the way Willa Rose was looking at you during Thanksgiving. Then she followed you out to the sunroom. I had to leave the football game to rescue your sorry self. That woman is bad luck. She arrives in town on Wednesday and the church burns three days later."

"Aunt Bernie!" Tripp scolded. "A rat caused the church to burn, not Willa Rose."

Although if she had kissed me in the foyer, it could have heated up things enough to cause a blaze.

"Maybe that rat came with her from Poetry and crawled from the old parsonage to the church," Bernie argued. "I say she is bad luck, and I'm going to do everything in my power to see to it that she doesn't stay here."

"That's not fair. I need Hank to be happy in Spanish Fort, and if she leaves, he might go with her since that's the only family he has," Tripp said.

"Are you going to drug her and send her off with the carnival?" Knox teased.

"Something like that," Bernie answered. "I'm going to introduce her to Finn and work my butt off to be sure they get to spend a lot of time together. After all, this is the holiday season, and magic can be conjured up."

A shot of hot jealousy shot through Tripp. "What if she doesn't like him, or what if I decide I like her and change her mind about staying here?"

"She is helping Rae and Endora with their Christmas programs, so she might decide that she loves it here," Knox reminded Bernie.

"That don't mean jack squat," Bernie protested. "I don't want her to stay here, and I don't even care if she takes Hank with her when she goes. She's not good enough for either of you boys, and I'm going to start something up between her and Finn. He's not as pretty as you Callahan men, but he'll work for what I need him to do."

Tripp pulled a bill out of his pocket and laid it on the table. "Want to put your money where your words are? I bet you that twenty that she doesn't like Finn."

Bernie's eyes twinkled. "Make it a hundred, but before you do, remember that I have power on my side."

"What power is that?" Knox asked.

"Christmas is when miracles happen, and then there's just my natural skill at manipulation. I know it's a bad word, but it's the truth. I manage to get what I want when I want it," she declared.

Tripp thought of the two kisses and laid out four more twenties. "Knox, you can be our bookie."

Bernie took a hundred-dollar bill from her purse and tossed it into the middle of the table. "I'll buy Pepper a whole new wardrobe of rhinestone-studded collars with your money, plus I will stand on the edge of the road and gloat when she leaves. Ringling, Oklahoma, is only forty-five minutes from here, so it won't be a bit of trouble for them to see each other often. Now, I'm going home, and don't either of you say a word about walking me out to my truck or taking me back. Bernie takes care of herself."

"Yes, ma'am," Tripp agreed. "Is it all right if I help you with your coat or open the door for you?"

"No, it is not, and it's not all right for you to flirt with Willa Rose," she snapped.

"All's fair in love and war, and bets," Tripp told her.

Chapter 8

Right out of the bucket, so to speak, Willa Rose had to goose the gas pedal to even get out of the driveway that Sunday morning. Then the SUV did a complete 360-degree turn before it straightened up. She had heard of cutting doughnuts on the ice, but she'd never been brave enough to try such a thing. But then she had never seen ice like this before. She'd been born and raised in Poetry and gone to college in Austin and could count on the fingers of one hand the times that ice or snow caused any roads to be closed in either place.

Her heart thumped in her chest. Her knuckles were whiter than the falling snow. And it took a few minutes for her to focus on anything in the almost whiteout conditions because it seemed like her eyes were rolling around in her head like she was on a Tilt-A-Whirl ride.

Another good reason to leave this place, she thought as she eased forward at less than five miles an hour.

She made it to the corner and gently tapped the brakes. Made that one. *Just one more to go and I'm at the Paradise.*

When she reached the tree-lined lane leading up to the house, she slowed down even more, terrified that she would begin a slide and wind up with the front of her SUV smashed all to hell against one of the huge pecan trees. She was breathing easy when she got to the front yard, but then a cat ran out in front of her, and she instinctively slammed on the brakes. How a vehicle could go forward and sideways at the same time was a total mystery, but it did—and came to a stop about five inches from the side of Tripp's pickup truck.

She felt like an elephant had parked its big butt on her chest, and her pulse had jacked up like she had just walked through one of those silly haunted Halloween houses. When she finally got control and looked around to see if anyone had seen the fiasco, Tripp was grinning at her from the front seat of his truck. He waved and crawled over the console and exited the vehicle on the passenger side. Then he walked all the way around both vehicles and slung her door open.

"I'm so sorry." She felt the blush heating up her cheeks before it ever appeared and hoped that he attributed it to the cold wind.

He offered her a gloved hand. "No problem. I like playing Houdini and escaping from my truck through an alternate door."

She put her hand in his and was glad for his firm grip. "I did that on purpose to box you in."

I will not let Tripp Callahan get under my skin, she silently vowed.

"Oh, yeah, you did. Your face was as white as what is layin' on the ground when you finally came to a stop, so don't go lyin' to me, Miz Thomas." He couldn't remember a single time in his life that he had enjoyed flirting so much.

"How do you know I'm not being truthful?" she shot back at him. "Maybe I'm just that good of a driver."

"And maybe you are simply that lucky. After all, you met me, didn't you?" He led her up to the door and dropped her hand.

"Don't be egotistical," she snapped.

"Okay, then maybe I'm lucky because I met you," he said.

"Or perhaps we are both unlucky because of the same reasons."

"Could be."

He raised his hand to knock but before his knuckles reached the wood, Bernie slung the door open. "Come on in," she said and then frowned.

"Mornin', Bernie," Willa Rose said.

"Same to you. Now get on in here out of the cold. I swear, I've never seen so much sleet, freezing rain, and snow all at one time." Bernie grabbed her by the arm and pulled her inside the warm house. "I've got someone I want you to meet. We've already graced the food, and everyone is just finding a place to park their butts and eat. Finn is out in the sunroom, and I think y'all are going to hit it off real good."

"What makes you think that?" Willa Rose asked.

"He's sexy as hell, and he owns a carnival."

You are losing it, Miz Bernie, if you think you can set me up with a carnival owner. *I didn't even want to move here. Why would I want to travel all over Texas and Oklahoma?*

They were halfway past a couple of long tables laid out with all kinds of good food that smelled amazing. Willa Rose loved fried chicken and there were three big trays of that, plus a sliced ham and two big lasagnas.

"Finn can wait because I'm starving. So, I intend to eat first and meet him afterward. Or else I might faint at the very sight of him."

"Oh, okay." Bernie frowned. "But don't dawdle. He might decide to go to his trailer, and I really want you to get acquainted with him."

"Why?" Willa Rose asked.

"I visited with him last night, and he's such a sweet person, and…" Bernie stopped for a breath.

Any elementary teacher worth her salt learned early on that too many *ands* out of a child's mouth meant they were covering up something for sure.

"Maybe I don't like sweet," Willa Rose said. "Maybe I like wild and wicked."

Bernie crossed her arms over her chest. "I've never met a carnival guy yet that didn't have a little wild and wicked in him."

Willa Rose threw an arm around Bernie's shoulders and whispered, "That's not nearly bad boy enough for me. If you are trying to play matchmaker and find me a husband, look for someone else. I'm going to make a plate now and find Endora. We need to talk about the Christmas stuff. I'm hoping she will come help me put up my tree tomorrow. If not, maybe I can talk the Callahan brothers and maybe Audrey into helping me and Daddy."

Tripp stood close enough that he could hear part of the conversation. As soon as Willa Rose had loaded her plate and carried it to the staircase leading upstairs, he nudged Bernie on the shoulder. "Want to concede right now and give me your money?"

"That's just one battle," she answered through clenched teeth. "I've got more cards up my sleeve. Did you tell her about the bet?"

"Why would I do that?" Tripp answered. "Remember though, Spanish Fort is a small place, and she's probably heard that you aren't liking the idea of a Callahan flirting with her," Tripp answered.

"You do *not* want to see my bad side." Bernie growled.

He fixed himself a plate and carried it out to the sunporch. He had never seen anyone, not even Brodie, stand up to Bernie like Willa Rose had done. Made him wonder, though, if she really liked bad boys, or if she was just tormenting Bernie.

Finn looked up from the picnic table at the end of the room. He had jet-black hair, green eyes, and a chiseled face. Willa Rose was going to be sorry that she blew off Bernie's suggestion.

"Hello," he said. "Miz Bernie told me to stay right

here. I have no idea why. Are you someone I'm supposed to talk to?"

"Yes," Tripp answered without blinking.

"Somehow I thought it might be a lady."

"No, it's just me. I'm Tripp Callahan. I don't really like big crowds. I guess she thought you might be in the same boat." He set his plate on the table and took a bite of the lasagna.

"Bless her heart." Finn chuckled. "She hasn't gotten to know me yet. I run a carnival, so I'm around crowds all the time. I think I'll go on back inside and see how my people are doing. Nice meeting you, Tripp. I really appreciate your family taking us in like this."

"They are that kind of people."

Finn stood up and took a couple of steps. "We don't run into folks like that very often. See you around. If you got kids, bring them out to the barn. They'll love the animals."

"No wife, no kids," Tripp answered. "But thanks for the offer. I'm sure that Rae and Gunner's twin girls will be excited about seeing them."

"I've already met those kids, and they've been out there a couple of times." Finn said and kept walking. "Well, hello!" His whole tone changed when he met Willa Rose coming out onto the sunporch.

"You don't bite the hand that is feeding you," a teenage girl right behind Willa Rose said in a scolding tone.

"Remember who feeds *you*, Ivy Jo," Finn's tone was almost as cold as the north wind, but it turned warm when he focused on Willa Rose and introduced himself. "I'm Finn Duffy, and I think you might be the very person Miz Bernie wanted me to wait for out here."

"I'm Willa Rose, and it's nice to meet you, but if you'll excuse me, I'm starving. I couldn't find a place to sit inside."

"Of course, but…" Finn flashed a brilliant smile.

"*But* move out of the way," Ivy told him.

Finn shot a dirty look her way and let them pass before he went on into the house.

"He's just a big flirt. He and Yasmin—she's the fortune teller—are together when we're in Oklahoma, but they're on again and off again on the trips. It all depends on who she catches him flirting with," Ivy growled under her breath.

"There's plenty of room over here," Tripp called out. "If you hurry, you might even get to eat dessert before Aunt Bernie finds out where you are."

Willa Rose led the way across the room. "Miz Bernie doesn't tell me what to do."

Ivy set her plate on the table. "I'm Ivy."

"Tripp Callahan," he introduced himself.

"Pleased to meet you," Ivy said with a nod.

"Likewise." He glanced away from Ivy and over at Willa Rose. She looked pretty in a blue sweater with her dark hair flowing down over her shoulders, but the easy banter and the kisses had to have been a fleeting thing. Bernie was right in saying that he didn't need a woman who wouldn't stick around.

But the heart wants what the heart wants, the pesky voice in his head whispered.

My heart wanted a BB gun for Christmas when I was five. I didn't get it, and I got over it.

To take his mind off Willa Rose, he glanced over at Ivy. She was about the same height as Willa Rose, but that's where the resemblance stopped. The girl had blond hair tied up in a ponytail, and if Tripp had a quarter for every freckle on her face, he would be a rich man. Her chocolate-brown eyes had a note of sadness in them.

"Finn is egotastic," she blurted out.

"Do you mean 'egotistical'?" Willa Rose asked.

"If you are *old*. Egotastic is the new word," Ivy answered.

"Ouch!" Tripp said with a chuckle. "What's the difference in the two words?"

"They both mean the same thing, but 'egotastic' is what we say now. Finn is all about himself," Ivy answered.

"Sounds like it if he can't be faithful to his girlfriend. Is she in the house?" Tripp asked.

"Yep, and he wouldn't dare flirt with Willa Rose if she was close by."

"So, what do you do in the carnival, Miz Ivy?" Tripp asked.

"I take care of one of the game booths, but this is my last trip. When we get back to Oklahoma, Finn will be the big boss man. He's already said that I'm fired. Zeb don't like it, but then he needs hip surgery and he's ready to retire, so…" She shrugged.

"Hey, this is where you are," Bernie said as she came out to the sunroom with a glass of sweet tea in her hands. She sat down beside Tripp and kicked him on the side of his leg. "Where's Finn? I told him to wait out here."

Willa Rose felt Ivy bristle, and the temperature in the room felt like someone had left the back door open. She glanced over at the girl to see that her mouth was set in a firm line and her brows were drawn down.

"He went back inside just as Ivy and Willa Rose were coming out here," Tripp answered. "There's a houseful of folks today. He might have to stand in line to get at one of the cobblers."

"So, you met him, Willa Rose?" Bernie sounded excited.

"Just in passing," she answered.

"Good-lookin' guy, ain't he?"

"He is that."

"The weatherman said this morning that we've got another storm coming right in behind what we're experiencing now," Bernie said. "This time it's supposed to put several inches of snow down on this ice. They're calling it 'global warming,' but there ain't one thing warm about any of this. Poor little Pepper barely gets off the porch to take care of his business now."

"What's that got to do with Finn?" Willa Rose asked.

"It means that the roads will be closed longer than any of us thought. Finn and the carnival folks will be here more than just a few days. So, we will get to know all these folks for at least a week."

"I wouldn't mind staying here that long," Ivy muttered.

Bernie turned to focus on Ivy. "Aren't you in a hurry to get back to Ringling and see all your friends?"

"I don't have friends outside of the carnival. My grandpa raised me and homeschooled me on the road, and now he's gone. He died a few weeks ago. The only thing for me to do in Ringling is to find a place to spread his ashes, and hopefully find a job." Ivy's chin quivered.

Willa Rose laid a hand on her shoulder. "I lost my mother almost a year ago. It takes a while to work through the grief."

"Thanks for that," Ivy said. "I've lost my appetite. I'm going out to the barn for a nap."

"Why the barn?" Willa Rose asked.

Ivy shrugged again. "I have a cot out there, and the animals don't snore like Inez when I have to sleep on the floor."

"Where did you sleep when your grandpa was alive?" Tripp asked.

"We had a little room with two cots at the back of the game booth. It's all packed up in one of the big trucks now," she answered as she started out the back door.

"Hey!" Tripp raised his voice. "Where is your coat? It's cold out there."

"Didn't need one until now. I'll be fine," Ivy said and waved over her shoulder.

And Bernie expects me to live like that? Willa Rose frowned.

Bernie picked up her glass along with the plate and cutlery that Finn had left behind. "I'll take all this to the kitchen and be right back. I need to talk to Mary Jane."

"About what?" Tripp asked.

"Not that it's any of your business, but that child does not need to be living in a barn," she snapped.

"She could be living in worse when she gets back to Oklahoma," Willa Rose said. "She told us that she has no family or friends, and Finn is going to fire her."

"Not if I have anything to do with it," Bernie declared. "And, Willa Rose, you stay away from that man even if he is good-lookin'. If he's going to put a teenage girl out on the streets, then he's not the man for you."

"Yes, ma'am. I hear he's egotastic anyway," Willa Rose answered.

"I don't care what religion he is," Bernie said. "That precious child is not sleeping in a barn full of animals when there are seven empty bedrooms upstairs."

Willa Rose watched her leave and then looked across the table at Tripp. "I might decide to like that woman if she'll stay out of my business."

"Matchmaking is in her blood. So as long as you are single, she considers you fair game."

"Does she try her matchmaking on you?"

Tripp nodded. "But so far I've been able to bypass the women she's thrown my way. She believes she has magical powers when it comes to putting men and women together."

"The magic ends with me," Willa Rose declared.

Chapter 9

A loud noise brought Tripp up out of a deep sleep. His first thought was that Endora had gone into labor in the middle of a blizzard. He rushed down the hallway in his bare feet and threw open the door to find what looked like the abominable snowman standing in front of him. Whoever it was rushed into the house without saying a word. When she removed her heavy coat and shook the snow from her dark hair, he realized that Willa Rose was throwing cold, wet snow everywhere.

"Hold on and let me get you a towel." He hurried to the bathroom without waiting to ask what she was doing out in this weather at nearly midnight.

Her teeth were chattering when he returned with a couple of big towels. "Take off your coat and hang it on the rack. I'll put a towel under it to catch the water. Here's an extra one for your hair. What are you doing out in this messy weather?"

"I came to watch a movie with Daddy," she answered. "I thought I could make it home, but the SUV started sliding and I wound up in your front yard. I couldn't get any traction at all, so I got out and tried to push. It didn't take but a couple of minutes before I was covered in this wet stuff, and how am I going to get home?"

"You aren't," Tripp told her. "You are going to stay in my guest room. You need to take a hot shower to warm up. There's a bathroom right off the bedroom. You can sleep in one of my sweatshirts and a pair of my boxers, but there's no way we can get your vehicle out tonight and possibly not even tomorrow. You are stuck right here."

Willa Rose left wet footprints across the room. "I'm ruining this lovely hardwood."

"It's vinyl planks and will wipe up. Don't worry about it. We've got to get you warmed up or you'll have pneumonia."

He opened a door and pointed. "I'll put some dry things on the bed for you and make some hot tea or chocolate. If you had stayed out there much longer, you would have gotten hypothermia for sure."

"Do you think we can take me home tomorrow?"

"Not if this doesn't let up," he answered. "The news tonight says it's going to outdo the Texas snowstorm of 2010, when Dallas got more than a foot of snow in twenty-four hours. And that was just snow on dry ground, not snow on top of ice. Roads are closed everywhere from here to south of Fort Worth."

"Bernie isn't going to be happy about me spending the night here," she said.

"Nope," Tripp agreed. "I don't reckon she will."

He closed the door to the guest room, heard the phone ring, and ran back down the hall. He barely got out "hello" when Hank started apologizing for calling him in the middle of the night.

"I'm worried about Willa Rose. She left half an hour ago in this storm and was supposed to call me when she got home. I hated to call you this late, but…"

"She's here," Tripp said. "Her SUV started sliding and wound up in my yard. By the time she got to the door, she was half-frozen, so she is taking a hot shower to warm up. She can stay in my guest room until the blizzard passes."

"That's great. If you can make it across the yards, I'll see you in the morning, and thank you, Tripp, for letting her stay." His chuckle held both humor and relief. "Bernie ain't goin' to like this. I've got a twenty ridin' on Willa Rose stayin' right here in Spanish Fort, but when it comes to women, a man never knows what they'll do."

"You are very welcome, and it's no problem. I've got lots of room, and Hank, you are right about women. I might be a little late tomorrow morning, but I'll do my best to get over there."

He ended the call, fished a pair of boxer shorts from a drawer, decided against them, and took out a pair of flannel pajama bottoms. When he'd added a sweatshirt, he went back to the guest room and laid them on the bed.

"It's not time for breakfast," he muttered when his stomach growled.

He got into bed and tried to ignore the hunger pains, but nothing worked. Finally, he pushed back the covers, put on a shirt, and headed to the kitchen for a bowl of cereal.

He grabbed the fruity kind and found nothing in the box. Same with three others. "Damn you, Knox. The grocery list is right there on the refrigerator. When you empty it, you write down what kind it is and throw the box away." He opened the refrigerator and removed everything to make an omelet, and there were even a couple of bags of frozen biscuits in the freezer.

"What's going on in here?" Willa Rose asked from the doorway.

"Hunger pains," he answered as he turned on the oven.

"Me too."

"Omelets or biscuits and gravy?"

"Both, and I'll help," she answered. "And thanks again, Tripp. I never knew a warm shower and a dry sweatshirt could feel so good."

Tripp cracked half a dozen eggs into a bowl and handed it to her. "You can make the omelets while I do the biscuits and gravy."

When he and Knox designed the house, they hadn't figured on more than one person being in the kitchen. Now Tripp wished he had made it into a big room like they had at the Paradise—where six or seven women could all be working at once. It seemed like no matter which way he turned, he brushed against Willa Rose's hip or shoulder.

"Shall we just eat on the bar?" Willa Rose asked.

"Yes," Tripp answered.

"You aren't one much for words, are you?"

"Other than my brothers, I've probably talked more to

you than anyone else in a long time."

She slipped one omelet onto her plate and handed the other one to Tripp. "Why is that?"

"You argue with me."

"So, you like the banter?" she asked.

"It does make things interesting," he admitted.

"And the kisses?"

"Yep, that too," he said and then filled his mouth with food.

"There's no banter if there's nothing but three- or four-word answers," she snapped.

"I'm hungry, and it's almost two o'clock in the morning. My alarm is set for eight so I can be at work at nine. I need sleep more than I need flirting."

"Oh!" She cocked her head to one side. "What makes you think I was flirting?"

"I'm not dumb." He turned and looked her in the eye.

"Well, you must be, because I was not flirting."

"And I don't flirt with women when I'm hungry and losing sleep," Tripp said and went back to his food.

Willa Rose was ready to scream when she crawled into the back side of the bed and pulled the covers up to her chin. All men, including her father, could be so infuriating sometimes. That's when she remembered she was supposed to call Hank when she made it home. She sat straight up and moaned.

"Are you all right?" Tripp's voice floated down the hall.

"I'm fine," she called out. "I was supposed to call my dad when I got home."

"He called here. Everything is good."

She fell back on the pillow and bit back a second groan. She fell asleep and dreamed of Tripp kissing her. The warmth of his broad chest against her body when he held her close created a ball of fire in her body. She leaned in even closer and laid her head on his shoulder. Then she woke up snuggled up to Tripp—for real.

"What the hell!" she squealed and moved to her side of the bed.

"Holy…" He rolled over, blinked a couple of times, jumped out of bed, and grabbed a pillow to cover his nakedness.

Only it was not Tripp who had slept with her. It was his twin brother, Knox. Thank God they weren't identical twins—or maybe that wasn't even the right thought.

"What are you doing!" she yelled.

Knox rubbed sleep from his eyes. "I could ask you the same thing."

Tripp was suddenly standing—bare-chested—in the doorway. "Knox? Willa Rose?"

Her eyes flipped so fast from one half-naked man to the one holding the pillow that it made her dizzy. Finally, she pointed at Knox. "He owes both of us an explanation."

Knox grabbed his pants off the floor, turned around, and put them on. "I didn't know…" He picked up the rest of his things and ran out of the room.

Tripp followed him, and Willa Rose jumped out of bed and trailed along behind them. "I was right there. How could you not see me?"

"It was dark," Knox said as he pulled a knit shirt over his head. "I didn't want to wake Tripp, so I used my key and…"

"Just got into bed with me? Didn't you see my SUV by the porch?" Willa Rose's tone was less inquiring and more demanding.

"Woman, I saw a big snowdrift. How was I to know it was a vehicle?" Knox countered.

"Why are you here, anyway?" Tripp asked.

"The electricity blinked several times over at my place and then went out completely. I figured there was heat here and a warm bed." Knox backed up to the wall and flipped on the light switch.

"No!" Willa Rose wailed when no lights came on. "This place is out of power too. Now what are we going to do?"

Tripp's phone rang and the little red bar at the top right told him the battery would be dead within an hour. "Hello, Mary Jane. Is your power out too?"

"No, and that's why I'm calling. It looks like the north side of town is all dark, but we've got four extra bedrooms here at the Paradise. If you can get here, we'll be glad to share our heat."

"We'll make it somehow, and thank you," he said.

"Be safe. Ivy and I are making breakfast for everyone," she said and ended the call.

"Make it where?" Knox asked.

"The Paradise," Tripp answered. "Willa Rose, call Hank and tell him that we'll come get him soon as we are loaded. We're all going to the Paradise until we have power again. We'll shovel what we can off your vehicle, Knox, and you can drive."

"All I have is what I wore in here last night," Willa Rose muttered.

"You and Mary Jane are about the same size, and you can do laundry there. It's only until the storm blows over," Tripp assured her.

"What if we get bogged down or slide off in a ditch?" Her whole body shivered at the thought of being as cold as she was the night before.

"Then Knox can warm you up," Tripp said.

"This is no time for jokes," she fumed, and stormed back to her bedroom. "I'm already sick of this place, and it hasn't even been a week."

You told Bernie that you wanted wild. Well, looks to me like your wish has been granted. Her mother's voice was loud and clear in her head.

"It's never ending." Tripp wiped snow from his face as he tried to clear the windshield on Knox's truck.

"We might as well stop trying to get it all off. The snow is coming down faster than we can get it swept away," Knox said.

"Think you can drive to the Paradise basically in the dark since the wipers will have a devil of a time keeping up?" Tripp asked.

Knox raised his voice over the howling wind. "No, but I'll give it my best shot. We might have to walk if I don't make the two turns, but it will beat staying here."

"Okay, then," Tripp started back to the house. "Thank God for the tall rubber boots that we bought when we were on the farm."

"Yep," Knox agreed, and slogged through the wet stuff that came halfway to his knees.

Willa Rose must have heard them coming because she opened the door and stood back. "Daddy called and said he has a bag packed and is ready to go."

"I'll go get him and then drive as close to the porch as I can to pick up y'all," Knox said.

"I'll get some things ready to go and we'll come out as soon as we hear you," Tripp said and then turned to Willa Rose. "Will you please make sure all the faucets in the house are dripping? That might save us from having busted pipes."

"Us?" She raised an eyebrow.

"You just spent the night with one Callahan and woke up with another. That should be enough to warrant an *us*, don't you think?"

"I hope you haven't bet too much money on me staying in this town," she shot back at him.

He headed back down the hallway, but stopped long enough to turn back and say, "Who says that I made my bet in that direction?"

Tripp was packed and ready when he heard a honk. "This

is it," he said and handed Willa Rose a pair of sunglasses. "Put these on."

"Why?"

"Woman, why do you have to question everything? They are to protect your eyes from the blowing snow."

"Where's yours?" she asked.

"I only have one pair."

"Do you have a coat to throw down for me to walk on?"

"No, but I've got a plan. Just don't fight me." He scooped her up in his arms, opened the door, and made a beeline for the truck. He shoved her into the back seat beside Hank and then went back for his bag.

By the time he reached the truck the second time, he was covered with snow. "Okay, Brother, let's see if you can navigate a blizzard and get us to the Paradise."

"Why did you carry Willa Rose out here?" Hank asked.

"The snow would have been up to her knees, and this is not going to be a short trip. Her shoes would have gotten wet," Tripp answered.

"Thank you," Willa Rose and Hank both said at the same time.

"Was there another reason?" Knox asked out the corner of his mouth.

"It was my turn to be hero." Tripp grinned.

Knox pulled out slowly. "I can't see where the yard ends and the road begins."

"You do it by feel, not sight," Hank told him. "The road will feel different. The trouble will be in finding the turns."

Knox was going a little too fast and slid forward half a city block when he finally made it to the road. "That was a close one," he whispered when the truck came to a stop, and he eased on at five miles an hour. "If there weren't fences, we could just drive between the trees."

"Oh, no!" Willa Rose gasped. "What about Remy and Ursula's cows, and poor little Pansy pig?"

"They're all in the barns. The cattle are in stalls at Remy's, and Pansy has been moved into the barn on Audrey's property." Tripp rolled down the window and stuck his head outside. "Turn now. This is where we go left."

Knox let up on the gas and took the corner in a long, greasy slide.

"Good job," Hank said from the back seat.

"Have you ever had to drive in this kind of weather?" Tripp asked.

"Couple of times when I was making a haul up to Vermont in the wintertime," he answered, "but I had the weight of an eighteen-wheeler working for me. Just take it slow and easy. Are there any signs that we can use to know when to turn at the Paradise?"

"I can barely make them out, but there's lights on the fences," Knox answered. "There will be a small break where the lane is. Tripp, help me watch for it."

"I will never pray for snow again." Willa Rose's voice sounded strained and scared. "A white Christmas or even a snowman isn't worth all this."

"It wouldn't be so bad if there wasn't a layer of sleet and

ice underneath it," Hank assured her. "We're closer by the minute. Every few feet means that we won't have to walk that far. And you've got some big strong men to carry you if we do."

"I can walk," she protested loudly. "I'm tough enough to take the snow."

"In those cloth shoes?" Hank chuckled. "You'll have frostbite before you reach the house. We've got to get you some rubber boots before winter is over."

"Hopefully, this won't happen again for another decade or more. I can see a break in the lights, so I'm going to give it a try right here." Knox made a hard right and only fishtailed for a minute before he got control and finally brought the truck to a stop at the edge of the back porch.

"Just when I get the hang of doing this, the trip is over," he said.

"You aren't fooling me one bit," Tripp said with a long sigh. "You were just as nervous as the rest of us."

"No, Brother, you are wrong. This drop in adrenaline testifies that I was twice as nervous as any of you," Knox admitted.

Chapter 10

"What happened last night?" Parker chuckled when Tripp came through the back door with Willa Rose in his arms.

"About what?" Tripp asked. Surely the whole family didn't already know that Willa Rose had spent the night at his place. Gossip traveled fast, but the whiteout blizzard should have slowed it down a little.

"You are carrying Willa Rose over the threshold. Aren't you rushing things a little? You've only known her a week," Parker teased.

Bernie jerked her head up and locked eyes with Tripp. "Explain why you are carrying that woman into the house. Is her leg broken?"

Willa Rose wiggled free of his arms, planted her feet firmly on the floor, and glared at Tripp.

"Calling her 'woman' in that tone is disrespectful, Aunt Bernie," Tripp scolded, "and her leg is not broken, but she would have had to wade through knee-deep snowdrifts to get to the house." Tripp did his best to keep laughter out of his tone, but it came through anyway. He'd heard that Bernie was a poker whiz, but he could read her face like a book—and the story did not have a happy ending.

"Well, pardon me." Bernie did a perfect head wiggle.

"When you know, you know," he said and put an arm around Willa Rose's shoulders. If Bernie could hang mistletoe on his porch, then he could tease her a little.

"What does that mean?" she shot back at him.

"Think about it, Aunt Bernie," Parker answered and winked at Tripp. "When you know you are in love, you know it. I knew the minute I laid eyes on Endora that I was going to marry her."

"And when you don't know, you don't pretend." Willa Rose shook off his arm and turned to face Mary Jane. "Thank you for taking us in, ma'am."

Bernie shook her finger at Tripp. "Don't joke with me on a day like this. I'm not in the mood for it."

"Who said I was joking? Maybe I'm like Parker. Willa Rose might not know her own heart just yet," he said.

"You are very welcome." Mary Jane crossed the room and hugged them both. "I'm glad y'all got here safely. I was worried about you."

"This place is a haven in a very real storm," Tripp said.

"We hope so," Mary Jane said. "Ivy is making a fresh batch of hot pancakes. The rest of breakfast is on the bar, so help yourselves. A little food and warmth will make all of you…" She paused and waved at Hank and Knox. "Y'all come on in, hang up your coats, and get some warm food in your stomachs. Everyone else has already eaten this morning. We're just sitting around the table having coffee and visiting."

Tripp helped Willa Rose with her coat and hung it on a

rack beside the back door before removing his and motioning toward the bar. "Ladies first."

"Who told you I was a lady?" she asked.

"If it walks like a duck, and all that." Tripp ushered her across the room with a hand on her lower back. When she had loaded her plate, he carried it to the table for her and set it down. Then he pulled out a chair and seated her right beside Bernie.

"Thank you," Willa Rose muttered.

"Any lady who spends the night at my place gets breakfast and treated like a queen," Tripp said.

Knox sat down across from Willa Rose. "But, Brother, she woke up next to me, not you."

The way Bernie was trying to focus on one after another of all three of them had to make her dizzy. But Tripp figured she had it coming after the mistletoe.

With that thought, he looked up and saw a sprig tied with a red ribbon hung above every single door. It was going to be a long few days for sure.

"I think I need a shot of good whiskey in my coffee," Bernie finally said.

"I think I need someone to explain to me what these three kids are talking about," Hank said as he took his place at the end of the table.

Willa Rose could have thrown both Callahan brothers out in the snow with the hopes that they would turn into Popsicles, but she would be damned if she let either one, or both, get the best of her that morning. Especially after the comments they had both just made. She would show them that she could hold her own even against double odds.

"It's like this, Daddy..." She took the time to slowly butter a biscuit before she went on. "I got stuck in the snow and knocked on Tripp's door. I hoped he would help by giving my SUV a push with his truck, but he was too big of a sissy to go out in the cold and insisted that I spend the night at his house."

No one needs to know that the chemistry between us was hot enough to melt all the snow in the state of Texas.

"Hey, now!" Tripp argued. "I was using good common sense and protecting you. You weren't complaining when you got into that warm bath, were you? If we'd tried to get your vehicle unstuck, then we would both have frostbite today."

She raised an eyebrow. "I'm telling this story, and it was a hot shower, not a bath."

"He's just holding the tail, right?" Bernie said.

"What does that mean?" Ivy asked.

"It's something old people used to say. It means that someone has bitten off more than they can handle. Like Willa Rose is wrestling with a tiger and all Tripp is doing is holding the tail."

"I'm picturing that in my mind, and it's funny," Ivy said with a giggle.

"My part of the story is that a gentleman does not throw a lady out in the cold," Tripp argued.

"But he should take his pansy ass outside and help push her truck out of the snow," Bernie shot back.

"He hasn't won that bet you've got going yet, Miz Bernie," Willa Rose told her.

"How did you… I don't know…" Bernie sputtered. "And you can call me Aunt Bernie. Miz Bernie makes me feel old, and I am not old."

"The lifeblood of small Texas towns is good, juicy gossip," Willa Rose said. "Everyone knows who did what, who they did it with, and if breakfast was involved the next morning. If I call you 'Aunt Bernie,' then everyone will think I'm staying in Spanish Fort, and you'll lose money," Willa Rose said, intending to draw out the story long enough to make both of the Callahan brothers' faces turn scarlet.

Ivy brought a platter piled high with pancakes and set it in the middle of the table. "So, you stayed all night in Tripp's house?" She sat down, propped her elbows on the table, and leaned her chin on her fists.

Willa Rose nodded and forked three pancakes over onto her plate. "I didn't have a choice. It was either stay or walk home, and I would have frozen to death if I'd chosen the latter."

"Like I said, it was the only sensible thing to do," Tripp added.

Willa Rose checked the brothers' faces. Neither had turned even a faint shade of red yet, but the best was yet to come, so she went on. "After living with snoring parents for eighteen years and then moving back in with them when

Mama took sick, I've learned to sleep through any kind of noise. And besides I was very tired…" She checked Tripp and found him grinning like he was enjoying the story.

"She's right," Hank agreed. "We had a tornado scare a while back, and I practically had to break down her door to wake her up so we could go to the storm cellar."

"This sounds like a happy-ever-after fairy tale," Ivy sighed.

"Maybe more like a love triangle." Parker chuckled. "I can't wait to hear the rest of it and then go upstairs to tell Endora."

"Yes!" Willa Rose exclaimed. "You are right, Parker. That's exactly what it was. Note that I said 'was' and not 'is.'"

"Dear Lord!" Bernie gasped. "Mary Jane, where are you hiding the whiskey? I don't even care if it's the cheap stuff. I need a shot."

"Not at this time of the morning," Mary Jane told her.

"Now, Aunt Bernie…" Tripp reached across the table and patted her hand. "You were wrong before when you tried to use your matchmaking magic on Brodie. Remember that fiasco with the woman who got mad when Audrey set Pansy down on the table at Tertia and Noah's café? And how about that other one—Lucy, no that's not right—Linda was her name. She was looking at wedding dresses before she and Brodie even went on a first date."

"I want to hear those stories when Willa Rose finishes this one," Ivy said. "Living here is like watching those reality shows."

Bernie shook off Tripp's hand and glared at him. "I was just testing the waters to see what kind of woman Brodie really needed. I never meant for him to actually get serious about either one of those two. And you are trying to change the subject here. What do you mean, Willa Rose woke up with Knox?"

"Did I say it was Knox?" Tripp asked with an innocent look on his face. "Brodie is my brother too."

"Mary Jane, why are you sitting there?" Bernie asked. "You're supposed to be getting out the whiskey. If you don't hurry, I might have a heart attack."

"Remember the rules. No hard drinking before evening," Mary Jane reminded her.

"But it really was me that slept with her, not Brodie," Knox admitted. "The electricity flickered in my trailer, so I went over to Tripp's house. I stay over there about half the time anyway. It was dark, so I figured he was asleep, so I let myself in…" He had everyone's attention, but he stopped midsentence. "I believe that in addition to selling antiques, Willa Rose could possibly write stories."

"Quit trying to get off track," Bernie demanded. "I want to know what happened. I've got a lot of money riding on this."

Willa Rose turned slightly and locked eyes with Bernie. "Put me down for twenty dollars on the side that I won't stay here for more than six months. And if there's another bet going on which Callahan brother I'll end up with, let's just say right now the jury is still out."

"You are amazing," Tripp whispered so softly that she was the only one who heard it.

"I believe you might have met your match, Bernie," Joe Clay chuckled.

Willa Rose buttered her pancakes and covered them with warm maple syrup. "Mama always heated up the syrup, didn't she, Daddy?"

Bernie fidgeted.

Hank nodded and gave her one of those looks that terrified her when she was a little girl. One such frown would do far more to correct her than grounding her for a week.

Sparks danced between her and Tripp.

Knox had finished his breakfast and was sipping on his second cup of coffee when she decided to talk again. He had to know what was coming, but dammit! He didn't have the faintest sign of a blush.

"Okay…" She took another bite of pancake. "So, there I was sleeping as sound as a bear in the winter when I rolled over and found Knox in bed with me."

Knox held up both palms. "In my defense, not only does she sleep soundly, she doesn't move at all. I didn't even know there was anyone on the other side of the bed when I went in the room. I turned back the covers and even groaned when I crawled into bed. Then a few hours later I woke up to someone screaming like a coyote with his foot caught in a trap."

"He jumped up like he'd been stung by a whole hive of bees and grabbed a pillow to cover…" Willa Rose smiled.

"Because even if there's snowdrifts piling up to the windowsills, he sleeps the same way he was born."

"You mean naked?" Ivy asked.

"Exactly," Willa Rose answered. "There I was trying to avert my eyes and scream at the same time when Tripp rushed in like he was going to save the maiden in distress. Then we figured out the power was off, and we came here. The end."

"That was a hell of a place to stop the story," Hank said.

"I'd say it was a perfect way," Bernie disagreed. "I think all of you just conjured up this story to rile me up. Well, you win. You got me."

Willa Rose leaned over and gave Bernie a sideways hug. "Of course we did. We made it all up on the way over here this morning. That's the real reason Tripp carried me into the house. We were teasing you just like, I'm sure, you are teasing us about that big bet going on about when I leave."

"Well, it's a good story," Ivy sighed. "I believed every word of it, and I don't think you should ever leave here. If I had a chance to stay, I would. This is like a little piece of heaven."

"Well, it *is* called the Paradise," Mary Jane told her.

"Soon as I finish these pancakes, I'm going upstairs to see if I can fool Endora into believing me," Willa Rose said.

"That will be a great distraction for her," Parker said. "She's so worried these babies will be born right here at the Paradise because we can't get her to the hospital."

Ivy cleared the dirty plates and put them in the dishwasher.

"If that happens, Yasmin is a midwife. She delivers a lot of babies when we are in Oklahoma and has even brought a couple into the world on the road. If the twins decide to make their appearance before this storm is over, she'll know what to do."

Chapter 11

Willa Rose opened her eyes the next morning and thought she was at home in Poetry. She focused on the ceiling, then looked over to the window only to find someone had replaced it with French doors. Whoever put them up had forgotten to take the film off the glass because everything looked blurry outside.

She groaned loudly, and everything flooded back to remind her where she was.

Thank goodness for the sister who left things behind, she thought as she removed Bo's nightshirt and dressed for the day. When she stepped out into the hallway, she came face-to-face with Tripp.

"Good morning to you," he said.

"Right back at you," she said.

"I believe that Hank was right."

"About what?" Willa Rose covered a yawn with her hand. "That it's going to snow forever? I've already checked outside, and it hasn't let up yet."

Tripp stepped to one side of the steps leading down to the foyer. "No, about you sleeping through a tornado. Ladies first."

"Aren't you going to carry me down?" she teased.

"No, ma'am," Tripp answered. "Aunt Bernie gets up at the crack of dawn and is probably already having coffee. She'll catch on if we keep lying to her."

"Did I hear my name?" Bernie said as she came out of a room behind them. Pepper tugged at the leash so hard that it was hard to know which one of them was leading the other. "That was quite a night, wasn't it?"

"What makes you…" Willa Rose stopped and then cocked her head to one side when she heard a strange sound coming out of one of the bedrooms. Was that a kitten or a puppy? Did that big mama cat that roamed around the house and tormented Pepper have babies last night?

"The whole household was topsy-turvy last night," Bernie said. "We've all been up since midnight waiting for the babies. I'm surprised that you didn't hear Endora cussing at Parker and telling him that he would be having the next baby."

"Endora cussed?" Willa Rose gasped.

"She did, but Parker has forgiven her. Still, in amongst all the carrying water up and down the stairs, and Endora trying to walk the babies out of her body, how did you sleep?"

"I really do sleep like the dead. I can't believe someone"—she cut her eyes around at Tripp—"didn't wake me up."

"You are awake," Mary Jane called out from behind them. "Do you want to come see the babies?"

"They came into the world at one o'clock this morning," Bernie said.

"You should have wakened me," Willa Rose scolded Tripp.

"If a tornado couldn't do the job, how could I?" he asked.

Bernie gave Tripp a gentle shove. "Go on with her. You know you are itchin' to see them again, but we need to talk—alone—sometime this morning. And, besides, Pepper needs to get outside or he's going to burst."

"Want me to take him out?" he asked.

"No, and now that Willa Rose is out of hearing, I'll say what I've got to say."

"Okay," Tripp answered. "Shoot!"

"I still don't think that woman is right for you," she said in a low tone, "and I intend to work harder at finding a suitable woman for you. I'm willing to let you get your heart broken, but don't come cryin' to me when it happens because I will tell you, 'I told you so.'"

"That's mighty nice of you." Tripp chuckled. "She's only been here a week. I don't know if I would ask her out if I *had* your blessing, but I will remember that you are saving that 'I told you so' especially just for me."

But a little harmless flirting and banter is more fun than I remember, he thought.

"Fair enough," Bernie said. "The bets are still on. If God spoke from the clouds and told her to make her home here, I don't think she would listen to Him. But I see the way she looks at you, and I can predict that she will ask you to leave with her, and that will break Mary Jane's heart."

"Not going to happen," Tripp said. "I'm happy here."

Bernie started down the stairs. "For now, but what about six months from now?"

"Can't predict the future," Tripp muttered and headed back to Endora's room.

Willa Rose slipped out into the hallway before he had taken two steps. "Yasmin is still here and helping Endora with breast-feeding techniques for twins. It's less stressful without a room full of people. She's even sent Parker off to have some breakfast and then bring up a tray for Endora. They are so beautiful, Tripp."

Tripp motioned again for her to go ahead of him. "How many newborn babies have you seen?"

"Plenty," she answered. "Sometimes Mama and I kept the nursery at our church. How about you?"

"No more than five or six, and they all look just alike to me," he answered.

"They do not!" she argued. "Endora's girls do not look a thing like Luna's son did when he was born."

"How do you know what Garrett looked like then? You weren't around these parts in October."

"Ever heard of *pictures*?" she smarted off. "Folks use their phones to take them these days. I'll teach you how to use yours for that purpose after breakfast. It's so easy that even a monkey could master the skill."

"Could a monkey carry you from truck to house?" he countered.

She kept walking toward the kitchen and dining area.

"Possibly, if he was trained." She stepped aside to let Parker pass through with a tray laden with food.

"Y'all check your phones in about two minutes. When I get back to the room, there's going to be pictures, and an announcement made. We're doing it this way so the whole family gets the news at the same time," he said with a broad smile.

"Can you give us a little hint?" Tripp asked.

"Just listen for the ping. Endora has set up a group that includes the whole family. She included you and Hank on it, too, Willa Rose."

"Thank you, but…"

"No buts. You and Hank are now family," he said as he disappeared up the stairs.

"If we are family, then that means you might have some monkey DNA in you, too," Tripp teased.

"I did not call you a monkey," she protested. "I said that one could be trained to take pictures with a phone."

"Close enough." He grinned.

Ivy was setting a pan of fresh biscuits on the counter when he and Willa Rose arrived in the kitchen. People were either at the table or standing in line for the buffet.

"Hey, does anyone know what this message thing is all about?" Tripp asked.

"I imagine since the rest of her siblings can't be here, Endora is about to announce the birth of her girls," Mary Jane answered.

"Has she named them yet?" Willa Rose got in line behind Luna.

"She's had them named since she found out they were twin girls," Luna answered, "but she wouldn't even tell me, which is just downright not right. I told her Garrett's name the day I found out I was having a boy. She and I are identical twins. We are supposed to share everything."

Willa Rose was standing next to Ivy when her phone pinged. She pulled it out of her hip pocket, touched the screen, and held it out so Ivy could see too. A picture of Endora and Parker each holding a baby showed up, and then a birth announcement: Sarah Jane Martin and Stella Jo Martin, born December 4, each weighing exactly six pounds. Sarah means "happy" and Stella means "star," and they're named after Mama and Daddy. We can't wait for everyone to meet them. A special thanks to Yasmin for her help.

Willa Rose heard a sniffle and glanced over to see tears streaming down Mary Jane's cheeks. Joe Clay pulled her close to his chest and buried his face in her hair. Willa Rose clicked on the camera icon and took pictures of the expressions on everyone's faces and then sent them to Endora.

"That was so sweet." Ivy's voice cracked. "When Grandpa was alive, I felt like we had a family with our carnival folks. Not so much anymore. I know there are bets going on about whether you should go back to your hometown, but I think you should stay here."

"Why?" Willa Rose went back to the message and looked

at the pictures of the newborns once again. Tripp was wrong about all babies, and if she could have one, she wouldn't care what it came out looking like.

"Number one"—Ivy held up a finger—"because of the way Tripp's eyes light up when he looks at you. Number two"—another finger went up—"because of the same thing happening when you realize he's in the room. And number three"—a third finger shot up—"because you would be crazy to leave all this love."

"Maybe there's love back in my hometown," Willa Rose said.

"Nobody has that kind of luck, to have a setup like this in two places," Ivy told her.

Luna nudged Willa Rose on the arm. "Those babies are darling, and I love that they named them after Mama and Daddy, but we were in line for food."

"You go on ahead of me. I'll just take one more peek at them," Willa Rose said.

"Are you getting baby fever?"

Willa Rose slipped the phone back into her hip pocket. "Of course not."

She didn't lie. She wasn't *getting* the yearning for a child of her own. She'd had it since last year when she found out that she could never have a child. That's what broke her and her ex up. He wanted and needed a son to carry on the family name since he was the last male in the Holton line. She had never told her father the real reason that their relationship ended, because he wanted grandchildren so much.

Erica had bragged when she came to Vada's funeral that she didn't intend to ever have a child. According to her, all they did was tie a person down, and she intended to be free until the day she died. Besides, any kids she produced wouldn't be Hank's kin anyway.

When Tripp sat down beside her, his shoulder brushed against hers. Sparks that flew around them were so hot that it was a miracle the folks at the table didn't see them—or at the very least feel the heat off them.

"Didn't your mama ever tell you that your face could freeze that way?" he asked.

"What way?"

"Like you are having a mental argument with someone, or maybe trying to work out a big problem?" he answered. "Pass the picante sauce, please. It makes scrambled eggs so much better."

She forced a smile and held up the half-full jar. "This picante?"

"Yes, ma'am," Tripp answered. "Knox makes that stuff, and it's better than anything you can buy at the store."

"Are you sure you want this picante?" she teased.

He reached for it. "Yes, I do."

Ivy sat down across the table. "Those babies are so, so cute. Yasmin has only helped deliver one set of twins before these."

Willa Rose held the jar out toward her. "Tripp tells me this is really good on eggs. Want to try some?"

"I was just about to ask you to pass it to me," Ivy

answered. "I had it yesterday, and he's right. It is good. Mary Jane told me that Knox makes it by the gallon and keeps her supplied."

Tripp leaned over and whispered, "I hope your face does freeze."

"It almost did yesterday, but a knight in…" She paused as his warm breath on her neck caused her to forget her own name.

"In shining armor," Ivy finished for her. "What did Tripp do?"

"He saved me from freezing to death," Willa Rose answered. "But he didn't ride out in the snow on a white horse."

Ivy poured sauce over her eggs and then set the jar back in the middle of the table. "Grandpa watched old western movies late at night when we were home in Oklahoma. I never understood why. From the first scene in the show, the bad guys' horses and hats were black. The hero always had a white horse and hat. Why not just see what color horse they rode and what hat they wore and then go watch something more modern? After all, the man with the white hat would be the hero in the end."

Tripp reached for the jar at the same time Willa Rose did. His hand closed around hers.

Dammit! Why is he such a big temptation? she wondered.

"Well?" Ivy asked.

"Because knowing the end isn't the important thing. It's the journey and what happens between the first scene and the last that matters," Willa Rose answered.

"So, this flirting y'all are doing is just the journey?" Ivy asked.

"We're not flirting," Tripp argued. "We are arguing, and I concede, Willa Rose. A gentleman lets the ladies go first. So, you go ahead and put a couple of spoonsful of Knox's picante sauce on your eggs."

Ivy giggled. "Y'all are so funny. Why aren't you dating? Life would never be dull if you did."

"I thought teenagers called it something different," Willa Rose said.

Ivy shrugged. "I watch Toks, but y'all are too old to go through all the talking, then sleeping together, and then dating. Just get with the program and admit that you like each other."

"Just how old do you think we are?" Tripp asked.

"Maybe about as old as my mama would be if she was alive."

"Aren't you sixteen?" Willa Rose asked. "If I was your mother, I would have had a baby when I was twelve."

"Then I guess you are about twenty-eight. It's way past time that you did more than flirt," Ivy said.

"Like I said, we aren't flirting." Willa Rose gasped. "We are bantering or maybe even arguing."

"Same difference," Ivy told her and set about eating her breakfast.

Chapter 12

WILLA ROSE DRESSED IN her own clothes on Thursday morning and took the bedding and Bo's things down to the laundry room. "Back to being plain old me instead of a sassy woman like Bo. It had to be the clothes that made me act the way I did," she muttered on the way out of the bedroom.

"Who says you are plain?" Tripp asked.

His voice startled her so badly that she dropped the basket, and it tumbled all the way to the bottom of the stairs. "Never sneak up on anyone that way."

"I'll admit I was quiet coming out of my room, which is right next to Endora and Parker's. I didn't want to wake the babies, but you must slip into your own world when you talk to yourself," he said.

"Doesn't everyone?" She headed down the stairs and realized that changing from Bo's jeans and shirts into her own didn't make her less sassy.

Tripp followed behind her. "Not me. I'm fully aware of my surroundings at all times."

"Yeah, right." She shoved what had landed in complete disorder back into the basket. "You are perfect."

"Thank you so much for noticing." He stepped over a

bra and two pairs of panties on his way to the laundry. "And it's *not* ladies first today. It's first come, first served."

"That's not very gentlemanly," she said.

"I want to get this done so Hank and I can get back to the shop, so today I'm not a gentleman."

"No one is going anywhere until we are all three finished," she reminded him. "Knox brought all of us in his truck."

"Hank got his laundry done last night while we waited on the babies. Knox said he doesn't mind taking us to the shop and coming back for you. Your dad is anxious to get to work."

"Him or you?" she asked.

"Maybe a little of both. Being cooped up has got us stir crazy," he answered as he led the way to the laundry room and shoved everything in his basket into the industrial-sized washer. "Still a lot of room if you want to put your stuff in with mine."

"Mixing my underwear with yours would be kind of personal," she said.

He raised an eyebrow. "Hey, you've spent the night with me and slept with my brother. What can be more personal than that?"

Willa Rose didn't even hesitate before she dumped her things in with his. "You are right, but just remember what's in there belongs to Bo, not me. I'll be sure to tell her husband that it was your idea to mix up her underwear with yours."

"You are one mean woman, Willa Rose Thomas," Tripp said.

"Don't ever forget it," she threw over her shoulder on her way to the kitchen.

Maybe it was the fact that the house was so cold that made it seem so empty when Willa Rose walked into it later that morning. She adjusted the thermostat and drew her coat tighter around her body. It seemed like she had been gone weeks instead of two days. She put on a pot of coffee and lit a gingerbread-scented candle, thinking that the scents would make it feel more like home.

She sat down on the sofa, removed her shoes, and propped her feet on a tapestry-covered hassock. Her phone rang, but she didn't recognize the number, so she didn't answer it. In less than a minute it pinged with a text that said: Answer your damn phone, Willa Rose. When it rang a second time, she hit the accept button and said, "Who is this?"

"Is that anyway to talk to your sister?" Erica asked.

Willa Rose bristled. "What do you want?"

A sister is someone who is there for you, like all the Paradise siblings, not one who calls or comes by when they need something.

"You haven't changed. You've always thought you were better than me."

"I'd say it was the other way around," Willa Rose snapped.

"I didn't call to argue." Erica's voice changed to almost nice.

Is there hope even yet? Willa Rose wondered.

"I haven't heard from you in nearly a year, and I've tried to call several times." Willa Rose dialed back her own anger.

"I changed my phone number a couple of times. Yes, men were involved," Erica said, "so don't go getting all preachy at me. Are you and Hank in Poetry still? Or have you finally talked him into selling that antique mall that Mama called home?"

Willa Rose bit back a groan but decided to try to be nice one more time. "No, we moved to Spanish Fort. It might or might not be permanent," she answered.

"Are you still with that rich guy?"

"No, we broke up just before Mama passed away, which you would know if you would keep in touch," Willa Rose told her.

"My bad," Erica said with a chuckle.

"Are you coming home for Christmas? If so, we are up near the Red River. Spanish Fort, just a little north of Nocona where our great-grandparents are buried."

"Not for Christmas but probably a little before. I'm pregnant and the baby is due any day. I planned to put it up for adoption, but…"

"You are what?" Willa Rose felt the room take a couple of spins.

"You heard me. I'm pregnant, and I do not want the baby," she answered. "Do you want to take the child?"

"You can't just give a baby away," Willa Rose whispered. "There's laws against that, isn't there?"

"Yes, I can, but since you are blood kin, I want you to have a chance before I sign adoption papers," she said.

"But…"

"I've looked into things and talked to the right people. There is a lot of paperwork, but you can be assigned guardianship, and then in a few months we'll go to court, and you can adopt the child."

"Erica, why don't you think about this…"

"I have, and I told you years ago that I do not want to be a mother. So, what do you say?"

Willa Rose felt as if all the air had left her body. What did she say? She couldn't let her mother's only grandchild be given to strangers, and yet, was she ready to take on that kind of responsibility? She was in a new town, a new house, and wasn't even sure about staying for more than a year.

"Of course, I'll take the baby and raise it, but are you sure about this?" she finally answered. "What kind of legal stuff is involved?"

"I've got a good lawyer who will help navigate me through the whole process. Since you are family, he says that it will require a couple of court visits. I'm willing to come back to Texas for those, and I will pay for everything." Erica sounded relieved.

"When is the baby due, and is it a boy or girl?"

"I don't know what it is, but it's due in two weeks," she said. "I don't want to see or hold it, so the arrangements might be made for someone else to bring it to you."

"Erica, that tells me that you aren't sure." Willa Rose's chest tightened at the very idea of having a child and not wanting to even see it. "If we do this, I couldn't bear to lose the baby if you change your mind."

"I will not change my mind," Erica said.

"What about the baby's father? Doesn't he have rights?"

"He's dead," she answered. "I have the death certificate to prove it. An aneurysm two months ago, but we had already decided that we didn't want to be saddled down with a baby."

"Grandparents?" Willa Rose asked.

"Also dead," Erica answered flatly. "Are you going to change your mind?"

"No, never, but…"

"Okay, then. Goodbye, Willa Rose," she said, and the screen went dark.

There's nothing to worry about or to even get excited about, Willa Rose told herself. *Erica has always been fickle, but she has Mama's genes, and she will never give up her baby once she holds it in her arms.*

Tripp was tapping in the last part of an intricate rose on a lady's belt when Willa Rose arrived at noon.

"Hello!" He looked up and smiled. "I'm glad to see you. This morning has been dragging."

"To me it's going by fast," Hank said and waved at her. "I'm just glad that the place has warmed up."

"Hello to both of you," Willa Rose set a slow cooker on the table. "I made a pot of chili and brought it for lunch."

"Bless your heart!" Tripp said.

"In a good or bad way?" she asked.

"The best," Tripp answered.

"There's corn bread, corn chips, and cheese in the vehicle. Daddy likes chili pie, so I brought everything we needed. If you'll go get it, I'll get out some bowls and spoons."

Tripp put on his coat and headed across the room. "Gladly. This is quite a treat from cold sandwiches."

Hank looked up and smiled. "How did you know that I've been craving chili for days?"

"You always said that it's cold weather food," Willa Rose reminded her father. She wanted to tell him about Erica's phone call, but she still didn't believe it would ever happen. No need in getting his hopes up about a grandbaby.

Tripp came back into the shop with a box in his arms. "I can smell the chili from here. It's best when there's a foot of snow outside."

Hank left the workstation and moved over to the table.

"Is the carnival is getting ready to move out?" Willa Rose asked. Anything to keep from blurting out the news of Erica's baby.

"Mary Jane and Joe Clay have invited them to stay until after the Christmas program. If they agree and the roads are clear, they'll leave on Monday," Tripp said.

"About this program…" Willa Rose said as she dipped out the first bowl of chili and handed the ladle to Hank. "Is it a big thing? How many people will attend? And while I'm asking questions, how come no one is putting as much emphasis on Brodie and Audrey's wedding as they are on the Christmas thing?"

"I don't know how many folks will attend the program.

We arrived too late to get in all that last year, so we haven't attended any of the events that go on during this month," Tripp answered and took the ladle from Hank. "The reason behind the wedding is that the house is already decorated, and the wedding is a small affair in the house. Audrey wanted the party to be their reception. Brodie told me that they would leave the next morning for their honeymoon."

"Where's that?" Hank asked.

Tripp laid a wedge of cornbread in his bowl and covered it with chili. "Brodie left that up to Audrey. She chose a place on the beach in Florida. Her old foreman lives down there, and she wants to see him on the way to the house that Brodie rented. Where would you choose, Willa Rose?"

"She's always wanted to go to England," Hank answered. "I told her that I would take her if they ever built a bridge from here to there. I don't like airports or the idea of shooting through the air in what amounts to an overgrown tin can with seats in it."

"I could fly by myself," she said.

"Where's the fun in that?" Tripp asked. "Sharing the experience with someone is half the joy."

"There has to be a marriage before there is a honeymoon," Willa Rose said. "Speaking of that, who's going to take care of Pansy?"

"From love to pigs," Tripp chuckled. "That's quite a jump, but just so you know, I volunteered you for that job. All you have to do is go out to the farm, clean out the little pen they built for her in Audrey's barn, and make sure she has food and water."

"Do I have to tell her bedtime stories, too?" Willa Rose barked.

"That would be great," Tripp answered. "You could choose one of Endora's children's books. I bet Pansy would love any of them."

"You can call them today and un-volunteer me," she said through clenched teeth. "I like Audrey, but I wouldn't clean pig poop for anyone."

Tripp pulled the tab on a can of root beer and took a long drink. "Santa Claus is putting you on the naughty list for that, and for your attitude."

Hank chuckled and took a drink of sweet tea from a bottle. "Y'all remind me of the way me and Vada used to banter. I miss that."

Willa Rose laid a hand on his shoulder. "I'm sorry, Daddy. I didn't mean…"

"Don't be," he interrupted her. "I love the happy memories. Carry on, Tripp. Tell me more about the pig that Willa Rose is going to babysit."

She shook her head. She couldn't be tied down to a pig when a baby would show up on her doorstep any day. "I am not going to do that," she declared. "She's cute, but I'm not going out to that farm and taking care of her. Tripp had no right to volunteer me."

"I'm sorry." Tripp's tone or the expression on his face did not match his words. "I overheard you tell Mary Jane that you were willing to do anything to help with the wedding. I assumed that meant the honeymoon too."

"I did not!"

"How about we bring the pig to your house? That way you wouldn't have to go to the farm in the cold weather, and I understand that she is trained to use a litter pan," Tripp suggested.

A pig in the house with a newborn baby—if Erica proved her wrong? That would never work.

"No!" Willa Rose raised her voice a notch.

"You are a hard woman," Tripp said with a fake sigh. "Since I volunteered you, I guess I'll have to be the one who takes care of Pansy. She's going to be so disappointed. I already told her that you would be there to visit her every evening. Will you at least go with me a few times, so she won't throw a fit and refuse to eat? It wouldn't be a date. That would make Aunt Bernie mad, and we don't want to ruin her holiday."

"I would never go on a date that involved a pig," she said, and wondered if he really volunteered her for the job. If he was teasing, she didn't like it—especially that day.

Yes, you do, the voice inside her head said. *You haven't had so much fun in years, maybe forever.*

Hank chuckled again. "I remember when me and Vada took Erica to the county fair, and she wanted to take a piglet and a lamb home with us. When I told her no, she got so angry that she wouldn't even tell me goodbye the next day when I left on the truck for a week." He glanced over at

Willa Rose. "A few years later, we took you to the same event and you wanted to take home a cow and calf."

"I remember that, and I cried all the way home," she said. "But that doesn't mean I'm going to babysit a pig."

"When you have kids, are you going to let them have pets?" Hank asked.

"That's something I'll never have to make a choice about," she blurted out—and wished she could put the words back in her mouth.

Hank laid down his spoon and raised an eyebrow. "You've always said that you wanted a big family. What changed your mind?"

Willa Rose blinked back tears. "The doctor did when he said that I would never have children of my own. That's the reason why Dillon broke up with me. Since he was the last Holton, he felt it was his duty to carry on the family name."

"Why didn't you tell me then?" Hank frowned.

"Mama was sick, and y'all always wanted grandchildren," she answered. The time was right, but she wasn't going to tell him until it happened. "I didn't want to disappoint either of you. Let's talk about this another time."

"Okay, but I adopted Erica and always felt like she was mine," Hank said.

Too bad she didn't feel like you were hers, Willa Rose thought.

"Knox and I were adopted when we were only days old," Tripp said. "We had wonderful parents, and now we have Mary Jane and Joe Clay. I've always wanted a big family, too, but it doesn't matter to me if they are mine through DNA or adoption papers."

"I don't want to talk about it anymore," Willa Rose said around the lump in her throat. "There is a little pan of gingerbread for dessert. Mama always made it for you during the holidays, Daddy."

"With lemon sauce?"

"Yes, sir." She finally managed a smile. "I'll heat it up in the microwave while y'all finish eating."

While the sauce heated, she wondered if she should even mention that she had talked to Erica earlier that day. Perhaps that would at least break the news gently. She really shouldn't wait until the child was there to tell her father, but she had no idea where to even start.

"No," she mumbled. "No use in getting Daddy's hopes up that she might drop in to see us."

Are you going to help Tripp babysit the pig? Her mother's voice was as clear as if she was standing behind her.

"No, I am not."

Chapter 13

"Endora, are you sure you're up to this?" Willa Rose asked. "I can finalize everything myself with help from Rae and Luna. You had twins less than forty-eight hours ago and haven't even seen a doctor yet."

"Yasmin says they are thriving, and I'm right on track for healing. As soon as the roads are clear, we'll go to the hospital and get checked out, but right now, I can sit on a pillow and help you go over the plans," Endora answered. "Parker is very happy to watch Sarah and Stella sleep. After the program on Sunday, we are going home. Mama wants us to stay a couple of weeks, but the girls need to get adjusted to their own space."

Willa Rose opened her sketch pad to show Endora what she had in mind. "Two little blond girls must bring back memories for her."

"Yes, they do," Mary Jane said as she joined them. "Did Endora tell you that Ivy wants to write books someday? I would love to mentor her, and I can do it from a distance, but…" She paused. "I would like to see her finish her education in a public school and then go on to college. If she goes with the carnival, I'm afraid..." A hard knock on the back door stopped her midsentence. "That will be Zeb."

She hurried across the kitchen and swung the door open. "Come in. Sweet tea or coffee?"

Zeb removed his coat and hung it on the rack. "Snow is melting, but it's still cold enough to aggravate this old hip."

"Can we get you some coffee or sweet tea?" Mary Jane asked.

"Coffee, please, and..."

Ivy peeked around the corner. "And black like you like to see the books at the end of the tour every year. Not running in the red. I'll get it for you. Do you want something, Mary Jane?"

"You are a good kid," Zeb said.

"Coffee is good for me, too, and I like mine with a spoon of sugar," Mary Jane answered. "Zeb, come on into the kitchen and have a seat."

Ivy brought two coffees and a glass of sweet tea for herself to the table and sat down across from Zeb.

Zeb held the warm mug in his hands for several seconds before he took a sip. "Finn said the roads aren't clear, but the bridges are open, so we think we can probably get out of your way tomorrow."

"Could you possibly stay a couple of extra days?" Mary Jane asked. "Our Christmas program is Sunday, and we'd love to have you and the animals here for the event. Plus, we want to have a big supper for the whole carnival in the barn as a farewell party for all y'all."

"We figured you'd want us out of your hair as soon as possible, but if we can be a help for your program, we'd be glad to stay over until Monday morning," Zeb answered.

Willa Rose started to say something, but Endora shook her head. "We can't see around the corner into the kitchen, but we can hear what's being said. Mama is about to ask Zeb about Ivy living here."

Willa Rose was reminded of all the times she hid in the shadows and eavesdropped on adult conversations. Like the day before Erica had stormed out of the house with what she could throw into a big, black garbage bag. Willa Rose still shivered at what she overheard that morning when her mother and sister were arguing in the kitchen. Erica had said that she was not a Thomas, and she was going to change her name back to her birth name, and that she was never coming back to Poetry.

Vada was crying so hard that Willa Rose finally left her hiding place and tried to console her mother, but all that did was make Erica scream at her and then stomp off upstairs. She did come back to Poetry a few times. There was hope when she arrived, but it always left with her, and Vada was sad for days afterward. Willa Rose usually wished that her sister would stay away.

"Zeb, since you are the nearest thing to a relative that Ivy has, I want to talk to you about letting her stay here at the Paradise when the carnival leaves," Mary Jane said.

He shook his head. "I don't know about that. I promised her grandpa on his deathbed *I* would take care of her."

"Is there legal paperwork, like a will or a trust fund?" Mary Jane asked.

"None of that," Zeb said. "Just a handshake between me and my old friend. He didn't have anything when he died. I'd been helping him pay for the medicine he needed, and he lived in my rental houses when we weren't on the road. I guess it would be up to Ivy, not to me."

Mary Jane stood up and brought a platter of cookies to the table. "A few years back I filed all the paperwork to foster children," she said as she sat back down. "Help yourself. Sometimes coffee sloshes around in my stomach if I don't have something to soak it up."

"Thank you." Zeb reached for a cookie and took a bite. "How does this work legally?"

"I called the caseworker who handled everything when I wanted to foster a child," Mary Jane said. "She says my standing paperwork is still good, so it would be legal, but there would have to be a court date for you to relinquish whatever rights you have to be her guardian. I will put Ivy in the public school where my daughter, Rae, teaches. When she graduates, I promise that I will send her to the college or university of her choice if you will let her stay here with us."

Mary Jane reminds me of Mama. She would have taken in a homeless child if Erica hadn't broken her heart so badly.

Tears welled up in Willa Rose's eyes. Mary Jane wanted to take Ivy and give her a good life, and Erica talked about giving her baby away.

"What do you want, Ivy?" Zeb asked.

"The carnival has been my home my whole life," she answered. "I'm third generation, and I don't know anything else. But Finn has already said that I won't have a job when we get back to Oklahoma."

"What if I told him that he had to keep you?"

"You will be laid up with your hip surgery, and then retired," Ivy said. "Finn doesn't like me, and to tell the truth, I don't like him much either. I don't want to be where I'm not wanted. So, the answer is yes, I would like to stay here. These people have made me feel like family."

"Then I guess I'm fine with that. But remember, Ivy, we are only an hour away from here. You will be welcome there anytime you want to come home, and you visit us anytime, and whenever things get settled, I'll come back for the court thing."

"Yes, sir." She beamed and circled around the table to hug him.

"Yes!" Endora pumped her fist into the air. "Now let's go over the plans for the program."

Willa Rose opened the book, but her mind stayed on what she'd just heard. Would she be willing to take in a basically homeless child? Was the Universe trying to tell her that she could be a mother even if she couldn't give birth to a child?

"You'll have to be in complete charge," Endora was saying when Willa Rose tuned in again. "We salvaged enough curtains from the church to use one last time. There's enough family to meet up on Saturday night and help move things from the yard here at the Paradise to the staging area. Daddy says he'll get the sleigh put in the middle part for the older folks to gather around."

"The cutouts of Frosty and Santa can go on the first part," Willa Rose said.

"And the back part will have the manger, the camel and sheep," Endora added. "We've got this all down well enough."

Willa Rose made a few notations on her sketch pad and closed it. "I'll be here tomorrow morning right after breakfast."

"Come for breakfast," Endora said. "Tripp and Hank have already volunteered to help, and Remy and Parker will be here. Your job is to give orders and make sure everything is ready for Sunday."

"I can do that," Willa Rose said.

Tripp picked up the phone when it rang, saw that it was Bernie, and answered it on the third ring. "Hello, Miz Bernie, how are you today?"

"You better get to the Paradise quick. I need help," she said in a frantic tone.

"What's happening?" Tripp asked, but Bernie had already hung up on him. "Hank, something is going on at the Paradise," he said as he shoved his arms down into his coat. "I'll be back as soon as I can."

Hank waved him away. "I'll hold down the fort. I don't expect many folks will come out today anyway."

"Thanks," Tripp said and rushed out to his truck. His mind ran in fast circles. Had something happened to Willa Rose, and the family needed him to break the news to Hank? From the way Bernie was talking, it might even be that Endora or the new twins needed help getting to the hospital. The roads weren't cleared yet, but he would do his dead level best to get her there if that was the issue.

He was careful to drive in the ruts already made by tires, but there was still a layer of ice under the snow that made him feel like he was hydroplaning most of the way. His phone rang again when he came to a long, greasy slide beside the back door. He picked it up and answered it without even checking the caller ID.

"Don't stop there. Come on down here. This is where the emergency is," Bernie shouted into his ear.

He put the truck back in gear and drove through snow down to her trailer. She looked like a homeless person, all wrapped up in a patchwork quilt and with the wind blowing her red hair across her face.

"Do you need me to take you to the hospital? Why didn't you call Joe Clay? He was closer," he yelled as he jumped out of the truck.

"Do you really think I'd go anywhere looking like this?" she barked. "It's Pepper, not me."

"Does he need a vet?"

"No, he needs rescuing. Brodie isn't answering his phone, and neither is Audrey. You are next in line so it's your job to get that pesky pig and save my dog," Bernie told him.

"I've had enough of Pansy leading my precious Pepper into trouble. For all I care, you can roast her for supper tonight. They're under the snow and…" She pointed. "There he is now. Every now and then he pokes his head up for air, but he won't backtrack and come to me."

"Looks like they're headed for the barn," Tripp said as he stepped out into the snow again. "You go on back inside and get warm. I'll run that rascal down and bring him straight to you."

"You better, or I'll match you up with a shrew of a woman," Bernie threatened.

The only time Tripp had seen a trail like the one in front of him was when he was a little boy. His mother had been furious when she saw what a gopher had done to her perfectly manicured lawn. The gardener had finally flushed the critter out by flooding the original hole.

"It's bigger than a gopher," he muttered, "and water wouldn't work."

Pepper's head appeared about ten feet in front of him, and the animal had the audacity to bark at him before he went back under to follow Pansy. Evidently the pig was the snowplow, and Pepper was running behind her. Like he thought, the animals were digging their way to the barn, so instead of following the trail they left behind, he headed off in that direction.

When he was inside, Willa Rose looked up from the area at the back of the building and frowned. "Are you stalking me?"

"No, ma'am," he answered and began checking the perimeter of the place. "I found it!"

"What did you find?" Willa Rose's voice echoed across the big, empty space.

"A hole," he shouted.

"You are telling me that you waded through all this snow to find a hole?"

"Yes, and any minute, Pansy and Pepper are going to come through it. As soon as they do, you chase them away and I'll plug the hole with a bale of hay," he said.

"Are you ordering me or asking?"

Tripp dropped down on one knee, took Willa Rose's hand in his, and said, "Miz Thomas, will you please chase a pig and a Chihuahua across the barn so I can cover up this hole? Aunt Bernie is about to have a heart attack because her dog is lost in the snow."

She jerked her hand back. "Get up off the floor. If someone comes in, they'll think…"

"That I'm proposing." Tripp chuckled. "Today I just need help with a pig and a dog, but we can talk about the joys of matrimony in the future."

She backed up and sat down on the bale of hay. "I will tell you no if that subject ever comes up."

He sat down beside her. "Is that because you can't have children?"

"It's because I'm not staying here, and you would never leave. Shhh…." She cocked her head to one side. "I hear Pansy grunting and Pepper yipping. They'll be here soon."

"Does that mean you are going to help me corral them?"

"Yes, I will, but I'm not trudging all the way to Bernie's place to take Pepper home," she answered.

"How about going with me out to the farm to take Pansy back?" he asked.

"Only if you don't get down on a knee again," she agreed.

"Fair enough. See that snow coming through the hole? They're on the final stretch now."

A white sifting landed on Willa Rose's boot. "How do they know where the hole is? They can't see it, and there's ice under the snow so they can't smell the trail in the dirt."

"The heart knows what it wants, and Pansy likes all these new critters the carnival brought with them. I wonder if she grew up on a farm and misses it," Tripp answered.

Pansy's snout came through the hole first. Her round little body followed, and she took off in a blur toward the pen with the other animals. Pepper stopped long enough to shake away the snow that had fallen on him, and then he followed her.

"My job is done," Willa Rose said.

"Oh, no, it's not," Tripp argued. "You said you would hold Pansy on the trip to the farm. She'll take off as soon as the door is open if you don't."

"I did not agree to hold that pig," she argued.

Tripp shoved the bale of hay over the hole and grabbed Pepper the next time he whizzed by. "Playtime is over. You have to go home now."

The dog yipped and tried to wiggle free, but Tripp held

on tightly. "I'll be back as soon as I can. Close the door behind me or we'll be chasing Pansy again."

"You will be running her down, not me," Willa Rose declared.

He heard the door slam shut when he had taken a couple of steps and smiled. Pansy could root out from under a pen, or into a barn with a dirt floor, but there was no way the silly pig could open a barn door.

Bernie met them on the porch and took Pepper from his arms. "If you ever do something like this again," she told Pepper, "I won't share my Irish coffee with you for a week. I'd invite you inside, Tripp, but you need to take that pig home before I see to it that she goes with the carnival on Monday morning. She's a bad influence on my poor Pepper."

"I'll tell Brodie that Pansy is on probation," he promised.

"Next time she goes straight to jail. She does not pass Go or get to romp around with Pepper," Bernie said and carried Pepper inside.

Tripp retraced his footsteps back to the barn and eased inside carefully so Pansy wouldn't slip past him. He blinked several times before his eyes adjusted from the sun's bright light creating a blinding effect on the snow. When he could fully focus, he couldn't believe the sight in front of him.

Willa Rose was sitting on the hard dirt floor with Pansy snoring in her lap. He tiptoed over to them and reached down to pick up the animal, but Willa Rose shook her head. "You go get the truck and pull it up close to the barn. I'll carry her out and pet her to keep her calm on the trip."

"You didn't like her when I volunteered you to watch her," Tripp said.

"I never said that. I just didn't want to babysit her for a whole week," she protested. "She's a sweetheart, but I've got an antique store to get organized so I can have a grand opening on Valentine's Day."

Pansy grunted a couple of times on the way to the truck, but she didn't open her eyes. Tripp opened the door for Willa Rose and eased it shut when she and Pansy were settled into the passenger seat.

"She must like you," he said as he started the engine. "Am I understanding right? You are warming up to the idea of starting your store?"

"I'm not sure, but all the stuff will be here, so I might as well give it a try," she answered.

He drove slowly and kept in the ruts. "Valentine's Day will be a good time to have a grand opening."

"Why do you think so?"

"It's on a Saturday."

"I didn't even think of that," she said, "but how did you already know what day it's on?"

"A customer ordered a saddle for her husband, and it has to be finished by Valentine's Day. I marked it on the calendar before the storm and saw that it was on a Saturday."

The pig's snores were the only noise in the truck for a few minutes. As if she knew Brodie was nearby, she woke up when Tripp saw Brodie coming toward them in the cab of a tractor with a grader on the front. Trip pulled up beside him and rolled down the window. "We found something at the Paradise that belongs to you. Bernie is so mad that flames are coming out her ears because Pansy led Pepper through the snow to the barn. You might want to chain her to your bedpost until Bernie gets over her mad spell."

Brodie got out of the tractor and took Pansy from Willa Rose. "Thanks for bringing her home again. We probably need to get some more small animals in the spring to keep her company. I figure if we buy few goats, they could keep the ground under the fruit trees cleaned up for me."

"Sounds like a good idea to me," Tripp said. "But on a different note, you do know that the sun is supposed to shine for the next few days and nighttime temps are going to be in the fifties. You don't really have to do this."

"Maybe not, but the weatherman has been wrong, and I want folks to be able to get to the Paradise for the program," he answered as he shoved Pansy into the passenger seat of the tractor. "And on top of that, Audrey is dying to hold Endora's new babies, and we're going there for supper tonight. See y'all later." He got into the tractor and started the engine.

"One more job well done," Tripp said. "You want to go on to the farm and visit with Audrey this afternoon?"

"Not really. Mary Jane invited me to have supper with the family tonight," she answered.

"Okay then. I'll drop you off and get back to work."

"You won't be coming in with me?" she asked.

"Only if you get down on one knee," he teased.

Willa Rose air slapped him on the arm. "I'm not that kind of woman."

"So, you don't propose to men?"

"I do not," she answered.

Chapter 14

Willa Rose had been to carnivals and state fairs where fortune tellers plied their charms, but she didn't believe in them. She always read her fortune cookies at the end of a very good meal of Chinese food, but she got something in return for her money those times.

"Your turn, Willa Rose," Audrey said when she came out of the brightly colored curtained-off section of the barn.

"No thanks."

"Scared of what she might reveal?" Audrey asked.

"Maybe," Willa Rose answered.

Audrey gave her a gentle shove. "It's all in fun. Go on in and see what tomorrow holds."

Willa Rose took a step forward. "What's around the corner for you?"

"A happy marriage, with four kids but not without arguments," Audrey beamed.

Willa Rose raised both eyebrows. "I bet she tells all the women that, and she makes the men believe they will find happiness after they finish sowing their wild oats."

"Probably," Audrey agreed, "but when she's telling it, she makes such a big production of it that it's a lot of fun.

Besides, she is kind enough to do this for free tonight. They even set up the carousel for the kids, even though there's only Rae and Gunner's girls and Clayton, who is just a year old."

Willa Rose nodded over her shoulder at Bernie, who was riding a black horse on the carousel. Then she opened the curtain and stepped inside the dimly lit area where Yasmin looked every bit the part of a fortune teller in her multicolored skirt, dangling bracelets, and scarf tied around her long, black hair. "Please have a seat and let's visit about your future."

Willa Rose sat down on the other side of the small card table covered with a turquoise cloth, and just as she expected, there was a crystal ball half the size of a basketball in the middle of the table.

"You are a nonbeliever, yes or no?" Yasmin asked.

"I don't believe in hocus-pocus. Not even Ouija boards or tarot cards," Willa Rose replied. "So, let's talk about Endora instead of me. Parker has taken her and the babies to the hospital in Wichita Falls. They're keeping them overnight to run all the tests. If you were reading Endora's future in this pretty ball, what would you see?"

Yasmin's blue eyes twinkled. "I can only work with the person in front of me, but I can tell you a little. To take her mind off the labor pains, I did a reading for her—with the cards, and just so you know, I don't put much stock in the Ouija board either. She will not have any more children, but those two girls will bring her great joy, both in the journey of raising them and in the grandchildren they will give her in her old age."

Her bracelets jingled as she reached across the table and took Willa Rose's hand in hers. She bent the fingers back slightly and studied the lines in her palm. "This line means you will live a long life"—she ran her finger along one of the wrinkles—"and this one tells me that you have had a heartbreak when it comes to relationships—maybe with a sibling or losing your mother, or both."

Bernie's been talking to you, or maybe Mary Jane or one of the sisters.

"But this one"—Yasmin traced a line close to Willa Rose's little finger with her long, purple fingernail—"tells me that even though you will never forget the pain, you will replace it with happy memories. This one right here says that you are destined for an extraordinarily long relationship that will bring joy to your heart, and you will live to be a grandmother and great-grandmother. When your five sons are grown, they will settle down close to you and your husband, who will always be the love of your life. You will see at least sixty years together before one of you steps into eternity." Her eyes shifted to the crystal ball. "Everything is not crystal clear and is a little foggy. That tells me that everything I see today depends on which path you take. This line is one future, but this one is a different one, and I get nothing from it but regret."

Now, I know this is a bunch of fresh bull crap. I can't have one child, much less five sons.

A cold chill chased down Willa Rose's spine, but she attributed it to the cold wind blowing outside. Everyone had two paths—sometimes daily—so that wasn't anything new, but what Yasmin said about regrets scared Willa Rose. Was there something every bit as wonderful in store for her outside of Spanish Fort? Or would she be sorry that she left something even more amazing behind?

"Which path should I take?" she whispered.

"That is your decision," Yasmin said. "I only tell what I see and feel. You have to make up your mind about what you do with it. Now, you are the last reading for tonight. Let's go get something to eat." She stood up and rounded the table. "This is so kind of Mary Jane and Joe Clay to have a going-away party for us. We are so tired of being cooped up with the weather that we are glad for a little escape tonight, and we are happy to help set things up tomorrow morning. Mary Jane says that we are to have our meals in the house—come-and-go buffets—all day."

"How many people are in the carnival?" Willa Rose stood up and followed Yasmin out into the noisy barn full of people.

"Thirty, last count," she answered. "I see Tripp standing on the other side of the carousel. I'm going over there to flirt with him."

A surge of red-hot jealousy shot through Willa Rose's body and settled in her chest. "I thought you were with Finn."

"I am, but if he can let Bernie think he's single and flirt with you, then it's time I taught him another lesson," she said with half a giggle. "Every now and then I have to remind him that it's my bed he sleeps in. Is that going to be a problem for you?"

"Why should it?" Willa Rose asked. "Did you see a flicker of something in the crystal ball?"

"No, but I have seen Tripp's eyes following you whenever y'all are in the same room. Don't close the door when opportunity knocks, or you might really have regrets later on down whichever path you choose. Have fun tonight and eat some of that delicious barbecue that Joe Clay has fixed for us."

Ivy grabbed Willa Rose by the arm and pulled her out into the crowd. "Come and meet my friend Dara who operates the carousel. Her husband is the mechanic for the carnival and makes sure everything is inspected and safe before we get started." She introduced Dara and Willa Rose and then hurried back over to the food table to help Mary Jane.

"I saw you come out of the makeshift fortune teller's tent with Yasmin. Did you like your fortune?" Dara motioned toward an empty table over against the far wall. "Let's get some food and then go sit down. I spent the whole day helping get that carousel out of the trailer and set up. I'm so hungry I could eat Clyde. Not really, but you get the picture."

Willa Rose had woken up that morning with intentions of spending an hour with Endora and then wrapping presents the rest of the afternoon. Thank goodness for online shopping and that she had brought several rolls of leftover paper from Poetry. The biggest problem had been finding gifts for everyone in the Paradise family when their tradition said that each one could cost no more than five dollars.

"Well?" Dara said as she loaded up her plate with two barbecue sandwiches, potato salad, and baked beans.

Willa Rose had been so engrossed in her own thoughts that it took a moment for her to remember the question. "My future evidently hinges on a choice I will make about which path to take. I must be at the fork of a road, and I'm not sure whether to go right or left."

Dara crossed the barn and set her plate on the table. "Do you know what is at the end of each one?"

"No, but the sign in front of me says that Spanish Fort is to the right and Poetry is to the left," Willa Rose answered. She pulled off her coat and hung it on the back of a chair on the other side of the table.

"You write poetry?"

"No." Willa Rose had been asked that same question several times. "Poetry is the name of the town where I was born and lived until right before Thanksgiving. My dad and I moved up here because he wanted to work for Tripp."

Dara fanned her face with the back of her hand. "That man is sex on a stick. If I wasn't married..."

Another rush of jealousy shot through Willa Rose. "What do you think of Knox?"

"He'd do for a one-night stand or maybe even a fling," Dara replied.

"Why do you say that?" Willa Rose asked and then bit into her sandwich.

"Knox is like an untamable lion. He'd be wild and fun, but he's a lot like Finn. He's pretty to look at, but there's not a lot of depth, so he wouldn't be one for the long haul," Dara said between bites. "Tripp might not be as sexy at first blush, but oh, honey, there's a fire brewing inside his heart and soul."

"Girl, you should be the one telling fortunes, or maybe writing hot, steamy romance books."

"Telling fortunes is Yasmin's job," Dara said. "And I read romance books, including Mary Jane's and Ursula's, but I could never write one. I love to study people, though."

"What do you see in this crowd?"

"A bunch of folks who are eager to get back to Oklahoma, and all y'all who will be glad when the snow is gone and you can get back to your lives. Mary Jane was worried earlier, but when she got word that everything was all right with Endora and the new babies, she was happy."

"What else?"

"Well," Dara glanced around the room. "Right now, Tripp isn't having any of Yasmin's flirting. His eyes were darting around the room, but now that he's found you, he is brushing past her and coming this way."

"Oh, really?" Willa Rose asked.

"Yep, and from what I see, I do believe I will finish my food over by the carousel. That way my sweet husband can have a break," she said with a broad smile.

"One more thing before you go," Willa Rose said. "What do you figure Knox is talking about to that woman over there?"

Dara picked up her plate and took a step. "Have you got something for him?"

"No, but since you study people…"

"Knox is chatting up Julie, who takes care of the cotton candy and popcorn booth. Her mama is retiring this year right along with Zeb. Maybe she'll go home with Knox tonight, but it won't be for anything serious. And now I'm looking at Finn and Yasmin. He got jealous when she was flirting with Tripp, so he will pay attention to her all evening. Anyone else?"

"Nope, that about covers it."

"Then it was right nice meeting you, and maybe we'll visit again when we're setting up for the program."

"Great visiting with you, and let's make sure that tomorrow we find a corner to 'study people.'" Willa Rose air quoted the last two words.

Tripp pulled up a chair beside Willa Rose and sat down. "Yasmin said that she read your palm. She tried to grab mine over there in the corner, but I shoved both of my hands into my jacket pockets. I didn't want Finn to think I was moving in on his property."

"So, women are property to you?" she asked.

"No, ma'am, I am not that kind of guy, but it's no secret that he has staked a claim," Tripp replied.

"That makes her an acre or two or maybe more of nothing but dirt?"

"I'm not going there," he answered. "Did Dara put you in this mood or did you hate the fortune that Yasmin told you?"

"I like Dara, and I don't believe in fortune telling," she snapped, "but she did make me aware of choices having consequences and to be careful that I don't regret my decision."

"About?" Tripp asked.

Before she could answer, Bernie brought two beers over and handed one to Willa Rose and one to Tripp. "I've got my liquor in this root beer."

"That sounds horrible," Tripp shivered.

"Don't knock it until you've tried it," Bernie said. "All the Cokes were gone, or I'd be having Rum and Coke. But there was lots of root beer left, and it's not bad at all with a little kick of Maker's Mark. I'm legal because it's way after five o'clock."

"I didn't see any hard liquor anywhere," Tripp said.

"There isn't any, but I carry a couple of little single serves in my purse. A crowd like this reminds me of my bar when things were hopping. I think we should figure out a way to use the carousel in the Christmas program so we get more use out of it."

"You are jumping from one topic to another, Aunt Bernie." Tripp chuckled. "How many of those little bottles have you had tonight?"

"Not that it's any of your business, but I started with one, and I had an extra that I put into this root beer," she answered. "If you want to go out to my trailer and get yourself a few, it might loosen you up a little."

"This beer will do fine." Tripp held the up the bottle and

touched her can of root beer with it. "Now what idea have you got about the carousel?"

"It's right about where the smallest kids will be singing about Santa Claus coming to town and about old Rudolph," Bernie answered. "They're always picking at their noses or their butts instead of singing, but if they were sitting on the carousel horses, it would make things easier. I asked Dara if the music could be turned off, and she said that wouldn't be a problem."

"That sounds wonderful," Willa Rose agreed—to Tripp's surprise. "Does anyone know if the choir robes survived the church fire?"

"All the costumes were stored in the same room, so I imagine they did," Bernie answered.

"Hey, Yasmin," Willa Rose yelled across the room and motioned her over to the table.

"Want me to redo your fortune?" Yasmin asked.

"Not right now," Willa Rose replied. "But I'm making a few last-minute changes to the program. This old barn has lofty ceilings and most of our sound equipment got burned up in the church fire. We need a backup choir to line up around the edges of the building and help us sing. We've got robes, or y'all can wear street clothes."

"You got it, but the robes might have a smoky smell. We'll just wear our regular clothing," Yasmin said.

"And can we have the carousel until after the program?" Bernie asked. "I know it's asking a lot for you to get it torn down in time to leave on Monday."

Yasmin shook her head. "After the kindness y'all have all shown us, we're glad to help anyway we can. I'll talk to Dara and tell her the new plan."

"Thank you," Willa Rose said.

"Could we do a little practice run tomorrow when we get everything set in place?" Yasmin asked. "That way we'll all know where our places are, and maybe you should print off some sheets with the songs on them. We go caroling in Ringling every year a day or two before Christmas, so we probably know most of them, but just to be sure, it would be good to have the music in front of us."

Willa Rose nodded. "Yes, we can. I'll ask Mary Jane to do that for us, and Ivy will hand them out just before the program."

"I love it!" Bernie said. "This is going to be the best program ever. I just wish I could ride the carousel while I sing."

"Why not?" Willa Rose said. "We can put the sleigh over to the left in the second staging area, and when we pull the curtains, whichever of you elderly folks who want to gather around it, or else take a place on the carousel."

Bernie narrowed her eyes into nothing more than tiny slits. "Who are you calling old? Yasmin told me I will live to be past ninety and that's a ways off. And honey, I'll be the one with the outfit that sparkles the most on Sunday. I think Ivy should do a reading in between acts. She's the new little sister in the family. Just before the last curtain is drawn, she can do that part out of the scripture about when Jesus was born."

"I might as well throw my notebook away," Willa Rose barked.

"Sounds like a wonderful idea to me. We've been needing some new ideas to spice the program up," Bernie said. "And while we're at it, rethink that business of a carousel and then the sleigh being fully visible when you pull the last curtain and there's the camel and sheep with baby Jesus in the manger."

"Sweet Lord! That won't work at all, will it?"

Tripp couldn't suppress his laughter any longer. This whole thing was fast turning into a circus. He wondered if Bernie would even remember what she had organized the next morning.

"I have an idea," he said when he got control of himself. "Why don't you forget about curtains up at the front part? Let the sleigh and carousel both be visible together with the cutout decorations around the sides where your singers will be standing."

"We have to have a manger scene," Willa Rose said.

"Yes, ma'am," Tripp said, "but you could close off the side over there where we have the animals already penned up. The congregation would only have to turn slightly to see what was happening in that staging area. Ivy could do her reading up front, then someone could swing the curtains back and there will be the animals and the manger. They'll be in a pen, but that won't be too bad."

Bernie patted him on the back. "You just proved that men are good for something after all."

"Some men," Willa Rose added.

"Hey, now!" Tripp snapped.

"I didn't call any names, and your idea is wonderful. We'll only have to rig up one curtain that way," she said. "I just hope Endora isn't disappointed."

Bernie turned slightly and laid a hand on her shoulder. "Honey, she is so wrapped up right now in those new babies that she wouldn't care if we had the program in Bo and Maverick's bar. Which reminds me, I'm supposed to tell you that Bo will hold a microphone and lead the singing."

"Sounds like we're all set then," Tripp said and turned to Willa Rose. "Since you don't have a ride home, I could take you."

Bernie finished off her root beer and tossed the bottle in a nearby trash can. "I figured you were spending the night so you could get an early start in the morning."

"I'll bring her with me and Hank," Tripp said as he stood up.

———

Willa Rose pushed back her chair. "I sleep better in my own bed, so good night, Bernie. And thank you for the reading, Yasmin. Even though I'm not a believer, I got some good lessons from it."

"Any time." Yasmin waved as she walked away. "Next year when we come to Nocona, I want to hear what path you chose."

"You got it," Willa Rose told her as she slipped off the

back of the chair. "Even if I don't decide to stay here, I'll come back for the holidays to visit my dad."

"Oh?" Yasmin whipped back around. "I thought that decision had already been made, and the crossroads had to do with romance."

"It might if I can find a suitable match for her," Bernie chimed in.

"Well, either way, I want to hear the story in a year," Yasmin said and disappeared into the crowd.

How Bernie could even walk a straight line, much less move across the barn floor as gracefully as a ballerina was a total mystery to Willa Rose. "That woman amazes me and scares me more than a little bit."

Tripp draped an arm around her shoulders. "You just proved you are a smart woman. And this show of affection is to throw her off, so don't be thinking that there will be a good-night kiss."

"My SUV is parked in front of the house, so you won't be walking me to the door, just across the yard. And if you are expecting a make-out session in the front seat…"

"Console gets in the way in the front seat, darlin'. Let's crawl in the space behind the back seats where there's more room. You do keep a quilt or a blanket back there, don't you?"

She shrugged his arm away when they were outside, but he scooped her up in his arms and carried her to her vehicle. "You have got to start wearing boots, woman."

She pointed toward her feet. "I am. See? You can put me down."

"My dad said that a good man always finishes a job he starts, so I'll take you to your SUV," Tripp said.

Even through his coat, his heartbeat sounded loud and clear in her ear. Maybe she should stay in Spanish Fort and see if the chemistry between them could lead to something.

No, no! That idea is terrible. I'm not taking the right fork in the road that leads to a permanent place in Spanish Fort. I'm going to run down the left one back to what I know. I will soon forget this whole area.

Yasmin's words about being sure she made the right decision and not having regrets later came back to haunt her, sending a shiver down her spine.

"Just a little bit more and you'll be behind the wheel and out of this bitterly cold wind," Tripp assured her. "I'll follow you home. Even though Brodie plowed a path from his place to the Paradise, the rest of the trip could be slippery. Don't want to find you have frozen in a ditch tomorrow."

"Why not?" she asked.

"I'm just worried about my youngest sister. Endora would be frantic if you weren't there to supervise the decorations for the program. We don't need to upset the new mama, do we?"

That settles a lot right there. Basically, you just said that I'm only someone to flirt with. When it comes time to get serious, you will want a woman who can give you a houseful of kids.

"No, we do not want to stress Endora out," she answered.

Somehow, he opened the SUV door for her without even

putting her on the ground and slid her in behind the steering wheel.

"I'll follow behind you. Are you going to invite me in for a cup of coffee or maybe hot chocolate?"

No! the voice in her head screamed.

"Of course," she answered. "After being carried across the snow, it's the least I can do."

"And maybe a movie or a couple of reruns of *Justified*?"

"Don't push your luck. But I won't walk you to the door and linger behind for a kiss."

He sucked in a lungful of air and blew in out in a huff. "I guess I can't ask for anything on the first date, now, can I?"

"This is not a date," she snapped.

"That's not what I intend to tell Knox and let him *accidentally*"—he grinned—"let it slip to Aunt Bernie."

"Well, in that case, maybe it is," Willa Rose said. "I'll see you at the house."

Chapter 15

WILLA ROSE LEFT THE door open for Tripp, kicked off her boots, and hung her coat on the rack in the corner. *Was she really teasing Aunt Bernie, or did she want to spend some one-on-one time with him?* she asked herself.

"Come on in," she yelled when she heard him on the porch.

He closed the door, left his boots on the mat, and removed his coat. He glanced around until he found the rack and hung it beside hers. There was something very personal about their coats hanging side by side, the sleeves touching as if they were holding hands. She felt a little heat in her cheeks at the silly idea.

"Coffee, hot chocolate, beer, wine from Ophelia's business, or sweet tea?" she asked.

"Maybe a glass of wine," Tripp answered. "Having anything with caffeine this late will keep me awake half the night. What can I do to help?"

"Last I checked, I was able to pour a couple of glasses of wine all by myself," she teased.

He sat down on the couch and leaned his head back. "I'm impressed. Most women don't master that art until they are a lot older than you."

"They lied when they told me that you were the quiet, almost shy Callahan brother," she said as she brought a bottle of wine and two stemless glasses to the living room.

"Who told such a thing?" he asked.

"All seven of your sisters."

"Guess I got them fooled."

She poured the wine, handed him a glass, and sat down on the other end of the sofa from him. "Well, you certainly have not pulled the wool over my eyes. I see you for what you are."

"Oh, really, what is that?"

"A big flirt hiding behind a shy man."

"Busted," he said with a grin. "What kind are we drinking tonight, and to what are we toasting?"

"It's strawberry, and why would we toast anything?" she asked.

"My favorite," he replied and touched his glass to hers. "To our first date. May it fool some of the people some of the time."

"Like Bernie?" she asked.

"Like whoever thinks I'm the quiet, shy brother," he answered.

"Why would they tell me that?"

Tripp took another drink of his wine. "That's the way most people see me. Brodie was the oldest and the hero. He went off to the military, did a couple of tours overseas, and got into some stuff that was classified. Knox was the good-looking wild, rebel son who didn't let anyone tell him what to do. He wanted to be a carpenter and build houses, so that's what he did."

Willa Rose thought of Erica, her wild sister who left home at eighteen and apparently never looked back. "And that left you to be the quiet one?"

"I felt like I had to pick up the slack and be what my parents wanted me to be—the next CEO of Dad's oil company. So that's what I did instead of putting in a leather-working shop. After all, they had adopted me and Knox. We owed them something for loving us and taking care of us all our lives."

Yasmin's words about Willa Rose having five sons came back to her mind. "How did you feel when you found out you were adopted?"

Tripp shrugged and finished off his wine. "It was no big deal. My folks set me and Knox down before we started kindergarten and explained adoption to us. They said that we were as much their sons as Brodie, and how we came into the family didn't matter at all. I didn't feel one way or the other. I was glad none of us was in trouble and that we could go back out and play on the jungle gym in the yard. Why are you asking?"

"My sister had problems with being adopted," Willa Rose said, and wondered if that was the reason behind Erica not wanting to give her child to strangers. "She left home when she finished high school and swore that she would never come back to Poetry. Sometime after that she changed her name from Thomas back to her birth name,

Williams. That broke Daddy's heart because he really loves Erica."

"Does that mean you would never consider adopting a baby?"

"That's a tough question," she answered and clamped her mouth shut. She still wasn't ready to say the words because when that child was born, Erica would probably change her mind—even though she swore that she wouldn't. "Erica was already a little girl when Daddy married Mama and adopted her. I would give some serious thought to a newborn. How did we get on this topic anyway? I thought we were going to watch reruns of *Justified*."

"The character, Raylan Givens, is not adopted, and he hated his father as much as you say Erica hated Hank," Tripp said.

"But he had good reason to be at odds with Arlo," Willa Rose argued. "Erica didn't."

"I'm just saying that each situation should be studied carefully. Maybe Erica loved her biological father even if he was a bad husband to Vada."

She picked up the remote and turned on the television, only to find that the storm had knocked out the cable, so all her streaming stations were gone. "Mama never talked about him, but Erica made him out to be a hero, so you are probably right."

"Guess we won't be watching reruns of anything tonight," Tripp said.

"Don't give up yet. I've got a box full of DVDs." She

stood up and everything spun around a couple of times before she could focus. "I guess Ophelia's wine has a little more kick than what I've had before."

"Yep, it does," Tripp said with a grin. "Need some help?"

"Nope, I've got it." No way would she let him think she was a total lightweight when it came to drinking—even though she was. "What'll it be? Old western? Romantic comedy? The first season of *NCIS*? That show is one of Daddy's favorites."

"What have you got in westerns?"

She pulled out *Quigley Down Under* and held it up.

"I haven't ever seen that one."

"Then Tom Selleck it is." She slipped the disc into the player and went back to the sofa.

Fifteen minutes into the show, she had slumped down and fallen sound asleep. Tripp remembered the story about her sleeping so soundly that a tornado—or even Knox getting into bed with her—hadn't wakened her. She was like a rag doll in his arms when he picked her up and carried her to the bedroom. He laid her gently on the bed and covered her with a quilt that had been draped over the back of a chair.

He tiptoed back to the living room, turned out all the lights, shut down the DVD player, and locked the door behind him as he left. The story he would spin tomorrow would involve lots of making out before she went to sleep.

After all, he had to live up to the image she had of him—and that was not shy and quiet.

Tripp stomped through what snow the sun hadn't melted across her yard and got into his truck. The distance from the parsonage to his house was only a couple of city blocks, but driving on still-slick roads took a little longer. He had just pulled into his driveway when his phone rang. Thinking that it was probably Willa Rose, he didn't even check to see who was calling.

"Tripp Callahan, where are you?" Bernie asked.

"I'm at home," he answered.

"I need you to come to the Paradise. I can't find Pepper. I've looked in the barn and he's not there. I'm afraid he's got some bad notions from Pansy or from those animals in the barn. I found him humping one of his toys yesterday," she moaned. "If you find him, I'm going to take him to the vet and have him neutered. I swore I wouldn't embarrass him that way, but he's got to stop running away like this."

"I'll drive out to the farm. I bet he's headed that way to find Pansy," Tripp told her. "You stay by the phone, and I'll call if I find him."

"Not *if*, Tripp, *when*," she said, and the screen went black.

"Why does she call me every time?" he grumbled as he backed out of the driveway and headed south. When he passed by the lane to the Paradise, something Remy had said clicked in his mind. One of his cow dogs had come in heat, and after he'd had her bred, he had penned her up in one of the barn stalls.

Tripp made a right turn and then another one at the next lane leading back to Ursula and Remy's house.

The place was dark and he didn't want to wake anyone, so he left the truck door open. Then he hopped over the fence and headed out to the barn. He heard yipping before he even opened the door and found Pepper trying his best to dig his way under the stall.

"Come on, old boy," Tripp said as he picked him up. "You've got great ambitions, but that's all you have. That lady dog is too much for a little fellow like you to handle."

Pepper whined all the way across the pasture and almost wiggled free when Tripp had to crawl through the barbed-wire fence with the dog in his arms. "Be still, or I'll take you to the vet myself right now and pay for emergency surgery on you."

Tripp didn't let go of the dog until the truck door was closed. Pepper snorted a few times and finally curled up on the passenger seat.

"Snorting like that means you've been around Pansy too much. I wouldn't be surprised if Aunt Bernie grounds you and that pig disappears when the carnival leaves," he said and picked up his phone.

"Did you find him?" Bernie answered on the first ring.

"Yep, I did and we're on the way to bring him back to you."

"Where was he?"

"In Remy's barn trying to dig under a stall door to get at Remy's cow dog."

"Good God!" Bernie gasped. "That animal could chew him up for breakfast."

"I don't think he was looking for a fight." Tripp chuckled. "The dog is still in heat. Remy had her bred before the snowstorm hit. Once she has puppies, he's going to have her spayed."

"Why has he started all this now? He's got to be several years old."

"Maybe he's got a dose of middle-aged craziness," Tripp answered. "He's got to prove that he's still got it."

"Well, he's going to lose it as soon as I can get him in for an appointment. I see your headlights coming this way. Want to come in for a good, stiff drink?"

"No, we've all got a big day ahead of us tomorrow. I better get on home," he answered.

"Well, thank you again!" Bernie said. "It was a good day when you boys appeared at the Paradise last Christmas."

Tripp parked but didn't turn off the engine. He got a firm hold on the dog, carried him up on the porch, and handed him off to Bernie. "We've got to stop meeting like this, ma'am. People will talk."

Bernie threw back her head and laughed. "Now, that's funny, and you're supposed to be the introverted twin."

"Sometimes it just takes the right woman to bring out the inner man."

"I'll find one who will do just that," Bernie told him and closed the door.

He could hear her fussing at Pepper the whole way back

to his vehicle. He was parking in his driveway for the second time that evening when his phone rang again.

"If that damn dog got out again, then you can hop the fence between the Paradise and Remy's ranch and get him yourself," he muttered as he answered it with a gruff, "Hello."

"Hello, Brother," Brodie said. "Where are you?"

"I'm not chasing down Pansy again," Tripp answered and went on to tell him about Pepper's escapades.

Brodie's laughter was so loud that Tripp had to hold the phone out from his ear. "What's so funny?"

"Pansy is locked down really tight," Brodie replied when he got control of himself. "Audrey and I came over to your house after the supper at the barn. You weren't home so we visited Knox a little while. I was just being a nosy big brother and wondering where you had gone."

"I had some wine and watched a movie with Willa Rose at her house," he answered.

"Good for you," Brodie said. "Good night, then."

"Good night to you," Tripp said and hurried inside the house.

"Aha," Knox said as he came out of the hallway. "Is this a walk of shame?"

"Nope, it is not, but I do have a story to tell you about poor old Pepper who wishes he got to take the walk of shame."

Chapter 16

Bernie met Willa Rose at the door when she arrived thirty minutes late on Saturday morning. "Well, well, well," she said with a head wiggle. "You're wearing the same clothes you had on last night when you left."

"I fell asleep in my clothes and overslept."

"In whose house?" Bernie asked.

"I'll give you three guesses and the first two don't count," Willa Rose answered.

"I'm so proud of you," Tripp whispered from right behind her.

His warm breath on her chilly neck sent a shot of heat through her body.

"You are late, too," Bernie said.

"What I was doing this morning made it worth an extra thirty minutes," he teased.

"One of these days you are both going to regret the decisions you are making, and you can write that in stone," Bernie said and then left in a huff.

Willa Rose smiled up at Tripp. "What do you regret about last night?"

"That I didn't get to see all that movie." His twinkling

eyes told her that he loved every minute of the bantering. "How about you?"

"That half a bottle of very good strawberry wine got poured down the drain this morning," she said and pointed to across the room. "But right now we're wasting time. You are on the schedule to help Joe Clay and Remy move the sleigh back into the barn."

"Do you remember what we talked about just before you fell asleep?" Tripp asked.

"No, I don't. What was it?" she asked.

"It will come back to you eventually. When it does, we can talk about it some more, but right now I should be getting outside to help the guys."

Dara and Ophelia seemed to show up out of thin air. But then, Willa Rose had almost gone into a trance trying to figure out what she had said the night before. Had she done something totally stupid like say she was considering staying in Spanish Fort? If so, she would blame it on the wine.

"We need to know if you want two curtains hung around the manger scene or only one," Ophelia said. "And what's going on between you and Tripp?"

"Two will give it more folds and make it tougher for folks to peek behind before it's time for that part of the program, but one looks more like a wall," Dara added. "Are you and Tripp just flirting or is there some feelings?"

"Two curtains," Willa Rose said, "and to tell the truth, I'm not sure about anything when it comes to Tripp."

"Bernie thinks y'all are already getting involved, and she's not a happy camper," Ophelia whispered.

"I know," Willa Rose said. "Ain't it a hoot?"

Folks often said that not liking Texas because of the weather was a sorry excuse, because it could change in thirty minutes. That thought came to Tripp's mind as the heat from the bright sun melted the icicles hanging from the roof of the house.

"Looks like the snow will be gone by the night of Brodie and Audrey's wedding and the Paradise Christmas party," he said as he helped load the sleigh onto a flatbed trailer.

Joe Clay winked at Tripp. "Looks to me like the heat between you and Willa Rose has already melted part of it."

"Maybe the rise in the temperature is the result of Aunt Bernie's anger instead of romance between Tripp and Willa Rose," Remy said.

"Could be," Joe Clay said. "She's determined to find Tripp a wife that is not Willa Rose."

Dara's husband Eli and Finn rounded the end of the house. "Hey, y'all need some extra hands out here?"

"Yes and thank you. We never turn down help, and this thing gets heavier every year," Joe Clay said.

"We're used to hoisting up heavy equipment," Eli said as he picked up the back of the sleigh and helped Tripp slide it onto the flatbed.

"Might be easier if you'd put wheels on it," Tripp said.

"That's a great idea for another year," Joe Clay agreed. "Maybe some that could be taken off and put back on easily."

That statement triggered Tripp's thought pattern into thinking about Willa Rose. Was she just having a good time with the matchmaking business, or did she possibly feel the chemistry between them like he did? Was she simply putting wheels on the idea of going back to Poetry to tease Bernie? Or was she seriously considering putting down some roots right there in Spanish Fort?

"You look like you are arguing with yourself," Finn said as he and Tripp took their places on the trailer and held the sleigh in place. "I'm glad we've got a few minutes alone. I have been meaning to tell you that I didn't know you and Willa Rose were an item when we first got here. Bernie seemed all excited about introducing me to her, and Yasmin and I were going through one of our rough spots, so…" Finn shrugged.

"No problem," Tripp said before Finn could finish.

"We get along very well the three months we're in Oklahoma," Finn went on, "but by the time we get to Nocona, we're having problems."

"Every year?"

"Yep. I've asked her to marry me, but she says she wants a family, and she isn't raising kids in a carnival. I'm unloading on you. I'm sorry."

"Don't be," Tripp said. "I'm a good listener, but tell me, what do you want?"

"I want to settle down in Oklahoma and do carpentry

work for a living. I'd like to have a house with no wheels, a place out to the side or at the back to build furniture—somewhat like Joe Clay has here—and have that family that Yasmin talks about."

"But? I hear a 'but' in that dream." Tripp thought of his own dream being fulfilled right there in Spanish Fort.

"But my dad inherited this business from his father, and now it's my turn to step up to the plate and do my duty," Finn answered.

"I feel you," Tripp said. "I was CEO of a big oil company for the same reasons you are talking about. When my folks passed away, my brothers and I sold it. Our dreams brought us here to Spanish Fort. Have you talked to Zeb?"

Finn shook his head.

"You might start there and be honest with him." Tripp suggested. "I wish I'd talked to my dad like Brodie and Knox did. But I was in the same spot you are—guilt and responsibility rolled into one big ball."

"Thanks for listening," Finn said. "I'm glad to have the air cleared."

"No problem," Tripp assured him, but he wasn't totally sure the air was cleared. He had feelings for Willa Rose, and he thought maybe she might have something for him. But the chances of her staying in Spanish Fort were slim to none, and Tripp had a home, a business, and more importantly, a family now.

Before Tripp could say anything else, Joe Clay had backed the trailer inside the barn. Finn and Tripp hopped off and half a dozen carnival workers jogged over to help get the sleigh set in place.

"Just a little to the left," Willa Rose yelled from the other side of the barn.

"That's just about right," Bernie shouted from the other side.

Tripp jogged back to where Willa Rose was standing and gave the moving crew a thumbs-up.

Bernie made her way over to them and smiled brightly. "This is for you, Tripp, and this is for you, Willa Rose." She handed each of them a piece of paper.

"What is this?" Willa Rose asked.

Tripp looked down at a name: *Melanie O'Dell*. "What does this mean?"

"I went home to check on Pepper and glanced through my online matchmaking site. I found the perfect matches for each of y'all and fixed each of you up with a blind date on Monday night. I would have invited Melanie and Zachary to the program and the potluck tomorrow morning, but I think you should each meet them alone the first time," she said with a bright smile.

"But…" Willa Rose stammered.

"No buts about it. You will meet Zachary," Bernie said.

"Not me," Tripp said.

"No, you won't meet Zachary, but you will have coffee and dessert with Melanie. I will not take no for an answer from either of you. You will each meet your dates at Noah and Tertia's café at five o'clock on Monday. I arranged a coffee and dessert date. Whether it lasts for half an hour or if maybe you take them home for a long evening is up to you. Noah and Tertia close up at six o'clock, so you have an hour to make that decision. Merry Christmas, and you are welcome."

"I can't go anywhere at five o'clock," Tripp said. "Hank and I will be working late."

"I've talked to him, and he says he'll finish up the evening for you," Bernie said.

Willa Rose crossed her arms over her chest. "I'm not going on a blind date with anyone."

"Thank you, Aunt Bernie," Tripp said after he got over the initial shock of being blindsided at that very moment. "Can you tell me a little about Melanie? Have our paths crossed before? Maybe at Bo and Maverick's bar or at church?"

"Nope," Bernie beamed, "I'm not handing out hints to either of you. The only thing I'll tell either of you is that Melanie is from Henrietta and Zachary lives in Saint Jo. The rest I will leave up to you to find out."

If Tripp was going on a date, then by damn, Willa Rose would do the same. "I've changed my mind. I will be at the café on Monday at five. It will be love at first sight."

No way in the real world, she thought. *Especially not with a guy named Zachary.* Willa Rose shivered. A little boy she'd had in her class when she went through her practice teaching was named Zachary. He picked his nose and wiped it on his jeans or else put it in his mouth.

"I expected y'all to fight me a lot more on this. You aren't going to wait until the last minute and cancel, are you?" Bernie gave each of them a shot of evil eye.

"No fight left in me," Tripp said. "I'll go on this one date, but only if you promise not to set me up with any more until after the holidays."

Bernie shook her finger at Tripp. "If you are nice to Melanie and truly give some serious thought to taking her out on a real date, I'll make that deal with you."

"What if Pepper gets lost and you need me to go hunt him down tomorrow night?"

"I promise I will call on someone else," Bernie said.

Willa Rose stuck out her fist. "I can spare one hour, but I don't want any more blind dates until after Valentine's Day. I'm going to be busy getting everything arranged for my grand opening."

Bernie bumped it with hers and nodded. "Agreed on both counts."

"Miz Bernie," Dara called from across the barn. "Will you come pass judgment on these curtains?"

"Of course." Bernie raised her voice. "I do wish we would have had time to do a practice run on the program like we did at the church. But the blizzard stopped that, so we'll just have to do what we can. Don't either of you forget. Monday at five. Oh, and Tripp, there will be a red rose and a sprig of mistletoe on your table, and Willa Rose, you look for a yellow one with a little mistletoe on yours."

"Yes, ma'am," Tripp said.

Yellow roses reminded Willa Rose of the flowers her ex always brought her, and she had come to hate them almost as much as she did the name Zachary. She turned to face Tripp and said, "I guess we're going on a date. Are you bringing Melanie as your plus one to Audrey and Brodie's wedding?"

"Hell, no!" Tripp answered. "I'm going to be polite, walk her to the door, and never call her for a second date."

"If that's your plan, then don't tell her that you will call," Willa Rose told him. "That gives a woman false hope."

"I'll keep that in mind. How are you going to handle your date?"

"If he calls or asks for a second date, I will be honest and say that I'm too busy for a relationship. Why did you agree in the first place?" she asked.

"So that Bernie would back off until after the holidays. How about you?"

"Same," Willa Rose answered. "And to throw her off track about me staying or going. Now the wagers will hold steady. After all, if it's love at first sight with Zachary, then I'll be moving out of Spanish Fort, and she won't have to worry about *us* getting involved. But"—she lowered her voice—"I hate yellow roses. I don't believe in that crap about mistletoe. And I would never even kiss a man named Zachary."

"Why?" Tripp asked.

"My ex brought me yellow roses. Mistletoe is a parasite. That should be enough of an explanation. And…" She went on to tell him about the little boy in her class when she did her practice teaching.

Tripp laughed so hard that all the conversations and noise in the barn ceased, and everyone stared at him. "Willa Rose just told me a funny kid story," he explained.

A few smiled, and the quietness ended.

Tripp turned his focus back to Willa Rose and asked, "What do we need to do next?"

"I've decided to leave the cutouts in the yard," Willa Rose said. "We'll have all our choir singers standing around the barn to help Bo with the singing, and of course the little kids on the carousel will be adding their voices.

"And then the older folks who will take their places for what I guess will be funny songs. I haven't seen the actual song list so I'm not sure what they'll sing," Willa Rose said. "After that, Remy and Joe Clay will open the curtains for the serious part of the program."

"Mary Jane is getting the smoke smell out of the costumes for that part," Tripp said. "She says for us to string twinkle lights around the barn door and hang a wreath on it. I've brought in several boxes, so if you tall guys will help me, we can all make it to the house to eat right at noon."

"While the guys are doing that, the rest of us can set up the chairs," Willa Rose said.

Dara grabbed the first folding chair and carried it to the back of the barn. "Should we reserve the first couple of rows for the parents of the little kids? That way they wouldn't have to chase through the whole congregation when their part is over."

"Great idea," Willa Rose said as she and several others

followed Dara's lead. "And we sure appreciate all y'all's help in getting this put together."

"Anything to get out of the trailers for a little while," Eli said.

"We are so ready to be home, but come spring, we'll be itchin' to get back on the road. It's the best of two lives," Dara said.

"So, would you raise kids in the carnival?" Tripp asked.

"Of course," Eli answered. "Dara was born in Oklahoma and taken on her first round when she was only six weeks old. We'll raise our family the same way she was—homeschooled and learning the ropes of the life."

"You weren't raised the same?" Willa Rose asked.

"No, ma'am." Eli chuckled. "I was a corporate lawyer in Austin, Texas. I took my nephews to the carnival down there and met Dara. It was love at first sight. I followed the carnival for six months and finally asked Dara to marry me. She wouldn't leave the carnival, so I left my job. I've never had a single regret."

"That's some story." Willa Rose felt the story rather than just heard it. Tripp would never leave Spanish Fort, but was she willing to change her mind? If so, would there be regrets? This really would be a good place to raise a child. Lots of loving family members around, but that was if Erica didn't change her mind once she gave birth.

Chapter 17

Willa Rose made coffee and two pieces of avocado toast on Sunday morning. She thought back over the past couple of years as she ate breakfast. Two years ago, on a freezing day like this, she and Vada had the same breakfast, then hurried off to the church to take care of little last-minute details for the program. One year ago, she had sat with her mother, who drifted in and out of sleep. Every breath was labored, and she seemed to be waiting for something or someone before she could make the transition from earth into eternity. Willa Rose had told her that it was all right to go on if she was tired, but the last two days of her life she kept asking for Erica.

"She never came, not once, and I'm not sure I'll ever forgive her," Willa Rose muttered.

A hard knock on the front door brought her out of her funk. She rushed over, thinking she might find her father on the other side, but it was Tripp.

"Are you ready?" he asked.

"Why would I be ready at nine o'clock?"

"The electricity blinked last night. Your phone is turned off and you didn't reset any clocks in the house. It is ten twenty-five right now, and the program starts at eleven."

She headed down the hall in a dead run. "Give me five minutes to get dressed and run a brush through my hair."

"If you can do that in five minutes, we need to call the Smithsonian or get in touch with whatever religion decides about saints," Tripp said.

She stopped and turned around. "What are you talking about?"

"It will be a miracle," he told her.

"That's not even funny," she said.

Tripp looked down at his watch. "Nine minutes, thirty seconds, and it is a little bit funny."

Willa Rose had never slapped on a bit of makeup, gotten dressed, and twisted her hair up into a messy bun so fast in her entire life. She shoved her feet down into a pair of cowboy boots and found Tripp finishing off a cup of coffee when she made it back to the kitchen.

"A miracle has happened. You made yourself even more beautiful than you were when I arrived, and you did it in four minutes and ten seconds. Shall we go?"

"As you can see, I'm wearing boots, so I don't need a knight in shining denim jacket to carry me to the vehicle," she told him.

"But parking will be at a premium with all the family vehicles plus a big percentage of the townsfolks' cars and trucks who are coming for the program. You might have to put your SUV out in the north forty, so to speak, and walk half a mile back to the barn. This denim jacket knight can take you right up to the door," Tripp said. "Don't worry. It's not a date. I don't have the energy to date two women at one time, and Melanie might be the jealous type."

"Then I will take you up on the offer," Willa Rose said as she put on her coat. "What is this big deal about Santa Claus?"

"Every year after the program, there's a potluck dinner in the fellowship hall," Tripp explained on the way outside to his truck. "Joe Clay dresses up as Santa Claus and pictures are always taken of the kids sitting on his lap. Each child gets a wrapped present and takes home a paper sack full of candy, fruit, and nuts."

"And where is this happening?"

He opened the door for her and then jogged around to his side of the truck. "While everyone is enjoying the potluck, Joe Clay, Brodie, and Knox will slip away and set the big Santa chair up in the barn. He'll come from behind the curtain where the animals are penned up and surprise everyone. Then the fun begins."

"If this is the first year you've been involved, how do you know all this?" Willa Rose asked.

"Seven sisters," he said with a shrug and started the engine. "I'm surprised that they haven't given you the rundown. But then there's a couple of brand-new babies that have them all spun up, and you've fit so well into the family that they probably forgot that you haven't been here that long."

He's right. You really are fitting into the community as well as you do in Poetry, her mother seemed to whisper in her ear.

"Looks like we've got a full day ahead of us," she said.

"Yep, and then tomorrow the carnival leaves."

"And Ivy stays behind to live at the Paradise," Willa Rose said.

"I'd forgotten about that. I was focusing on today and the fact that we both have a date tomorrow evening." Tripp groaned. "I am not looking forward to making small talk for an hour."

She reached across the console and patted him on the shoulder. "We will survive and then we don't have to worry about Aunt Bernie's matchmaking for a while."

"Why don't you just marry me, and then we would never have to worry about it," Tripp asked.

"Are you serious?" Willa Rose gasped.

"No, but Aunt Bernie wouldn't have to know," he answered. "We could say that we are going to have a long engagement. Then she would move on to Knox and leave us both alone."

"It's a great idea, but to make it work, my dad would have to believe it, and I couldn't do that to him."

Tripp turned into the lane to the Paradise. "You are right, and I could never lie to Hank. I guess we'll have to be satisfied with Aunt Bernie's promise to lay off for a little while."

"That's right, and maybe when she sets us up again, we can renegotiate a new deal, like no more until Easter or Mother's Day." She opened the door and got out as soon as Tripp stopped the vehicle. "Thanks for the ride. You were right about the parking."

"You are welcome, and I'm always right."

"Until it comes to a fake engagement," she shot back.

Willa Rose had to stand still inside the utility room to adjust to the noise of a dozen children lined up in the kitchen, while a bunch of older folks practiced their songs in the living room. When she had adjusted from a quiet morning—except for the race to get dressed—to the total chaos in the house, she caught Rae's eye and asked, "What do I need to do?"

"Daddy is taking the children to the barn on the flatbed trailer so they don't get their shoes all muddy," Rae answered. "You and I can ride with them. You will start everything at exactly eleven o'clock, which is ten minutes from now."

"'Start everything'?" Willa Rose asked.

"Either Parker or Endora gives a little welcoming speech before the program begins and reminds everyone that the potluck begins when it's over and after dinner Santa Claus will arrive… That kind of thing," Rae answered. "Gunner will film the whole thing so those of us who are in the house getting things ready for the potluck can watch it. We didn't expect so much food to get brought in, but then the blizzard kept folks holed up for weeks. We've all got cabin fever. Oh, and you might need to entertain a little while the little kids are leaving and we bring out the older group."

Mary Jane came into the kitchen and handed off a microphone to Willa Rose. "When you finish the introduction, give this to Bo. Y'all will hand it off to each other as needed, and it will finally end up in Ivy's hands. Everything is coming along better than we thought it could. Thank you for stepping in for Endora."

"You are welcome, but it's been a team effort. Hopefully, next year they'll have the church ready to go back to normal," Willa Rose said.

"From your lips to God's ears," Mary Jane said and disappeared back into the foyer.

Rae clapped her hands to get the kids' attention. "Okay, here's the rules. We are going to stay on the path that has been cleared. You are going to let either me or Miz Willa Rose help you up on the trailer, and then you are going to sit down on one of the quilts. When we get to the barn, we will help the little kids get up on the sleigh, and the bigger ones will ride on the carousel."

"But…but…" one little guy started.

"This is for the program, and there are no buts, but afterward if we can talk Santa Claus into coming with presents, then everyone who wants to ride the carousel will have a turn. Any more questions?"

One little girl's chin quivered. "I don't remember all the words to the songs."

"You just look pretty and sing what you do know," Willa Rose said. "There's going to be plenty of others singing with you. Now let's get in line and remember what Miz Rae told you."

The little girl beamed. "Yes, ma'am."

Tripp peeked out from between the curtains circling around the animal pens when everything went quiet in the barn full of people. Rae led the little children down the aisle between two rows of folding chairs, and Willa Rose followed behind them. She had been beautiful that morning when he arrived at her house. Her hair had been going every which way. She still had sleepy eyes and was wearing a tattered robe that looked like it had survived a couple of world wars. But in less than five minutes she had transformed into someone who could have won a beauty contest. Her thick, dark hair was twisted up on top of her head. A bright-blue sweater made her skin glow, and her slim skirt hugged her curves.

"Damn it," he said under his breath.

Why did he have to have real feelings for her, and why did she think they were just playing around with all their banter? Ever since those kisses in the old store, he had felt something he couldn't describe between them.

"Are you swearing in church?" Ivy whispered from beside him.

"This is a community center today," he informed her. "But damn it anyway."

Ivy giggled under her breath and held up a Bible. "I'm reading straight out of this, so for a little while, it's a church. And what are you so upset about?"

"Then forgive me for swearing in church, and it would take a couple of hours to tell you why I was talking that way," he answered. "Right now, Willa Rose motioned for us to take our places."

"Lead the way, and I will follow," Ivy said.

Tripp didn't lead the group, but Ivy was right behind him so that she would be in a good position for reading. When all the singers were in place, Tripp was lucky enough to only be a few yards from Willa Rose.

She helped several of the little children onto the sleigh and then stood in front of the carousel. "Good morning, everyone. Welcome to the Spanish Fort Christmas program and potluck dinner. We are so glad to see a full congregation today. We are fortunate to have the carnival folks staying on the grounds and helping us with decorations, singing, and pure old elbow grease in getting this program ready. They were gracious enough to stay a couple of extra days to lend us their carousel and animals as well as their singing voices today. Let's give them all a big hand."

She waited for the applause to end and then went on. "The growth of any community depends on the next generation, so let's hear it this time for our children who will begin the program with their songs."

She handed the microphone to Bo, who touched a button on a karaoke machine in front of the carousel, and the music to "Santa Claus Is Coming to Town" began.

Willa Rose sat down on a chair off to the side and expected echoes to resound off the walls of the barn when the singing started. But to her surprise, the place had fairly decent acoustics. As soon as that song ended, "Rudolph the Red-Nosed Reindeer" started. The kids were warmed up by then, and several of them began to wiggle their heads and bodies to the tune.

When that song ended, the older children got off the carousel and helped the younger ones down from the sleigh. Then Bo led them in "Little Snowflake" and some simple choreography. The little girl who had worried about not knowing the words did her own dance, spinning and twirling. When the music stopped, Bo smiled at the audience. "Let's give our littles another big hand. They've done a great job, especially considering that they haven't had much practice."

When the folks stopped clapping, Willa Rose stood up again and took the microphone. "A while back, I made the mistake of calling Miz Bernie an elderly person. I won't ever do that again."

That brought on several chuckles.

"So, that said, the next part of the program is presented to you by our *fabulous adults* who are coming down the aisle right now. They look like they are ready to give us a show, so I'm going to sit down and watch with the rest of you."

Well said, Tripp thought with a smile. *The first lesson I learned was to be careful what you say to Aunt Bernie.*

All the senior citizens wearing choir robes came in slowly from the back of the barn, some using walkers, a couple in wheelchairs, and the rest leaning on canes.

"Maybe I wasn't wrong when I called them elderly." Willa Rose chuckled.

An even dozen of them—six men and an equal number of women—finally made it to the front and lined up in front of the carousel and sleigh.

Bernie's voice carried through the barn when she said, "Be careful who you call such blasphemous names, young lady. We might have wrinkles, but we've still got the Christmas spirit."

"Then show us," Willa Rose teased.

The familiar old stripper music started, and with shaking hands, the folks began to unzip the robes. Tripp glanced down at the next song and could not believe that Bernie would have actually led her posse in the Ray Stevens song "Santa Claus Is Watching You."

Tripp locked eyes with Willa Rose, and it was evident they were both thinking the same thing. *Surely Bernie had not run this by Endora and Parker.*

The senior citizens twirled the robes around their heads a couple of times and then tossed them to the side. They all wore red sequin vests, but Bernie had gone a step further and had on matching pants. As the music started, they pulled Santa hats from their pockets and put them on. Then they started a high-kicking routine that would have put all Las Vegas dancers to shame.

Tripp was so speechless that he couldn't open his mouth to sing until after the first chorus. If that was their lead-in, then it was downright scary what would come next. At the end, each of the gentlemen kneeled with a lady on a knee.

And they aren't even out of breath, Tripp thought.

The second song started with someone ringing a doorbell, and then "Redneck 12 Days of Christmas," in true Jeff Foxworthy style started. They tossed their Santa hats on top of the robes lying on the floor and picked up flannel shirts and quickly donned them. They didn't even change the lyrics about twelve packs of beer and so much chewing tobacco, which surprised Tripp, but then again—like he told Ivy—this was a community program. He would have bet dollars to cow patties that Parker would have nixed that song if it had been in the church. But when he looked out over the crowd, Parker was laughing as hard as everyone else.

At the end of that presentation, the seniors all threw off their flannel shirts and put on reindeer antlers just as the old Chuck Berry song "Run, Rudolph, Run" started. Folks were really getting into the spirit of fun and began to clap in time with the music. Bernie led the group in the running man dance and the rest of the choreography. Those who probably didn't get the moves down right, rode the carousel ponies and waved at the audience. At the end of the hilarious production, the whole group held hands and took a deep bow. They put their robes and Santa hats back on, got a firm hold on walkers and canes, and shuffled out of the barn.

Willa Rose took the microphone from Bo and said, "I'm as close to speechless as I've ever been. I kept looking for lightning streaks to come shooting through the roof, but evidently since this is a community program and we aren't in church this Sunday morning…" She let the sentence hang while the people gave the group a standing ovation.

"But now," she said when the place was quiet again, "it's time to get serious. Ivy will deliver a reading to take our minds to the real meaning of Christmas, and then we'll hear some songs from the live manger scene. We've often seen plaques and even pillows embroidered with 'Jesus is the reason for the season.' Well, now is the time to remember that."

Ivy took a step forward and hopped up on the seat of the sleigh. Willa Rose handed her the microphone, and she pointed toward the curtained-off area. "Please look to your right and enjoy our live nativity scene while I read."

Luna and Shane played Mary and Joseph, and their son, Garrett, was in the manger. The wise men stood in front of the kneeling camel, Clyde. The shepherds, each with their staff, had places in the pen with the sheep, goats, and even the potbellied pig lying in the corner with his snout pressed against the wire fence.

Tripp held the laughter inside when he saw Pansy sitting on the outside of the pen with her snout against Porky's. Both pigs looked like little statues while the group sang, "Mary, Did You Know" and "O Holy Night." There wasn't a dry eye in the place, including Tripp's, when the last song, "The Manger," ended. Pansy didn't even stir when the curtains were closed.

"And that brings our program to an end," Ivy said. "Thank you for coming out today. The potluck dinner is ready in the house, and then I understand that Santa Claus was seen coming this way, but first Parker wants to say a few words."

Parker made his way down the center aisle. "I'm grateful to see everyone out for the traditional program—or maybe

I should just say 'program,' since part of this one wasn't what we normally have in the church. But I've got to admit, Bernie and her posse sure lifted our spirits, and that's what these programs are supposed to do." He chuckled. "I want to announce that we will begin to have our services right here in this barn next Sunday morning at the regular time. Hopefully, the church will be put back together soon, and we will appreciate any help all y'all can lend to make that possible. It will take a lot of elbow grease to get the job done. Just get with Knox Callahan if you have a Saturday or even a few hours to donate to the project. Could we please close with a word of prayer before we go into the house for food and fellowship?"

As soon as he heard "Amen," Tripp closed the distance between him and Willa Rose. "You were amazing," he said.

"It went off well, but like I told Mary Jane, the whole thing has been a team effort. I was shocked out of my mind at Bernie's performance. We have misjudged that woman. She is a force to deal with."

"Amen to that," Tripp agreed. "But she does keep her word, so after tomorrow we don't have to worry about her hanging mistletoe on our front porches."

"Doing what?"

"She has these little subtle ways of telling a person that she is not going to give up on finding a mate for them." Tripp told Willa Rose about finding the mistletoe on his porch. "I'm sure she meant it for kissing a woman, but I took it as a miracle that I met Hank less than an hour later."

"If a little sprig of that stuff can make miracles, I'll hang one on my porch," Willa Rose said.

"And what would you wish for?"

"That I could have the five sons that Yasmin predicted when she looked into my future," Willa Rose answered.

"Forget about what happens tomorrow or even next year," Tripp said and headed up the center aisle. "Let's talk about the here and now. Someone brought a whole slow cooker full of chicken and dressing to the potluck, and I want to get in on it before it's all gone."

She fell into step beside him. "You need to practice your lines before tomorrow evening."

"I wasn't trying to be romantic and cheat on Melissa," he said.

"If you want a second date with Melanie—not Melissa—you should remember her name," Willa Rose scolded.

"If you want to get through the evening with…" Tripp paused and tried to remember the man's name, but it wouldn't come to mind. "Whatever his name is, you should try to keep the arguing to a minimum."

Willa Rose grabbed Tripp's arm and jerked him to a stop. She raised up on her tiptoes, wrapped her arms around his neck, and kissed him—passionately, long and lingering. When it ended, she took a step back.

"That settles it. I'm telling 'whatever his name is' that I have cheated on him and the relationship is over," she teased.

Tripp was speechless for a split second and then he began to laugh. Willa Rose looped her arm in his and giggled. "You can tell Melissa or whatever her name is the same thing, or you can beg her forgiveness and ask for a second chance."

"Did you only kiss me to have a reason not to go out with Zachary?"

She snapped her fingers. "That's his name. I'll have to remember that and not call him 'Whatever.'"

"You didn't answer my question," Tripp said.

"I'll have to think about that and get back to you with an answer."

Chapter 18

"Is there still some chicken and dressing left?" Willa Rose asked as she got in line behind Yasmin at the buffet line. She liked all seven of the sisters and Audrey, but she had formed a special bond with Dara and Yasmin in the few days they had been at the Paradise. Maybe it was because they were not family, or the reason might be that they were simply easy to talk to.

"Right now, there is still half a cooker full, but I am about to dip into it. I'll leave you a few bites," Dara answered from up ahead of them.

Willa Rose turned around and winked at Tripp. "I'll share mine with you if it's all gone."

"Rumors will fly if we do that," he teased.

"What can I say? Might as well hang for a sheep as a lamb, as the old saying goes. I've already cheated on Zachary once," she said with a grin.

"Sharing food with you is worth getting into a duel with your intended, and I am a fairly good shot. If he chooses swords, I'm in big trouble, though."

"You would fight for my honor?" Willa Rose asked.

"I'm not sure, but I would definitely fight for chicken and dressing."

"At least he's honest"—Dara giggled—"but I had no idea that you were engaged."

"I'm not, but Bernie has fixed me up with a blind date tomorrow evening that she really hopes turns into something serious," Willa Rose explained.

"I heard that she was a matchmaker," Dara whispered and nodded toward the dining room where Bernie was talking to Zeb and Hank.

"She even has a website and hosts those speed dating events," Tripp explained. "So far she has a ninety percent positive outcome."

"Then I'll look for an invitation to your wedding in the next few months," Dara said.

"Don't hold your breath or start shopping for a new dress. I've already cheated on what's-his-name." She lowered her voice. "I kissed Tripp."

"If the man loves you, he might forgive you," Dara joked. "But you have to be honest with him from the beginning. Do you have feelings for Tripp?"

"I'm not sure," Willa Rose answered and took a big serving of chicken and dressing, "He kisses pretty good, but he has roots here in Spanish Fort."

Dara added a hot roll to her plate. "If a person is going to settle down, this seems like a lovely place to do so, but if you have a wandering soul, I can always find a place for you with the carnival. Finn has already hired my cousin, Adam, to help maintain the machinery for next year's tour. Y'all would make a cute couple."

Willa Rose moved on down the line as they talked. "Thanks, but no thanks. If I don't stay here, I'll go back to Poetry, where I was born and raised."

At least she said 'if' and not 'when', Tripp thought.

"Well, the offer stands if you change your mind, and I expect you to keep me posted about the new feller who's about to be in your life," Dara said. "Are you just a little jealous, Tripp?"

He laid his free hand over his chest. "I'm all broken up over the new guy. I thought that kiss proved that she and I had something real. But I guess she was just toying with my poor old heart."

"Who kissed who?" Bernie asked as she passed by on her way to the dessert table.

"My last girlfriend's goodbye kiss was short and sweet. Then she told me that she had found someone who wasn't a stick in the mud like me and she was breaking up with me," Tripp lied. "It was horrible, Aunt Bernie. That's the reason I haven't wanted to date anyone. My heart is still in pieces over that final kiss she gave me."

"I can tell by the twinkle in your eyes that you are full of crap and lying to me," Bernie fussed. "But Melanie is going to cure you. One look at her will make you forget all about that kiss."

"So…" Dara shot a wink over her shoulder at Willa Rose. "Are y'all double dating?"

"No, but that's not a bad idea. Maybe if Felix and Melissa aren't attracted to us, there might be chemistry between the two of them," Tripp answered.

Bernie put a piece of coconut pie and half a dozen cookies of one kind or another on her plate. "It's Zachary and Melanie. At least try to remember their names, or I won't hold up my end of the deal we made."

"Yes, ma'am. Zachary it is," Willa Rose declared.

"That's better," Bernie said.

"She's fierce," Dara whispered when she had left the kitchen.

"Yes, she is," Tripp said in a low tone. "She owned and operated a bar up in southern Oklahoma for half a century or more. She could outdrink all of us, and she likes a cigar on Sunday nights. She says it keeps her from ever getting dementia."

Dara reached the end of the line. "I'm going to go find my husband. But Miz Bernie doesn't need to worry about losing her mind. She's too ornery for that. I want to grow up and be just like her."

"Heaven forbid!" Willa Rose gasped.

Dara just giggled and disappeared into the crowd, moving toward tables that had been set up in the living room.

"Let's take our food out to the barn," Tripp suggested to Willa Rose when they had filled their plates.

"And miss out on all this noise?"

"Exactly," Tripp said. "Besides we can be the first to see Santa Claus and his elves and helpers."

"Oh, there's more than just ho-ho-ho?"

"I've heard that there might be," he answered.

"Then, by all means, lead the way," Willa Rose said.

"From the footprints in what's left of the snow, I will say that we aren't the only ones who have this idea," she said when they had passed through the sunporch and found it full of folks.

Tripp glanced down and saw dozens of footprints going toward the barn. "Guess everyone else had the same idea. At least we can sit on chairs out there and not have to find a square foot of floor space." But his mind was on what Willa Rose said earlier about *if* she left, not *when*.

"Where did all these people come from?" Willa Rose whispered when they stepped inside the barn. "This has to be the entire population of Spanish Fort."

"Yep, and the grandparents and aunts and uncles from as far away as Gainesville, Nocona, and Saint Jo. Everyone is sick of being stuck inside. Today gives them a cute program to watch, and also a potluck dinner, and their kids that couldn't go see Santa earlier because of the weather get to see him today."

"Is that..." She clamped a hand over her mouth and blinked several times.

"Yes, again, the elves today are presented to you by Knox

and Shane. The helpers dressed in those little red velvet costumes are Ivy and Tertia," Tripp answered. "Let's sit here in the back row out of their way."

Pansy waddled over to Willa Rose, sat down, and raised her fat little neck up as far as it would go.

"Here you go, baby girl," Willa Rose crooned and fed her a bite of ham.

"You do know that makes her a cannibal, don't you?" Tripp joked.

"We don't care, do we?" She raised her voice an octave when she talked to the pig. She dropped a bite of sweet potato casserole and Pansy caught it midair. "There now, that makes you a vegetarian."

"That animal will be running away from the farm to stay with you if she ever finds out where you live," Tripp said.

"She's cute, but not that cute," Willa Rose said.

"Oh, I thought maybe you wanted a potbellied critter for Christmas." Tripp finished off the last of the food on his plate.

"I'm going to sit on Santa's lap and ask him to put two under the tree for me," she said without a moment's hesitation. "That way I can raise them and have lots of fat little babies in the yard, or maybe I'll buy a house and fence the backyard special for them."

Tripp chuckled. "Do you want red bows on them?"

"Don't you dare," Willa Rose said. "Honest, I do not want a pig for Christmas."

"What do you want?" he asked.

"Five sons like Yasmin said," she whispered.

"Santa might not be able to locate five, but miracles happen during the holidays," Tripp said.

"I didn't mean to say that out loud," she said. "And I would be happy with one baby, but that would require more than a miracle. It would have to be pure magic."

"Does it have to be a baby boy?" Tripp asked.

Bernie sat down beside Willa Rose. "The kids are all on the way out here to see if Santa Claus is really coming. Did I hear you say something about a baby boy? Are you pregnant?"

"No, ma'am, I am not. I'm not going on the date until tomorrow," Willa Rose answered.

"Well, who is expecting?" Bernie asked.

"I don't know, but Pansy is getting fatter. Do you think Pepper is about to be a daddy?"

"Good God!" Bernie shivered. "I'd hate to see what those animals would look like. Besides, Pansy and Pepper are just friends."

Is Tripp my friend or is he merely an acquaintance that I'll forget in a few weeks if I leave this place? Willa Rose wondered.

Chapter 19

ALL HELL HAD BROKEN loose when Tripp walked into the café promptly at five o'clock. People were lined up at the cash register with take-out boxes in their hands. Two little boys were in the middle of the floor using a red rose and a yellow one for swords. A lady with a couple of red rose petals left on the table looked past the two kids and waved.

Willa Rose peeked around him into the room. "What is going on in there?"

"World War III," Tripp answered. "I see Felix sitting in a back booth, but there's only a yellow petal on his table. There's two little boys using what used to be roses as swords to fight each other. They are jumping from booths to tables, and everyone is leaving as fast as they can."

"You have got to be kidding." Willa Rose stepped around him and into the café for a better look. "Holy crap on a cracker," she gasped. "Who do those wild kids belong to?"

"Either Felix or Melissa," he answered.

One kid ran by and jabbed the rose at him. "Leave or suffer the death of an enemy."

Tripp was glad that the other little boy wasn't holding a real sword because he poked him twice in the thigh before he tore out after the first one. The only people who were still seated in the café were evidently his date, who seemed to be oblivious to the kids, and the guy who had his head down like he was hungover.

"Everyone is checking out except for our two dates," Willa Rose whispered. "I bet you five dollars that those wild boys belong to my date. A woman wouldn't let kids act like that in a restaurant."

"I'll take your bet and hope you are right." Tripp pasted on a fake smile and crossed the room to meet Melissa—or was it Melanie? He and Willa Rose had joked around so much that he really couldn't remember.

The lady slid out of the booth and stuck out her hand. "I'm Melanie and those are my two boys, Forest and Smoke."

"Tripp Callahan," he said as he shook her hand and waited for her to sit back down. There went five bucks and the first two sons that Willa Rose could lay claim to, but Tripp would have paid her double to have been right.

"Have a seat," Melanie said. "You don't have to be a proper gentleman. I believe in equal rights and free spirits. I can see that the people in this place don't agree with me letting my sons explore their spontaneity, but that's their problem, not mine. Now, tell me a little about yourself. I know you like to work in leather. That is impressive. I do astrological star charts for some of my customers. I am a Wiccan and have a small store in Gainesville where my coven is located. I sell crystals, feathers, plants, and herbs, and I believe that we get our energy from nature. If you are prejudiced against my beliefs, I'll take my sons and go home. No use in wasting our time if that's the case."

Bernie should give me a whole year of no blind dates after this, Tripp thought and glanced across the room to where Willa Rose was sitting across from Zachary. She rolled her eyes when she caught him looking.

The last person at the checkout counter paid out, said a few words to Tertia, and hurried outside. Tripp wished he could do the same and checked his watch. Fifty more minutes might have just as well been eternity plus three days.

"Now about you?" Melanie raised her voice above the two kids who were now crawling over the booths and under the tables like the whole place was one big jungle gym.

"I'm your basic boring guy. I work, spend time with my extended family, and read a little when I have time. I'm not much for television, but I do like old movies."

"There's never a dull minute at my house." Melanie pushed back a strand of brown hair.

"I can imagine." Tripp tried to smile, but it wouldn't materialize. "Is the boys' father in the picture?"

Melanie shook her head. "I told you that I'm a free spirit. Each of the boys has a different father, but I have no idea who they are. Therefore, they are mine and mine alone."

"I see." Tripp checked his watch again and thought it had stopped because only three minutes had passed.

A familiar grunting noise took his attention across the

room. Pansy had slipped past the last person leaving the café and was on her way across the room toward where Willa Rose was sitting. The two boys stopped what they were doing and gave out a war cry as they each picked up a knife from one of the vacant tables.

"Kill the pig," one of them yelled.

"Roast him for supper," the other screamed.

"Aren't you going to stop them?" Tripp asked Melanie.

"Why should I? A dirty pig does not belong in a café," she answered.

Tertia threw her order pad across the room and shouted. "Noah, come out here right now!"

The boys yelled.

Pansy squealed and ran to Willa Rose who grabbed her up and held her tightly against her chest. "You will not touch this pig. She's a pet."

One of the boys raised the knife and said, "That's a wild pig from Africa, and we're going to mount its head on our wall of fame."

Tripp grabbed the boy by the arm and took the knife from him. "That pig is my brother's pet, and you don't have any business with a knife, anyway."

Melanie was suddenly at his side. "Don't you talk to my child that way. I told you that I'm a free spirit, and so are my boys."

"You can raise your kids however you please, but it would be in their best interest later in their lives to give them a little training in public places."

Tertia folded her arms over her chest. "And I would ask… No that's not right. I'm telling you to keep them out of *this* public place from now on."

"Come on, boys," Melanie said. "We're going home."

The younger boy threw himself on the floor and began to kick and yell, "I want that pig's head on my wall!"

"Let's go home and you can hunt pigs in the backyard. If you catch one, we'll roast it for supper, I promise," Melanie said.

Her other son pocketed the knife he had been holding. "We'll put an apple in its mouth and have popcorn with it, right, Mama?"

"Of course, sweetheart," she said.

Tripp pointed at the child and said, "That knife…"

Noah touched him on the shoulder. "It's worth the price of that thing to get them out of here. Come into the kitchen with me and Tertia. I think we all three need a shot of whiskey to calm our nerves."

"Make mine a double," Tripp said.

Willa Rose carried Pansy over to the booth where Zachary waited and sat down with the pig in her lap. "Poor baby. You have got to stop running away like this. Someday you are going to get hit on the road or stolen by someone like those two hoodlums."

"Don't you call my sons names!" Melanie yelled and shook her fist at Willa Rose.

"The fact that they are horrible is your fault for not giving them any direction."

Before Melanie could say anything else, Tertia gave the woman a gentle shove outside and locked the door behind her. "Thank God that's over. I hope we don't lose our customers over it, and I wonder how many places she's been asked to take those boys and leave."

"Pansy and I both thank you," Willa Rose said and turned to Zachary. "Now, where were we before everything happened?"

"I was telling you that…" He snarled like he smelled a rotten egg. "How long are you going to hold that thing?"

"Her name is Pansy, and she really is a pet. The poor baby is still trembling from coming close to getting stabbed, so I'm going to hold her until she feels safe. Then I'm going to take her back to the farm. Maybe this scared her so bad, she will stop running away. Now, you were telling me what?"

He shrugged and set his mouth in a firm line. "That I'm a banker like my father before me, and my grandfather before him, and that…" He paused and pushed back his chair. "I can't do this, Willie Ruth. I'm sorry, but I just can't date a woman who thinks nothing is wrong with holding a pig in a restaurant."

"It's Willa Rose," she corrected him and giggled. "But you are forgiven. I kept calling you Felix, so we are even." She turned her head and shouted, "Tertia, you can unlock the door. Zachary is leaving."

Zachary stood up. "I'm sorry, but…"

Willa Rose waved him away with a flick of her wrist. "No 'buts' necessary. If you don't like Pansy, then you won't like me anyway. Have a safe trip back to wherever you are going, and better luck next time."

As soon as he was gone and the door was safely locked again, Tripp brought a bottle of whiskey to the table and poured two fingers in an empty coffee cup. "I've had a double already, so you'll have to drink alone, but I figure you need something to calm your nerves."

Willa Rose threw back the whiskey in one gulp. "Bernie owes us both at least six free months. I'm going to call her first thing when we get out of here."

"No need," Tripp said, "She called Tertia to see how things were going, and Tertia is giving her an earful. With all the people that were here, I'm sure the gossip vines are already so hot that they're melting what snow is left on the ground."

"Did all that really happen?"

"Ask Pansy."

"Poor little thing was terrified," Willa Rose said.

Tripp poured another shot and threw it back like a gambler in an old western saloon. "So was I."

"I owe you five dollars."

"Keep it. I'm just glad that the dates are over, but what ended yours so quickly?"

Willa Rose shook her head and sighed. "The third-generation banker didn't think he could stand to be around a woman who had a pig in her lap. I don't even need to ask what caused your date with Melissa to fail."

"Melanie." Tripp chuckled. "She was a Wiccan. That I could handle. She believed in being a free spirit. I couldn't fault her for her religion or her beliefs. But, five more minutes with those kids…"

Willa Rose held up a palm. "Say no more. I was just glad they weren't Felix's kids, and figured losing five bucks was well worth it."

"I vote that we take Pansy home. I'll drive if you'll hold her," Tripp said.

"Of course I'll hold her," Willa Rose agreed. "If this keeps happening, we need to get her a harness that we can use in the back seat. I bet she was headed for the Paradise. She would have been so disappointed to find that the carnival left this morning," Willa Rose said. "Maybe we should go show her that her boyfriend has gone home."

"Boyfriend?" Tripp asked.

Willa Rose stood up. "Of course, and now she'll be heartbroken that the daddy of her babies won't be around to help with them."

Tripp chuckled. "I never thought of that being the reason she kept running away the past few days. I can't wait to tell Brodie and Audrey."

Tertia rolled a cart out of the kitchen and began to clean off the tables. "Can you believe that?"

"It's still like a nightmare, but thanks for the whiskey," Willa Rose answered.

"You are so welcome. We all needed a shot after that. I'm going to buy one of those signs from an online store that says, 'Wild children will be given espresso and a puppy. You will find both in the pen in the backyard.'"

"I'm not sure a fence with razor wire around the top could hold those boys," Tripp said.

Noah rolled a second cart out of the kitchen to help Tertia. "What happened here would make a person wonder about having kids. I've never seen so many customers ask for take-out boxes and be in such a hurry to get the hell out of Dodge."

"I don't blame them one bit," Willa Rose said. "I shudder to think what might have happened to poor little Pansy if we hadn't been here."

Chapter 20

Brodie met Tripp and Willa Rose at the door before they could even knock. "I thought y'all might be bringing Pansy home again. Come on in out of the cold."

Willa Rose handed Pansy off to Brodie. "Bernie must have already called."

"Yep, she did and said the pig ruined your blind dates," Brodie answered. "But she also said the dates weren't a total bust because Willa Rose's date called Aunt Bernie immediately afterward and asked her to fix him up with Melanie."

"And…" Audrey came out of the kitchen. "I just got off the phone with Tertia, who said Pansy wasn't the whole cause, but also two little boys who almost destroyed the place. I told her to post a sign inside the front door that says, 'Misbehaved children will be sold to the circus.' She declares that she will do it and drive them up to Ringling and give them to the carnival folks. They can charge a ransom for the kids if Melanie wants them back."

"That reminds me of that O. Henry story Mama read to me when I was a little girl," Willa Rose said.

"'The Ransom of Red Chief,'" Audrey said with a chuckle. "I loved that story."

"Me too, and I wouldn't sell them to the carnival. I would write Melanie's phone number on their foreheads, drop them off on Zeb's porch, and speed away. Got to admit that even though we had a couple of dates that surpassed every fiasco on record, we have to say thank you to Pansy for helping get us out of those disaster dates."

"What are you going to do with the pig to keep her off the roads and away from the Paradise and café?" Tripp asked.

"We've decided to keep her in the garage," Audrey answered. "Hopefully, she won't find a way to root out of that place. Brodie, take her on out there, and y'all take off your coats. I've set the table for four, and you are having supper with us. The stew is ready, and I just took the bread out of the oven."

"Thank you." Willa Rose hung her coat on the rack inside the door. "I'm starving."

"It's just beef stew and hot rolls, but after what you've been through, it might settle your nerves. Tertia told me all about it. I can't believe that a mother would allow her children to act like that—especially in public." Audrey led the way into the kitchen.

Tripp laid a hand on Brodie's shoulder as they followed the women. "You have no idea how horrible it was. All the customers were checking out with to-go boxes. Tertia and Noah were ready to close up the café for good by the time my date got offended and left."

"All my blind dates combined wasn't that bad." Brodie chuckled.

"I believe you. Not much could top tonight. You can mark it on the calendar that on this very day, I vowed that I would never go on another blind date. Not even if Aunt Bernie cries and promises me the moon." Tripp pulled out a chair for Willa Rose, seated her, and then sat down beside her.

"At least those wild boys didn't stab Pansy," Willa Rose said. "If I see Melissa…"

"Melanie," Tripp corrected her with a grin.

"Whatever! I don't like either name, and if she ever brings those two kids toward my store, I hope I see her coming in time to lock the doors and hang the CLOSED sign out," she finished.

Audrey filled four bowls with stew and passed them around the table. "You are too nice, Willa Rose. I'd hate to think what I might do if they ever came to the farm."

"From what I hear, they could tear up a tractor with a feather," Brodie said.

"They wouldn't need a feather," Tripp declared. "They could do it with their fingernails and not even break one. But we've got news that goes beyond those wild boys."

"You are dating?" Audrey asked.

"No," Willa Rose declared before Tripp could form a single sentence.

"It's even bigger than that," Tripp teased.

"Aunt Bernie will be glad to know that this evening didn't create such a catastrophe that y'all decided to fall into each other's arms for a little comfort," Brodie said between bites.

Willa Rose held out her bowl for Audrey to fill. "If she ever gets it in her mind to set me up again, I'll move to Alaska, or maybe even Siberia."

"I'm going to tell her that I'll go with you," Tripp said. "That should make her move on to Knox."

Audrey passed the breadbasket around the table. "Okay then, if that's not the news, what is?"

"Pansy is most likely pregnant," Willa Rose said. "If I'm right, she will have a litter sometime around Easter, and she'll have about anywhere from six to a dozen little piglets."

"Maybe you should get in touch with Finn and tell him that he owes you pig support," Tripp teased. "Or perhaps it should be Zeb since he was the actual owner of the carnival at the time."

"What are we going to do with a dozen piglets?" Audrey groaned.

"Give them away, and then take Pansy to the vet," Tripp answered. "Unless you want to take her now, and not have any babies next spring."

"No!" Audrey said without hesitation. "She has weathered snow and a long walk every time she ran away. Taking her babies away from her wouldn't be fair. We will keep one little girl piglet and have her fixed early on. That way Pansy will have a friend and maybe stop running away."

Audrey's words stuck in Willa Rose's head: *have a friend and stop running away.*

Since a few days before Thanksgiving, she had made more friends in Spanish Fort than she had left behind in

Poetry, Texas. And then there was all the chemistry between her and Tripp.

So, why are you still running away from this place? Vada's voice whispered in her head. *Don't be too stubborn to admit that you are as happy here as Hank is.*

Tripp nudged her on the shoulder and set off a whole room full of sparks. "Earth to Willa Rose."

"I'm sorry," she said. "I was off in another world. What did I miss?"

"Brodie wants to know how many of the piglets you want," Audrey said.

"Depends on a lot of things, but don't give them all away before I make up my mind," she answered.

"The deciding factor is whether you go back to Poetry or stay here, right?" Tripp asked.

"No, it's whether I can take care of a pet properly wherever I land permanently," she answered, but her mother's words kept playing through her head.

"Why would you worry about taking care of a little piglet properly?" Tripp asked on the way back to the café parking lot that evening. "I'm told that they are easy to train to a litter box. They're kind of like a cat that way."

"Maybe I don't want anything to remind me of Spanish Fort if I leave," Willa Rose answered.

"Oh, honey, those kisses we shared will often come back to your memory."

"What makes you think so?"

"Because you will dream about them," Tripp replied.

"Will you?"

"I already do," he answered as he parked beside her SUV, got out, and jogged around to open the door for her. "But just to keep me from forgetting how hot they were…"

She barely had time to moisten her lips before his mouth closed on hers, and heat filled her whole body. She leaned in to his chest and felt his heart racing through both their coats. When the kiss ended, she wrapped her arms around his neck.

"Just to be sure I don't forget," she murmured as she kissed him again.

They were both panting when she took a step back. Tripp scooped her up in his arms and carried her to the back of his truck. With a free hand, he unlatched the tailgate and hopped up on it.

"It would be a terrible thing to have trouble remembering something this good," he said with her in his lap.

"I'm really good at forgetting what I don't want…"

He cupped her cheeks in his hands and brought her lips to his again. Willa Rose's mind swirled in circles as the whole world disappeared. She and Tripp were the only two people on the earth, and nothing—not weather, people, or even other thoughts—could make her jump down off his lap and hurry over to her own vehicle.

He finally drew back and took a couple of long breaths. "Think you will forget that?"

"Your place or mine?" she asked.

"Are you serious?"

"Yes, I am, but don't think this is anything other than a fling."

"Then neither your place nor mine," Tripp answered. "But I will follow you home to be sure that you make it, and then I'll go on to my house, take a cold shower, and dream of this."

She hopped down off his lap. "You are a strange person, Tripp Callahan."

"What makes you say that?"

"Most men would jump at a chance to have a sexual relationship with no strings attached."

"I'm not most men," he said. "Seems like a waste of time to me."

"Maybe it would be good enough that it wouldn't be a waste."

He walked her to her vehicle. "I'm not arguing that idea, because it probably would, but the aftershocks of the heartbreak wouldn't be worth it."

Her hand brushed against his, but he made no effort to lace his fingers with hers. She had never made such a bold suggestion before in her life—not even with her fiancé. With them things had just progressed slowly to the spending-the-entire-night stage. But after a make-out session with Tripp, her whole body screamed for more than kisses.

"Good night," Tripp said as he opened the door for her and then headed for his truck.

She slapped the steering wheel several times on the drive

home and stomped into the house like an angry second-grade kid. She made herself a cup of hot chocolate, drank one sip, and left it on the table.

What are you waiting for? Her mother's voice was back in her head. *You know what you want. Own it. There's no reason you can't stay in Spanish Fort, other than your pride. So, take a deep breath and listen to your heart.*

"But what if I make a big mistake?" she muttered.

Vada didn't have anything more to say, but rather left Willa Rose on her own to make her own choice in the matter.

"You used to preach that every choice had a consequence."

Still nothing.

Willa Rose took that to mean her mother was through talking. She grabbed her coat, put it on, and hoped that she wasn't making the biggest mistake of her life. She got into her SUV and started the engine. Before she backed out and headed toward Tripp's house, she made the decision that if Knox's truck was there, it would be an omen that she should turn around and go back home.

No vehicle other than Tripp's was in front of the house, so she did what Vada had told her. She took a deep breath, made her decision, and marched up to the porch. That's when she lost her courage and told herself that she was acting on impulse just like Hank did when he made the decision to move from Poetry.

"But he *is* happy, and I don't know where I stand on that issue." She quickly made a mental list of pros and cons about staying in Spanish Fort. The pros outweighed the cons by a long shot, so she raised her fist to knock on the door, but it seemed so forward, even for a modern-thinking woman.

Tripp made the decision for her when he swung the door open and stood before her in nothing but a pair of pajama bottoms. "Is everything okay?" he asked with a concerned expression.

"No, it's not. I want more than a fling, too, and I've made up my mind to stay in Spanish Fort," she blurted out, "and I don't care if Bernie loses all her bets."

"Are you sure about this?" Tripp asked.

"Not really, but my heart tells me if I leave, I'll regret it for the rest of my life. Are you going to invite me in, or do I have to ask again: my place or yours?"

"Well," Tripp stood to one side and motioned for her into the house, "since we're both already here at my place, I'd say that my place would be the better choice."

When she was inside, she removed her coat, tossed it over on the sofa, and took his hand in hers. "Guest bedroom or yours?"

"You choose," he said and pulled her to his chest, then started a string of long, lingering passionate kisses.

"Your room it is then. The bed would get crowded if Knox came sneaking in the house in the middle of the night."

Chapter 21

Willa Rose awoke the next morning in her own bed and felt more at peace than she had since her mother had passed away. Tripp had wanted her to spend the night, but she wasn't quite ready for that step yet. Making the decision she did, and being so bold as to lead him to the bedroom, had taken all her courage for one time.

"But it would have been nice to wake up next to him this morning," she muttered as she threw the covers back.

Her phone rang, and thinking it might be him, she answered it without checking to see who was calling. "Good morning," she said.

"Good morning to you. This is Cooter, and I'm on the way to your place with everything that was in your mama's house. I should be there in an hour, and it would be real nice if I had some help getting all this unloaded. I need to be in Wichita Falls to pick up my next transport to Phoenix at noon."

"I'll rustle up however many folks I can and meet you at the old store. It's on the west corner of the T in the road. You can't miss it." She pulled on a pair of jeans while she talked.

"Be there soon then," he said and ended the call.

She scrolled down, found Tripp's number, and called him.

"Good morning," he said. "I wished you were beside me when I awoke this morning."

"Me, too, but that's moving too fast," she told him and then said, "My antiques will be here in an hour. The truck driver, Cooter, needs help unloading."

"I'll take care of that end if you want to go on to the store," he told her. "And honey, we can move as fast or slow as you want, as long as we're going forward and not standing still."

"Thank you for that, Tripp."

"See you at the store in a few minutes, and I'll bring Hank. He'll want to visit with his buddy while we're unloading."

"Thanks."

"The family will be glad to help. You saw what they all did when the church burned."

She didn't know how to end the call, so she finally just said, "See you there."

Thirty minutes later she was standing in the middle of an empty store wondering how in the world she would ever get a whole truckload of stuff arranged in the place. By the time the big rig had backed up to the porch, the area was full of vehicles. As soon as Cooter had the back doors open and the ramp pulled down, the men of the Paradise family started unloading furniture, boxes, and still more boxes.

"I never figured on all this," Cooter said.

"I told you guys that I was moving to a wonderful place," Hank told him. "While the boys do this work, I want to show you around the leather shop and my apartment. It's just across the street in that big old barn."

Willa Rose tried to tell the guys where to put things, but she finally gave up and said, "Just find a place. I'll get it all organized later. I'd forgotten how much was in that house."

Tripp brought in a box marked GLASSWARE and set it against one wall. "There is definitely enough merchandise to stock the store."

"Hey," Ivy called out. "I'm here to help you all day if you need me. Looks like you have plenty of help unloading, but I'll lend a hand to get some of it unpacked."

"Thank you so much. Just looking at all these boxes bewilders me," Willa Rose admitted.

"I'm a pro at unpacking," Ivy said with a smile. "When they get it all out of the truck, we'll run them off and get busy. You can boss. I follow orders real good."

The guys were unloading the last two pieces of furniture when Cooter and Hank came back across the road. Willa Rose met them at the front of the truck and gave Cooter a hug.

"Thank you so much for doing this for us," she said. "What do I owe you?"

"Your dad took care of that a long time ago when he moved my daughter from California to Oklahoma in the back of his empty truck. We'll just call this a return favor. Y'all have a good thing going here, Willa Rose. Don't mess it up. Hank is happier than he's been since Vada passed away. He's found his place."

"So have I," she whispered.

"For real?" Hank asked.

"Yes, but don't say a word. We wouldn't want to mess up Bernie's Christmas," she answered.

"Now I'm even happier. What happened to make you change your mind?" Hank beamed.

"Something that Yasmin said when she told my fortune. We'll talk about it later. For now, Ivy and I've got lots of work to get done."

"And I need to get on the road," Cooter said.

"Thanks again for everything," Hank told him. "If you are coming near here again, give me a call and I'll meet you for a beer. One of the family members owns a bar in Nocona."

"I'll do it," Cooter promised on his way back up into the cab of the truck. He stuck his arm out the window to wave goodbye.

"Hey, everyone," Hank shouted. "Before you all split to leave, I want to thank you for everything you've done. Willa Rose and I owe you."

Joe Clay crossed the yard and laid a hand on Hank's shoulder. "Family takes care of family."

"Well, know that we appreciate all of you."

"Likewise," Joe Clay said and headed toward his truck. "Ivy wants to help, so I'm leaving her here. Will you see that she has a ride home when y'all call it a day?"

"I sure will," Willa Rose answered.

Within minutes, her SUV looked lonely sitting in the

driveway all alone. "But I won't ever have that kind of feeling again," she whispered as she headed back into the store.

"You are glowing," Ivy said. "You've made up your mind about whether to stay here or go back to your hometown, haven't you. Or maybe you are pregnant?"

"I'm not pregnant and never will be," Willa Rose blurted out.

"I figured you liked kids."

"I do, but my doctor said it would take an absolute miracle for me to have a baby of my own. The odds are about one in a million that I would ever produce a viable egg," Willa Rose confided in Ivy. "You are right about me deciding to stay here in Spanish Fort. However, keep that under your hat until after Christmas."

"I can keep a secret," Ivy declared. "I hear Bernie has a betting pool going on. I might do a little of that insider trading, though."

"What do you know about that?"

"I've lived a lot more than most sixteen-year-old kids," Ivy answered. "Don't tell Mary Jane, but I've actually finished my home schoolbooks through the twelfth grade. I really want to go to public school for the next two years and learn about the social side. If you'll keep my secret, I'll keep yours."

"It's a deal."

"Now that you have made up your mind to stay here, I hope you and Tripp get past the flirting stage and get on down to the business of a relationship," Ivy said.

Willa Rose handed her a pair of scissors. "You are sixteen going on thirty."

"That's what Zeb used to tell me. Now, which boxes do we work on first?"

"If we unpack the breakable stuff, we could put it on the shelves," Willa Rose answered. "Then we would have room to scoot things around a little. I thought we'd have a living room set up at the front of the store, then a dining room with kitchen stuff, and a bedroom on past that."

Ivy nodded and opened the nearest box. "I used to get bored packing and unpacking stuffed animals. This is going to be fun. I've always loved things like you've got here and all the stuff at the Paradise. In the carnival business we make minimalists look like hoarders." She stopped for a breath and unwrapped an antique crystal and silver ice bucket. "You should pick out a beautiful piece like this to give to Audrey and Brodie for their wedding gift."

Willa Rose hadn't thought of a gift, and the wedding was happening on Saturday. That only left Thursday and Friday to shop, and she would have to drive all the way to Wichita Falls if she really wanted to find something nice.

Ivy held up the ice bucket to catch the sunrays coming in the window. "This would be a fabulous gift. Put it with a couple of bottles of Ophelia's wine, and you've got a high-dollar present. Someday I'm going to let Bernie find me a husband."

"You are right about that making a good gift, but why would you ever let Bernie pick your husband?"

"She's done very well with all seven sisters and Brodie," Ivy answered and then lowered her voice. "I think she really wants you and Tripp to get together. It's some of that reverse stuff that she did with Tertia and Noah. She says it's not, but I don't believe her. I want to have a relationship like they all have when I'm about thirty and decide it's time for settling down. And I want to come back to Spanish Fort to live when I do."

At sixteen Willa Rose hadn't been thinking any further in the future than the next weekend. Now she was looking thirty right in the eye, and making the decision to stay in town had been difficult. She couldn't imagine having a path or a goal planned out when she was just a teenager.

"You look like you're seeing ghosts." Ivy giggled.

"Not ghosts, just Willa Rose of the past."

"I don't know what that means," Ivy said. "But let's talk about you and Tripp while I unload this box and put the pretty things on the shelf. Are you ever going to get serious with him? Or have you already?"

"That's a secret I don't want to share right now," Willa Rose answered. "I will spill the beans after the deadline is over for all the bets."

"Then it's a yes you have gotten serious, or you would have said no in a loud voice."

"How did you get so smart, girl?"

Ivy shrugged. "Watching people for nine months out of the year. You think Yasmin was the only fortune teller in the carnival?"

"So, what do you see in my future?" Willa Rose asked.

"A happy marriage and lots of babies," Ivy said.

"Yeah, sure!" Willa Rose said with half a fake laugh.

Chapter 22

Willa Rose had been to several weddings and had even been a bridesmaid at more than one. Some had been elaborate church weddings that took a year or more to plan. Others had been spur-of-the-moment ceremonies performed by a judge in a courthouse. But she had never been as impressed with one as she was that evening at the Paradise.

"I told you so," Ivy whispered when Brodie took his place in the front of the fireplace.

"That he was handsome?" Willa Rose asked in a low tone.

"Well, there is that, but mostly this place is filled with love. Even when two of them disagree, it doesn't last very long. Can't *you* feel it?"

"Yes, I can. I don't know if it's real or just the result of the Christmas season."

Before Ivy could answer, Audrey entered the room on Joe Clay's arm. White daisies were entwined in her dark hair, and she carried a matching bouquet sprinkled with baby's breath and a few sprigs of wispy greenery. Her dress hugged her curves and stopped at midcalf to show off white boots.

"This is what I want when I get married," Ivy said.

I'd just as soon go to the courthouse, or maybe a chapel in Las Vegas, Willa Rose thought.

The ceremony took all of twenty minutes, and there was even a song—"Forever to Me" by Cole Swindell—that brought tears to Ivy's and Willa Rose's eyes. Brodie bent his new bride back in a true Hollywood kiss and then it was over except for the applause and whistles.

You should at least have this much of a wedding so you will have some memories and pictures. Besides, family is important. Vada popped back into Willa Rose's head.

"Parker is here. Shall we make this a double?" Tripp asked from right behind Willa Rose.

"What have you been drinking or smoking?" She fired back at him.

"Nothing yet. I'm saving the champagne for the honeymoon."

"You are engaged?" Ivy gasped.

"No, we are not!" Willa Rose said.

Tripp laid a hand on his chest. "My heart is broken, Ivy."

Bernie stopped in her tracks. "Who broke your heart? Have you been dating someone behind my back?"

Tripp draped an arm around Bernie's shoulders. "No, but I've been sleeping with a gorgeous lady. Let's go congratulate the bride and groom. You did a fine job of reverse psychology on them."

Willa Rose's hand brushed against Tripp's, and for a brief second, he locked his little finger with hers. She was sure glad that Bernie was focused on Tripp and didn't see the blush on her face.

"It wasn't that at all," Bernie declared. "When I got to know Audrey and realized that she wasn't like her aunt Hettie, I figured Brodie would be a good match for her. Now who have you been carrying on with?"

Tripp stood to the side and let the three ladies get in line before him. "I don't kiss and tell."

Bernie stomped her foot on the hardwood floor, but there was enough noise in the room that it didn't even turn a head. "You are enough to make a holy lady cuss, and I've never been accused of being that kind of woman."

"Oh, no!" Tripp faked surprise. "I thought you had moved down here from a convent."

"You"—Bernie poked him in the chest with her forefinger—"are a wolf in sheep's clothing. You were just pretending to be all shy. I will have to rethink my approach to finding you a bride."

Amen to him just pretending to be an introvert. Willa Rose could feel the vibes between them even though there was a foot of air between them.

"Please don't tell me that you're setting me up with another woman like the last one. If so, I'm moving to Alaska, or maybe Siberia," he said.

"That woman has been blocked from ever putting a profile on my dating service," Bernie assured him.

After what seemed like a hundred or more photos were taken, Mary Jane picked up a microphone. "The actual annual Paradise Christmas party begins in half an hour, and there's already a yard full of waiting vehicles. So, Audrey and Brodie are going to cut the cake now and have their first toast—with a bottle of their favorite wine from Ophelia and Jake's winery, of course. Then Brodie will throw the garter to the next groom. Knox, you and Tripp both can take your hands out of your pockets. After that, Audrey will throw the bouquet."

"Aunt Bernie swears that she doesn't want it." Endora raised her voice.

"That's right!" Bernie shouted. "And don't tell me to take my hands out of my pockets. I've always been too much woman for one man to handle."

Tripp moved up a few inches in the crowded dining room to watch the newlyweds cut the cake, feed each other, and then loop their arms together for a toast. *I want this*, he thought. *Not just the excitement of the day, but a love like they have.*

"What are you thinking about so hard that it makes wrinkles on your brow?" Willa Rose asked.

"You want the truth or a story about how much I love wedding cake?"

"The truth."

"I want something like what Brodie and Audrey have," he answered. "But I do love wedding cake, and I intend to have a slice before the party begins and I lose out altogether."

"Then take your hands out of your pocket and catch the garter when he throws it. That will be an omen that you are next in line for a wedding."

"I don't need to be next in line. I'm not in a rush. Knox can have the garter. Maybe you'll catch the bouquet. After all, you've already slept with him. You left me long before daylight, so he must be the more important brother," Tripp teased.

Willa Rose bumped him with her hip. "Bernie can have that bouquet, even though I am partial to daisies, and just for future reference, I hate yellow roses."

Tripp tucked that away in his list of things about Willa Rose and felt a slight puff of wind as the garter whizzed past his face. Knox reached up to grab it but instead batted it back at Tripp, who instinctively reached up and caught it.

Willa Rose was staring up at Tripp's expression when Audrey crossed the room and handed off her bouquet. "Aunt Bernie threatened me, so I have no other choice but to make you the next Paradise bride. No one wants to wait a decade for Ivy to grow up and get married." She gave Willa Rose a hug and whispered, "Please don't leave Spanish Fort. Tripp's eyes have never twinkled like they do when he's around you."

"I'm not going anywhere, but don't tell Aunt Bernie. It would ruin the rest of her holiday if she lost the bet," Willa Rose said in a low tone.

Bernie nudged Tripp on the arm and frowned. "I wanted to catch that bouquet. But I guess Willa Rose should have it if

I want to keep my matchmaking crown. It looks like I've got my work cut out for me. We'll have two more weddings by this time next year."

"Knox and mine, right?" Tripp asked. "He touched this before I caught it, so he gets to move up in line, right?"

"Hey, now," Knox protested. "I wouldn't think of taking your place, and you are the one holding it. So, Aunt Bernie, I will gladly wait my turn."

"That's good," Bernie said with a broad smile. "Willa Rose, darlin', don't you worry, I'll find a husband for you who loves potbellied pigs. But for now, let's open the door for the party and reception to begin. Save a dance for me, Brodie."

He gave her a thumbs-up sign, and when the people began arriving for the party, he and Audrey were having their first dance as a newly wedded couple. When several of the sisters and their husbands joined them, Tripp put the garter on his upper arm and held out a hand to Willa Rose. She put her hand in his and listened to the lyrics of the slow country song, "Me and You" by Kenny Chesney.

"I understand what wedding fever is now," Tripp said as he drew Willa Rose into his arms. "My mama and daddy danced to this song on their wedding anniversary a few years ago. They would have loved to have lived long enough to see Brodie this happy."

"What about you and Knox?"

"Absolutely, but he's in the spotlight tonight, not us," Tripp replied.

The song ended, and Joe Clay picked up the microphone. "Mary Jane and our family would like to welcome everyone to the party tonight. The buffet is ready, and the wedding cake has been cut, so feel free to have a piece of that. Y'all all have a good time."

Willa Rose took a step back. "You were right. This is a big event. It's more than a little overwhelming. How do you feel about dessert first? We could sneak away to the back porch..."

"Yes, but I've got a better idea about where to go."

"Oh?"

"Just follow my lead," Tripp said. "And by the way, you look gorgeous tonight."

"I never know if you are joking or if you are serious."

"I'm always serious. Ask either of my brothers if you don't believe me. If you will get two pieces of cake, I'll steal a bottle of champagne. I'm told that only family is allowed to go upstairs. Meet me at the top of the steps."

She saw him pick up two flutes and a bottle and disappear up the staircase as she stepped up to the table and picked up two small plates of cake and added a spoonful of nuts and mints to each one. Then, feeling like a little girl sneaking a fistful of cookies, she slowly made her way up the dark stairs to the second-floor hallway.

What am I doing? she asked herself when she reached the top. *There's nothing but bedrooms and a bathroom up here. I'm not sure I can trust myself with Tripp with a bed so close by.*

Tripp reached out and pilfered a mint from one of the plates. "Just follow me. I've already got the champagne set up."

"Are you sure about this? What if Bernie comes hunting for us?"

"She will find us on the balcony off the room I used to have when Brodie, Knox, and I stayed here," he answered and led the way to a bedroom with an open door. "I didn't think to grab our jackets, so we'll have to snuggle up together under the quilts."

They went through a dark bedroom, but she could see a dresser, a four-poster bed, and a desk as she followed him through double doors out onto the balcony. He took the two plates from her and set them down on a small table in front of a wicker love seat. She eased down on one of the cold cushions, and Tripp covered her with a quilt, then added another one on top of that. Then he lifted up the end and joined her.

"If we snuggle up together, our body heat will warm us up under these covers," he said. "But then no matter where I am, being close to you creates a lot of steam."

She moved over closer to him. "That's a good pickup line. How many times have you used it before tonight?"

"Well…" he said and slipped an arm around her shoulders. "There was that time in Paris…"

"Texas or France?"

"I can't remember, but then, I can't remember who I said it to either. Maybe it was in a bar, or while I was standing in line at the taco wagon. If that was the case, it was Texas. The folks who run that joint make some fantastic food. Or…" he hesitated. "Maybe I was talking to the tacos. They were really spicy."

"Do you have such a sense of humor with everyone?"

"I don't know how to answer that," Tripp said. "If I had any humor in me, it was well tamped down and hidden until you came along and we started teasing Aunt Bernie. I kind of like the new me, though."

She pulled the covers up closer to her neck and unbuttoned his shirt so she could warm her hands on his chest. "I like this version of you too."

"Do you know what you are doing to me?"

"I have an idea, because the same thing is happening to me." She withdrew her hand. "Maybe it's time for cake and champagne since we are warmed up."

"If these bedroom doors had locks on them, I could think of something better to do."

"We could always sneak out to my place or yours."

"If we leave before cleanup is done, Bernie will have a stroke," he told her. "So, we'll have to do with making out under the stars and getting tipsy on a bottle of very good champagne."

"How do you know it's all that wonderful?"

"Because Knox and I volunteered to stock the bar for the party and reception, and we wouldn't buy cheap for our brother's wedding."

"Well, then, let it be known that I'm a lightweight when it comes to drinking, so if you plan to take advantage of me…"

He brought his hands out from under the quilts and poured two flutes full of bubbly and handed one to her. Then he touched his glass to hers and said, "To us and whatever this journey is that we are taking together."

She took a sip and motioned toward the cake. "If I drink all this on an empty stomach, you will have to carry me out of here."

Tripp took the glass from her and exchanged it for a plate of cake. "Fork?" he asked.

"Where's the romance in that?" she said with a smile as she broke off a piece and fed it to him.

"When we get married, let's do it just like this," he said.

"What makes you think I'll marry you?"

"Because someday you will fall in love with me," he answered.

"You sound pretty confident about that. Why do you think so?"

He picked a piece of cake from the slice and fed it to her. "Because it will take a rich man to pay all the adoption fees for five little boys. That means you will marry me to get that big family of sons that Yasmin predicted. If you don't love me when we say our vows, you will in time. And like I told you, I'm a patient man who doesn't mind waiting."

"We'll see about that, Mr. Tripp Callahan. I might refuse when you propose but rest assured that I will not ever get married for any other reason than pure old-fashioned love."

They took turns feeding each other until both plates were empty, and then he handed her glass of champagne back to her. "Are you just feeding me a line about not being able to hold your liquor?"

"Nope, I am not," she said and downed the rest of what was in her glass. "No more. I don't even like that stuff."

"Me, either," he admitted and pulled her even closer to him. She gazed up at the stars and he focused on the contours of her face, her full lips and thick eyelashes. Then suddenly her eyelids drooped, and her whole body relaxed.

"Holy smoke!" Tripp remembered how difficult it was to wake her. He gave her a gentle shake, but she just muttered his name and eased under the covers to curl up with her head in his lap.

"Willa Rose, you need to wake up. If Hank finds us like this, he'll get out his shotgun," he said.

She began snoring so softly that it sounded like a kitten purring.

"Willa Rose!" He raised his voice and shook her a little harder.

Nothing.

He threw the covers off both of them and shivered when the freezing wind blew against his warm skin. She slipped her hand up and tucked it inside his shirt and moaned ever so slightly.

"Darlin', you have to wake up." He bent down and kissed her on the forehead.

Still nothing.

Finally, he scooped her up in his arms and carried her through the bedroom and toward the bathroom. He was about to open the door when she giggled, looked up at him with those lovely brown eyes, and said, "Gotcha!"

"You are awful!" He set her down on the floor.

"Why were you taking me to the bathroom?"

"I was hopeful that a little cold water on your face would wake you," he answered.

"If you had ruined my makeup, I would never have married you."

"If you had really been asleep and Hank brought a shotgun out, you might not have had a choice."

She giggled again. "Honey, we are living in modern times, not in the old days. Besides, even though we are both fully dressed, you might need to button your shirt before we go back down to the party."

Chapter 23

With Ivy's help for the past couple of days, the antique shop was looking less like a jumbled mess and taking on the shape of a real store. Willa Rose had been in dozens and dozens of antique places all over the state of Texas with her mother. She wanted her place to look like the ones that were all shiny and arranged by rooms.

"You would be proud of this, Mama," she whispered as she took one more look around the store. "After the holidays, I'll have a sign made to go above the porch roof: Vada's Antiques." She imagined the fancy scroll on the upcoming project as she turned out the lights and locked the door. She intended to go straight home, take a long hot bath in the claw-foot tub, and read a chapter in the romance book she had started before she moved to Spanish Fort.

She was locking the door when her phone rang. She fished it out of her back pocket and answered without even looking at the caller ID.

"Can you meet me at the Montague County Courthouse in an hour?" Erica asked. "I know it's short notice, but my lawyer had to move heaven and earth to get this arranged. If we don't do this today, then it will have to wait two weeks, and the baby will stay in care of foster parents until then."

"This is really happening?" Willa Rose was filled with mixed emotions that brought on tears. She hated that Erica was still the self-centered person she had been. But in the same moment, Willa Rose was about to be a mother. Still, she wouldn't believe it until she held a baby in her arms.

"It definitely is," Erica snapped.

"I'm going to ask you one more time. Are you sure about this? You know how attached I can get. Please be sure so my heart doesn't get broken." She looked at the time—one o'clock. She barely had time to rush home and change from sweatpants into something presentable for court.

"I'm positive. Have you told Hank?" Erica asked.

"No, I have not. I was sure you would change your mind, and I can't believe that you got all this arranged in such a brief time, anyway." Willa Rose raced out to her vehicle and slid behind the wheel.

"It's all in who you know, and my lawyer has lots of connections," Erica said. "Can you be here in an hour? From the map I looked at, it's only a thirty-minute drive."

"I'll be there." She braked in front of her house and jogged to the porch. "Do you have the baby with you?"

"It's in a separate car."

"Why aren't you saying 'him' or 'her' instead of 'it'? That sounds so cold." Willa Rose rushed into the house, leaving a string of clothing behind her, and hurriedly dressed in the outfit she had worn to the Paradise for Sunday dinner.

"I don't know if it's a boy or girl. I don't want to know."

"Did you pick out names?" Willa Rose asked on her way back through the living room and outside again. "Surely you put something on the birth certificate."

"Since it's close to Christmas, I told them to put Nicholas on the certificate if it is a boy. Holly if it was a girl. You can change it in a year when we come for the legal adoption stuff. And my lawyer says you will have home visits, and you will work with a caseworker during the year," she said.

"Why did you even have the baby if you didn't want it?"

"Mama wanted a grandchild, and it doesn't look like you are ever going to find anyone to help you out in that area. And I wanted a little piece of me left behind when I die even if I don't want to be the one to raise it," she answered. "But just to be totally transparent, I had my tubes tied, so this is the only mistake I will make. See you at the courthouse and, Willa Rose, my lawyer had to move heaven and earth to get this done legally, so if you bail on me, I will turn the kid over to the courts for adoption."

If Erica really does this, Yasmin was wrong about me having five sons.

"Now that's a crazy thought right now," she muttered.

"What was that?"

"Nothing. I'll meet you there," Willa Rose answered.

"I'll be waiting," Erica said and ended the call.

Yeah, right! Willa Rose thought. *This is just another of your scare tactics or promises that you will break. When I get there, you will laugh at me and say you changed your mind and can't bear to give up the only child you will ever have.*

She checked the time when she got into her SUV and headed out of town. Erica had no conscience when it came to keeping promises. In the past she had promised their mother that she would come for a holiday, or even for a few hours as she was passing through the area, and then she wouldn't show up—without a word of explanation. Sometimes for several days or even weeks.

She figured she would show up at the courthouse in time for another call saying that Erica had changed her mind. That's why she hadn't gotten all excited about having a child, or even worrying about the consequences of accepting the enormous responsibility of raising a child as a single mother. It was also why she hadn't even mentioned the whole idea to Hank.

"This is going to be a trip for nothing," she told herself when she made the turn at Nocona.

Willa Rose parked her car with a few minutes to spare and hurried into the courthouse. She asked the security guard which way she should go to court and then walked right past her sister who was sitting on a bench with a middle-aged man beside her.

"Willa Rose!" Erica snapped.

Willa Rose whipped around and stared at her sister. "You've changed your hair, and…"

"I've had some plastic surgery, but it's me," Erica said with a smile.

Willa Rose recognized the voice, if not the woman. "I can see that. What now?"

"After you sign the papers, we go inside," Erica answered.

"I am Raymond Desmond, Erica's attorney. First, I need to see some identification to know that you are really Willa Rose Thomas."

Willa Rose sank down on the bench beside her sister and pulled her driver's license from her purse. "Will this do?"

"Yes, ma'am," Raymond answered. He opened his briefcase and drew out a stack of papers.

Good Lord! This is really happening. Erica wasn't bluffing. For the first time since her sister asked her if she would raise the baby, Willa Rose thought this could be real, and she only had minutes to get ready.

Willa Rose answered the few questions directed at her, and then the judge signed off on what the lawyer presented to him. She had come into the courthouse as a doubting sister and was leaving as a mother to a child that she had never seen and didn't even know if it was a boy or a girl. Outside on the lawn, the lawyer handed her a thick folder with copies of pages and pages of paperwork.

"What do we do now?" she asked. "Do I hug you or…"

"No!" Erica said. "Now Raymond will take me to the Dallas airport. The lady from the Texas Department of Health and Human Services will put the baby in your car. The birth certificate is in the folder, but just so you know,

I gave birth nine days ago in Austin. The DHS people have had charge of it since then. Goodbye, Willa Rose."

"Surely, you can say 'baby' rather than 'it,'" Willa Rose said.

"That's now your job," Erica said as she got into the vehicle and slammed the door.

The car was well out of sight when a tall, thin woman with gray hair opened the back door of the SUV parked next to Willa Rose's and removed a baby seat. "You are Willa Rose Thomas, right?"

"Yes, ma'am." Willa Rose opened the back door to her SUV.

"I am Loraine and let me say that it is a good thing you are doing, stepping up to take a little guy like this and raise him. We are always so glad to see relatives become guardians," she said as she took care of settling the seat into the vehicle. "The folks who've fostered him for the past week said that he's a good baby."

"Thank you," Willa Rose said, still unsure if she was awake or dreaming.

"I'll be in touch after the holidays to set up a schedule for home visits," she said. "Until then, happy holidays."

"You too," Willa Rose murmured.

"Oh, I almost forgot to give you the diaper bag and a letter from the foster parents telling you what kind of formula he uses and other little details to make your job easier," Lorraine said and handed the bag to Willa Rose.

Willa Rose set the bag on the passenger seat and rounded the front of the vehicle. She crawled into the back seat, unfastened all the straps holding the baby into the seat, and took him out. She touched his hair, dark like her mother's, and unwrapped the blue blanket from around him.

"You are mine," she whispered as she held him close to her chest. "Your name is Nicholas, but I'm going to call you Nicky, and I promise I will love you so much, even more than your grandfather, Hank, who is going to cry when he sees you."

The baby opened his eyes wide and snuggled down deeper into her chest. Tears flowed down Willa Rose's cheeks. She understood Tripp's love for his mother now and believed that a woman could love a child even if she hadn't given birth to him.

"Okay, baby boy, it's time for you to go back into your seat. Let's go home," she said as she settled him back into the carrier and kissed him on the top of his head.

In one respect, the trip back to Spanish Fort took forever. On the other side of the coin, it seemed like she had just driven away from the courthouse a minute before she parked in front of the leather shop. She took Nicky out of the seat and slung the diaper bag over her shoulder.

"We are here, and from the way you are chewing on your fist, I'd say it's about time for a bottle," she said as she made her way to the barn.

She stepped out of the cold and into warmth and soft Christmas music filling the shop. Her father worked on one side of a workbench, and Tripp on the other. Both looked up, saw that it wasn't a customer, and motioned her inside.

"Close the door, girl," Hank called out. "You are letting out all the bought warm air, and it don't come cheap. Are you babysitting one of Endora's twins today?"

"No, Daddy, I'm not. I want y'all both to meet Nicky." She went on to tell them everything. "I glanced at the birth certificate, and it says Nicholas Thomas. When I adopt him, I'm not changing his name."

"Oh, Willa Rose, I'm so proud of you for doing this."

"I've known about it for a while, but I didn't think she would give him up," Willa Rose said. "So, I didn't mention it to anyone or get my hopes up. Right until the time that she drove away from the courthouse, I figured she would change her mind."

"And now you are a mama," Hank said.

"Yes, I am." Willa Rose remembered that Endora's twins had been born on the same day as Nicky. That was the very morning that she had been envious and wanted a baby of her own.

Hank swiped tears streaming down his cheeks with the back of his hand. "I like shortening his name to Nicky. Are you going to stare at him all evening or let me hold my new grandson?"

"Nicky does fit him better, and yes, Daddy, you can hold him while I make a bottle for him. He's been chewing on his fist for the last few minutes," Willa Rose answered. "But I really want to be the first one to feed him."

"Of course you do," Hank said without taking his eyes off the baby.

"Looks to me like you just got the first of those five boys that Yasmin promised you," Tripp said.

Willa Rose handed the baby to Hank and then panic set in while she made the bottle. "My mind is spinning in circles. What if I can't do this? What if I said yes too quickly?"

"Stop worrying. You are going to make a fantastic mama." Tripp reached out to touch the baby's hand, but Nicky latched on to his finger. "Welcome home, baby boy. You are a mighty fine Christmas present. And Willa Rose, we've got this covered. There are three of us and only one of him. How much trouble can one little tiny boy be anyway?"

"I will never understand Erica," Hank whispered, "but I'm so glad she gave us a chance to raise him. Even if she doesn't claim me, they are blood to my Vada. I'll help you, Willa Rose, any way I can. He is family and an answer to prayers for you."

"I never thought…" Willa Rose said as she reached for the baby and sat down in a nearby chair to feed him.

When he had sucked down an ounce of formula, she looked up at Tripp. "Do you know how to burp a baby?"

"Yes, ma'am, I sure do."

The look of amazement and pure love for a baby that he had just met quelled all of Willa Rose's fears. She handed Nicky to him and knew that the three of them could give this baby all the love and support he would ever need.

Hank moved closer to Tripp. Willa Rose took a mental picture of her father's big, callused hand and Nicky's tiny one bonding and could already see them walking across the yard together when Nicky was older.

"His name seems to fit him well, and since he has my last name, that makes him mine too."

But someday I might add another name to the end. He could very well become Nicholas Thomas Callahan, but that's a long way in the future.

Was this the way that Tripp's mama felt when she held her adopted children for the first time? Even after going through the birth experience with Brodie, did she have the same maternal instincts with the adopted twins? If so, she fully understood Tripp's attitude about not caring if he had biological kids or if they were adopted.

"He is perfect," she said as she pulled back the blanket and kissed his little toes.

Tripp pulled up two more chairs and sat down in one. "Well, our worlds just turned upside down in five minutes. But you could let me and Hank hold him for a minute? We promise to give him back."

"This is like a Christmas miracle for me and Willa Rose, but what is it really to you?" Hank asked.

"He isn't really mine, but since I'm going to help with him, I can officially tell Brodie that he beat me to the marriage thing, but I got a son before he did."

"If I'm dreaming, don't wake me up," Willa Rose whispered.

"Oh, no!" Tripp said. "What if the baby's cries don't wake you? I mean, after all, you can sleep through a tornado, right?"

Hank chuckled and gave Nicky to Tripp. "I bet all that changes starting tonight."

"I think we should bring the crib from your antique shop to my house. I'm a light sleeper," Tripp said.

"Endora said something that makes sense when she went home before Mary Jane wanted her to. She said that the twins needed to get acclimated to their own place. I want Nicky to be in his own home from now on."

"That makes sense," Hank said.

"But, Daddy, I'm scared," she admitted. "What if…"

"That what-if game is a black hole that will swallow you whole. You will adjust, and Tripp is going to be there to help you at night for these first few weeks." Hank shifted his focus from the newborn to Tripp. "Right?"

"Yes, I am."

"And, Willa Rose, you have to promise to give me the same thing I gave you," Hank said.

"What's that?" she asked.

"One year. I gave you a year to decide if you wanted to stay in Spanish Fort or go back. These first months are not going to be easy, so if you decide you can't do this and follow your dream of taking care of the shop both, then we'll more or less put the houses in Poetry up for sale at the same time we give him up for adoption," Hank said.

"The houses, yes, but I could never do that to this baby," Willa Rose said.

"If you did, I'd be the high bidder," Tripp said.

"How can you say that when you just now met him?"

"When you know, you know, and I do," Tripp said. "I'll help get him into the SUV and then take my truck over to your shop and get that crib and cradle."

Knox pushed open the door and stopped right inside. "I figured you would have closed up shop by now. What is this? Are you babysitting for Endora? I thought they had one of those fancy strollers."

"Merry Christmas to me," Willa Rose answered. "I am a new mother."

"You are what?" Knox frowned.

"He is partly mine since I'm going to help Willa Rose take care of him," Tripp said and reached out toward Hank, who slipped the infant over into Tripp's arms.

"Come meet Nicky, Uncle Knox. If Willa Rose decides to sell him in a year, then I'm at the top of the list to get him."

Knox sank down in the empty chair. "Will someone explain what is going on here? Is this a joke? Are you holding a real baby, or is that one of those lifelike dolls?"

"It's not a joke, and he is very real," Hank said and went on to tell him what had happened.

"I see, but Brother, you do know it's illegal to buy a child," Knox said.

"I do, but Willa Rose and I will figure something out if it comes to that."

Knox chuckled and then threw back his head and guffawed. "Can I be the one to tell Bernie?"

"Why her?" Willa Rose asked.

"She told me last night that she is going to settle up all the bets today. She heard through the gossip mill that Willa Rose is staying in Spanish Fort. Bernie is about to have a big loss in the matchmaking game. She was sure she could find a husband for Willa Rose—who lives miles away from here. She may be so distraught that she won't even try to fix me up."

Tripp smiled and winked at his brother. "Don't bet on it, Brother."

"Y'all knew that she was staying for weeks, didn't you? There's no way you would be this relaxed and agreeable to having a child dumped in your laps without knowing. That's what all the whispering in the shadows has been about, isn't it? Why did you keep it from me? We're twins. We share things."

"They had no idea about Nicky," Willa Rose assured him.

"Like I said earlier, this is our Christmas miracle," Hank whispered. "A son born in December. Seems fitting, doesn't it?"

"I can't have children of my own, but I already feel that he is mine right here." She touched her heart. "I've got a good support system, so I can do this. We were about to take him home. Want to come with us?"

Hank shook his head and headed across the room. "You might need me as a daytime helper, but I'm the grandpa, not the parent."

"What can I do to help?" Knox asked.

"You can go with me and help me take a crib and cradle from the antique shop over to Willa Rose's house. We might need to tear it down to get it inside, so bring tools," Tripp answered.

Knox pushed his shoulder-length blond hair back and took a long look at the baby. "He's got your dark hair, Brother. Are you sure y'all are telling me the whole story?"

"We are, but no one can ever say that the night you slept with Willa Rose marked him, can they?"

"That's enough," Willa Rose barked. "And if either of you say a word like that to Bernie, I will ban you both from spending time with Nicky."

Chapter 24

"We have four granddaughters and only three grandsons," Mary Jane said as she rocked Nicky. "You sisters who don't have babies yet or haven't told me that you are pregnant need to catch up."

All the seven sisters began pointing at one another and talking at once. The smile on Mary Jane's face testified that she had deliberately stirred up that hornet's nest. Willa Rose couldn't make sense of all the blaming until Ursula clapped her hands loudly and swung her forefinger around at four of her sisters.

"I got the ball rolling when I had Clayton, and y'all were still sitting on the sidelines when the two youngest sisters had children. So, Mama is talking to all y'all, not to me, Luna, Endora, or Willa Rose."

"You can redirect your pointing to Tertia, Ophelia, and Bo. I brought two daughters into the family, and that's all I can handle," Rae told her.

"Oh, no!" Endora argued. "You got yours already sleeping all night and potty trained, so you have to have one yourself. No offense, Willa Rose. You get a pass because Nicky came to you as a newborn and you have to go through sleepless nights, teething, and potty training."

"None taken. My dad used to say that he got one daughter with a marriage license and one with a birth certificate, but it was all just paper. Now, who is volunteering to be next?" She wouldn't have believed Jesus, Himself, if he had told her how much her life would turn around in one short holiday season. She snapped a mental picture of the scene that reminded her of the front of a Christmas card—a blaze in the fireplace, Mary Jane rocking the newest baby and humming a lullaby, and a toddler staring down at Nicky.

Ophelia raised both palms. "I'll take this one for the team. I'm not pregnant but Jake and I are going to try to start a family after the holidays are over."

Knox and Tripp came into the living room, and Knox shook his head in mock disappointment. "With all that dark hair, he has to be yours. I was kind of hoping…"

Tripp slapped him on the arm. "If you want one born with a blond ponytail, then you'll have to find a willing partner, but before you do, you need to bank a lot of sleep."

Willa Rose covered a yawn with her hand. "Sleep appears to be a thing of the past."

"I remember those days," Mary Jane said. "Try having two sets of twins with only a year between them. Willa Rose, you and Tripp look like y'all are about to drop. Go upstairs and take a nap. There's plenty of us to babysit Nicky."

"No boys upstairs," Ursula said.

"That rule got changed when Brodie knocked on our door last Christmas," Mary Jane reminded her.

Tripp stood up. "Thank you. I'll take you up on that offer. Nicky is a good baby and only wakes up every four hours to be fed. Our trouble is that we are afraid we won't hear him even though he sleeps in the cradle right beside the bed. Willa Rose is a sound sleeper, as we all know from the night Endora's twins were born, and she's terrified to close her eyes."

"I understand," Ursula said. "It took a full month before we trusted the baby monitor, and even then, we checked the batteries every single day."

"I'm fine." Willa Rose could hardly hold her eyes open and the conversations among all the family members around her were only a buzz in her ears.

"No, we are not." Tripp took her hand and pulled her up. "Someone will come get us if Nicky fusses. We both could use an hour's sleep."

She let him lead her to the same bedroom they had been in on the night of the wedding. *How could that be only four days ago?* she wondered as she removed her shoes and curled up on top of the covers. That night she had wanted to fall back on the bed and drag Tripp down on top of her, and now all she could think about was a nap.

Tripp kicked off his shoes and shook the folds from a quilt that had been lying at the foot of the bed. He crawled into bed, snuggled up against her back and covered them both.

He kissed her on the neck and said, "Sweet dreams."

"Are we going to survive this?"

All she could think about was sleep, but her body reacted to his warm breath and lips on her neck. No surprise there—none at all.

"Of course." He hugged her a little tighter. "When we readjust our sleeping habits, we'll be fine. All new parents go through a time like this, but I must admit, I have a whole new respect for Endora and Parker. One at a time is enough."

"You are counting yourself as a parent?"

"Of course, I am," Tripp answered. "Someday when you decide to marry me, I'm going to adopt Nicky."

You have to ask me first, she thought.

The room was dark when Tripp awoke. He eased out of bed, picked up his shoes, and tiptoed downstairs. The house was so quiet that he could have heard a feather floating down from the ceiling, right up until Bernie stepped out of the living room. She stopped right in front of him, popped her hands on her hips, and gave him a go-to-hell look.

"What did I do?" he asked.

"I'll tell you exactly what you did," Bernie answered. "Like most men, you are blind to what's right in front of you, Tripp Callahan. You are sitting up there on your big white horse to save the damsel in distress. I bet this is your MO, as they say on the cop shows I like to watch. You have such a soft heart that you want to help women who have problems. Well, I'm about to shoot your horse if you don't turn it around and ride away from Willa Rose."

"With all her sass, Willa Rose definitely does not need saving."

"Of course she doesn't, but somewhere in your heart, you think she does, and that's a deadly attitude. And"—she poked him in the chest with a bony finger—"we are talking about you, not her."

"Can we have this conversation later? I'm starving." He tried to walk around her, but she moved backward and stayed with him.

"Food can wait. I've got you alone and you are going to listen to me."

"Yes, ma'am, but can you fuss at me over a sandwich?"

"No!" she answered. "You'll tune me out if you are eating. You'll pay attention, so sit down on the stairs and listen."

"Can you make it fast? I might fall over dead from starvation if you plan on talking until the world ends."

"You are exasperating me. Do you have any idea what happened to my customers who aggravated me when I owned my bar?" she asked.

"You threw them out?" His stomach growled loudly, but he sat down on the third step and stretched his long legs out to the bottom one.

She began to pace from one end of the foyer to the other and back again. "I'm as serious right now as when I threatened them with my sawed-off shotgun."

"Okay, don't have a heart attack or a stroke. Just spit it out."

"You had a case of transference when you looked at that baby and remembered that you were just like him at one time—homeless and about to be an orphan," she said.

"When did you get a doctorate in psychology?" Tripp asked.

"Running a bar for fifty years will take care of that as well as a piece of paper," she barked. "And besides, Dr. Charles on *Chicago Med* is one of my favorite people, and he taught me a lot."

"Are you protecting your betting interest or your matchmaking business?" Tripp asked.

"I settled the bets this morning, and after seeing that baby, I'm not even going to bitch about my losses," she declared. "I'm trying to make you see your problem when it comes to women. Your big, old kind heart is walking into a heartache. No, change that part about walking. You are running into it like a firefighter into a burning house."

He stood up and wrapped his arms around Bernie. "Thank you for caring enough about me to try to protect me, but right now it's my stomach that is a problem. Let's go out to the kitchen and see what we can do about taking care of that issue. We'll revisit the heart issue later."

"You are the most exasperating Callahan of the three of you. You come off as the reserved one, but that's on the outside. Underneath all that quietness you're as stubborn as a cross-eyed mule."

Tripp headed on down the foyer toward the kitchen. "Thank you for seeing all that, and next time you watch *Chicago Med*, thank Dr. Charles for me."

"This conversation is not over, but I can see I'm not making any headway with you."

"Remember that sprig of mistletoe you hung on my porch? I do believe it has come back to bite you."

Bernie threw up her hands and gave him another dose of stink eye. "I'm changing the subject because you can't see more than a foot in front of your eyes, especially since that adorable baby arrived. Are you sure you weren't playing knight in shining armor with Willa Rose's sister about nine months ago? That little boy looks a lot like you with his dark hair."

"Nope, been right here in Spanish Fort for the better part of a year and never met a woman named Erica, and if you take another look, Nicky looks more like Willa Rose than me. Speaking of that, who is watching Nicky? Did one of the sisters kidnap him?"

Bernie picked her coat up from the hall tree and slipped her arms into the sleeves. "Ivy is keeping an eye on him and writing in a notebook that she carries with her all the time. Mary Jane and Joe Clay went to Nocona, and the sisters all left about half an hour ago. There is a slow cooker full of potato chowder on the cabinet. I've already had a bowl of it. Promise me, you will think on what I told you."

"I will think on it, but I've never ridden a white horse. Once at summer camp I mounted up on a paint, but I didn't have a desire to save one of the girls who was having trouble controlling her animal," he said.

"You are going to be the death of me," she said as she closed the door behind her.

"No, ma'am, I'm saving that honor for Knox." Tripp chuckled.

Glad that the conversation was over, he went to the kitchen, dipped up a bowl of soup and carried it to the living room. Ivy looked up from her notebook and smiled. "He's been sleeping ever since Mary Jane fed him a bottle in the middle of the afternoon. Did you have a nice nap?"

"Yes, I did. Thanks for keeping an eye on him, but if you've got something else to do, I've proven that I can eat and watch him at the same time."

She slipped her notebook into a worn backpack, stood up, and stretched. "Ursula invited me over to her house to talk about writing, but I can stay until you finish eating."

"You go on with your plans," Tripp told her. "I can eat and watch Nicky at the same time."

"When are you going to ask Willa Rose to marry you?" she blurted out.

Tripp almost choked on a bite of soup.

"Don't look so shocked," Ivy said. "When Nicky arrived, y'all became a family. It's time to own it all the way."

"I don't want to rush her, so I'm waiting for the right time," he answered. "First, she had to decide whether to stay in Spanish Fort. Then the baby came, and it's all happened so fast that sometimes I think I'm dreaming."

"Well, don't wait too long. Grandpa used to tell me that when opportunity knocks, it's better to open the door and invite it to come right inside than it is to chase it a mile down the road."

"That's good advice. I'll remember it."

"See you later, and remember me if you ever need a sitter. I love babies, and Nicky is just the cutest little guy ever. I told him that he can call me Aunt Ivy," she said and blew the baby a kiss as she left the room.

You need to do some soul-searching. His mother's voice was clear in his head.

He nodded in agreement. As much as he hated to admit it, Bernie had made some very valid points. Could he be mounting up on a white horse for the first time? In the beginning, what he had going on with Willa Rose had been a flirtatious game that he figured wouldn't go anywhere since no one believed she would ever stay in town. Then the chemistry began to build—at least for him—and now there was Nicky.

Am I mistaking love for wanting a family? he asked himself.

"Hey, what happened to everyone?"

Willa Rose's voice almost made Tripp drop his bowl of soup. She went straight to the sofa where Nicky slept and asked, "Are we the only ones here?"

"Ivy left a few minutes ago. Everyone else has gone, but she stayed behind to keep an eye on him while he slept. Mary Jane gave him a bottle sometime around two, I would guess, and it's probably about time for another one. Should we wake him to keep him on schedule?"

How had they gone from enemies to friends to lovers and now parents in less than a month's time? Tripp wondered. "I'll fix him a bottle and feed him while you get something to eat. Did your nap help?"

She nodded. "More than words can say. I believe Endora now more than ever, though."

"About twins being double work?"

"Yes, and that they are the best birth control on the market," she answered. "Even if I could get pregnant, we're both too tired to even think about sex."

"Speak for yourself, woman," Tripp growled. "I can think about it even if that's all I can muster up the strength to do."

She bent down and kissed the baby on the forehead. "I still can't believe that you were ever inhibited. While you get his next bottle ready, I'll have some soup and then we should probably go home. Maybe we can catch a movie while we wait for his next feeding."

"Or make out a little, then doze through the movie," he said.

"That, too, or whichever comes first."

Everything had turned upside down, or perhaps a better saying would be that it had turned inside out, or so it seemed to Willa Rose. She and Tripp had been about to find some solid footing in their relationship when Nicky showed up. Now they were sliding into a four-hour routine without the benefit of a romance, a wedding, or a honeymoon. The proper sequence should have been flirting, lovers for several months, then planning a wedding for a year and a wonderful honeymoon. All that should have happened two years at the very least before a baby made them a family.

Surely, he was teasing about marrying her in this crazy, mixed-up world like they had been tossed into. How could he love someone who was constantly worn out from lack of sleep?

Whoa! Wait a minute. He hasn't said those three words to me yet. He's skipped around the bush and kidded me about being parents together, but the words, "I love you, Willa Rose Thomas," have never come out of his mouth.

"What are you thinking about?" he asked as he shook the bottle containing formula and water.

"Eating this bowl of soup," she lied. "My energy level is so low that I don't know if I can chew the potatoes."

"No one ever said that parenting is easy." He set the bottle on the table and hurried into the living room when he heard Nicky whimper.

He is making a wonderful father, the annoying voice in her head said.

"Yes, but I want more than that," she muttered under her breath, and admitted to herself that she wanted the excitement of the banter, or the long looks across the room, the sly winks and sneaking away to be alone for a little while. She wanted that tingle when his fingertips brushed hers at the dinner table and to feel the thrill of his naked body lying next to hers after making love.

"Want me to feed it to you like I did Brodie and Audrey's

wedding cake?" he asked when he came back with Nicky in his arms.

"I like you better when you are flirting," she blurted out.

Nicky latched on to the bottle nipple like he was starving. "What do you think I was doing? Don't you think eating from my fingertips is flirting?"

"How are you going to feed me soup from your fingers?" she fired back at him.

"Very carefully. Are we having our first fight as new parents?"

"No, we're having a discussion about flirting," she answered, "I am committed but you can walk away from this."

"I'm not going anywhere," Tripp told her.

"Remember to burp him after every ounce, or else he might get colic."

"I thought these bottles were supposed to prevent that, and how do you know so much about babies?" He held the bottle up, checked the milk level on the side, and set it down.

"On the Sundays that Mama and I kept the nursery at church, I didn't learn a lot about God, but I did learn quite a bit about babies. Tell me, and answer honestly, what happens when you get tired of playing daddy?"

"Trust me." He put Nicky up on his shoulder and patted him on the back. "I loved this baby the first time we threw back the blanket and looked at him, and I'm just as much in the game as you are."

"What happens if we get swallowed up by that love, and forget…"

The baby burped loudly, and Tripp repositioned him in

one of his big arms to feed him again. "Are you breaking up with me?"

"No…maybe… I don't know. Besides how can we break up when we've never been on an official date?"

"Ivy said she would be more than happy to babysit, so I can remedy that in a hurry. Willa Rose Thomas, will you go out with me Friday night on a real date? Dinner in Nocona and a walk in the park?"

"If Bernie hadn't already given up on us, she would flip out."

"Do either of us really care at this point what Bernie says?" he asked.

"I certainly don't, so yes, I will go with you if Ivy can come to the house and babysit, but between now and then I want *you* to stay at your house. You can pick me up at six."

"Can I see Nicky both days?"

"Of course, but I need a couple of days to sort out all this, to figure out if there is time for us when the dust settles from all this newness."

"You got it."

"Why do you have to be so agreeable?" she snapped.

"Because in this case, I need some time to think over what you said too. The chemistry between us could be rebound feelings for you and merely a flash in the pan for me. Or maybe it's just been having a good time for both of us. We need to figure out where this is going and if what we have is for *us*, or is it for Nicky?"

"I agree," she said in a softer tone.

Chapter 25

A MONTH BEFORE WHEN Hank showed up at his shop, Tripp would have been worried about whether he could get all the Christmas orders finished on time. But that evening his mind was on a merry-go-round, comparing Willa Rose's words to what Bernie had said. Just before he crawled into bed and turned out the lamp, he noticed the sprig of mistletoe still lying on his nightstand.

"If you have any power left at all, give me a sign," he muttered.

At two o'clock in the morning, his phone rang and awoke him from a dead sleep. "Hello," he mumbled.

"Tripp, I have no water and there's a strange hissing sound under the house." Willa Rose's tone was one of pure panic. "What do I do?"

"The parsonage is an old house, and the cold front that hit us yesterday has probably frozen the pipes under the house. What you are hearing is water spewing out when they burst," he answered. "If you'll pack bags for you and the baby, I'll come get you. I will turn off the water at the meter, and you won't be able to stay at your place until we get a plumber."

"But Nicky's things, his cradle and…"

"We can bring what he needs tonight to my house and worry about what else we need to move tomorrow."

"Okay, then I'll start getting things ready, and thank you, Tripp."

"No problem." He ended the call, picked up the mistletoe, and kissed the red ribbon. "I will never doubt you again."

A bitter north wind whipped through the tree limbs and sent a couple of huge tumbleweeds toward him when he stepped off the porch. He looked up at the sky, half expecting to see clouds that promised another snow or ice storm, but stars twinkled around a waxing moon.

Lights shone out Willa Rose's windows, leaving long strips of yellow on the crispy grass. He saw shadows moving around through the lacy curtains, but didn't go straight for the house. Instead, he parked on the road, hefted his toolbox over the truck bed, and found the water cutoff. He thought of Brodie back last spring when he had to do the same thing after the tornado blew away their house and all their belongings.

"At least I'm not having to do this in the rain and with no clothes on." He chuckled.

When he finished, he backed the truck up to the porch. Willa Rose slung open the door and said, "The hissing stopped."

"Good," Tripp said. "That means only whatever water is in the pipes will flood out under the house when they unfreeze. You are lucky…"

"How can you say that?" she butted in. "It's the middle of the night."

He drew her close to him for a quick hug. "Lucky that the pipe didn't burst inside the house, or you would be walking around in ankle-deep cold water. As it is, there is most likely a lake under the floor that will have to dry up before a plumber can even get to the problem. If this cold front hangs around, that could be days or weeks since it's close to the holidays, so you will have to stay with me for a while."

She stuffed even more baby clothes into a second diaper bag. "Do you believe in signs?"

He thought of that little sprig of mistletoe. "Sometimes. Do you?"

"Yes, I do," she answered as she took Nicky out of the cradle. "I asked for an omen just before I went to sleep. A sign of some kind to help me sort all of this out, and I woke up to that noise under the house. At first, I thought it might be a den of rattlesnakes."

He picked up the cradle and headed for the door with it. "What does this mean to you?"

"That we need to figure it out together, not apart," she answered.

"Absolutely," he told her, but he did not mention the mistletoe. After the holidays he was going to have that bit of greenery encased in a square of Lucite or preserved forever in a glass bubble.

Chapter 26

"My favorite memory as a little girl was driving through Poetry and then over to Terrell to see all the Christmas lights and decorations," Willa Rose said and whipped her head from one side of the road to the other all the way from Spanish Fort to Nocona. "I don't want to miss a thing, but I've got to admit none of them are as fancy as the Paradise."

"My folks took us all around Bandera and down to San Antonio to the River Walk to see it all lit up every year. Now, that's a town to visit during the holidays."

With his deep Texas drawl, Willa Rose could have listened to him read *Moby Dick*, and that was a compliment because she had tried to read it twice and didn't get past page fifty.

"Since you enjoy driving around and looking at lights, how would you feel about getting some fast-food burgers at the Dairy Queen?" Tripp asked. "That wouldn't take as long as a sit-down meal, and then we could drive over to Saint Jo to see all the Christmas decorations. They tell me that the square is pretty impressive during the holidays."

"I would love that."

"Then that's our new plan," he told her.

"Are we *really* on a date?" she asked.

"If you call a cheeseburger with bacon, fries, and a chocolate shake a date, then yes, we are. If you call it two friends who are raising a baby together on an evening out, then you will make Bernie very happy."

"I guess Bernie is going to be angry, or maybe she's been playing the two of us all this time," Willa Rose said.

"I don't think so." Tripp could easily visualize the expression on Bernie's face when she confronted him. "She thinks you are going to stay, but now she believes that if we got together, it would be for Nicky, not for us."

"I wonder if that's why my mama didn't say yes to my dad all those times he proposed," Willa Rose said.

"Because she liked hamburgers?"

"No, because she had to be sure that he wasn't looking for an instant family and that he really loved her for herself." The fact that Tripp had never said the words pricked her heart.

Neither have you, the niggling voice inside her head reminded her.

A guy is supposed to say them first, she argued.

In what world? the voice asked.

She brushed the thoughts away and pointed out the front window. "We're coming into town, and it really is lit up like Christmas, but not as much as the Paradise."

"I don't image there's a town in the whole county that can top the Paradise."

"Maybe not in all of north-central Texas."

"But not in the whole state," Tripp said. "My dad used to say that the astronauts could probably see San Antonio from outer space. That reminds me of something the old gentleman who taught me about leatherworking said when his wife passed away. They had been married sixty years, and he didn't seem to be nearly as saddened at losing her as I thought he would be. I asked him why, and he told me that everyone dies two deaths. One when their body is tired and leaves this earth. The second is when everyone stops telling their stories. With that in mind, when I remember something either of my parents said or a story that they used to tell…"

"That's a variation of what Ernest Hemingway supposedly said, something like: 'Every man has two deaths, when he is buried in the ground and the last time someone says his name. In some ways men can be immortal.' But how did you get that out of astronauts seeing a city lit up from outer space?"

"What my dad said about it, and what old Gus told me about remembering those who have passed away. If I remember their stories, their spirit is still alive. Do you remember things that your mother said?"

Willa Rose smiled at all the memories she had of her mother, and at the times when she still popped into her head to give her advice or argue with her. "Yes, I do, and I like what Gus told you. That's a comforting thought."

Tripp turned left and found a parking spot in front of the Dairy Queen. "Gus read all the time, so he probably just paraphrased what Hemingway said."

"What do you read?" she asked.

"I'm an eclectic reader—so the answer would be everything from Faulkner to the back of the cereal box. How about you?"

"Mary Jane Simmons and your sister, Ursula, here lately. If they don't have anything new on the market, then I like historical romance," she answered. "Don't give me that look. Men could learn a lot from reading steamy books."

He opened the truck door and asked, "When did you start reading that kind of book?"

"When I was twelve. I found one that Erica left behind."

"What did your dad say about that?"

She chuckled. "We had a five-page rule. Before you ask, it went like this: and then he kissed her, turn five pages and keep reading."

"And you followed the rule?"

Willa Rose giggled out loud. "Oh, hell no, but I did feel guilty a few times."

"That surprises me."

"What?"

"Both that you went against what Hank said, and that you felt guilty," he answered and slid out of the truck, closed the door, and jogged around the front to help her out of the vehicle.

"Thank you, kind sir," she quipped as she put her hand in his. "Why would you be surprised at me being a rebel or repenting?"

"You seem more like a woman who was born knowing

her own mind." He kept her hand in his and led her into the café.

She gave his hand a gentle squeeze. "Lot of good that did me. I was dead set against moving to Spanish Fort, and even more so against liking you or any of the Paradise family. Yet here I am."

"And happy?" He opened the café door for her.

"Yasmin told me to choose a path when I came to the fork in the road," she answered. "My dad used to tell me that I couldn't ride two horses with one ass, so the advice is pretty much the same. I refuse to have regrets concerning the path I chose."

The aroma of burgers cooking wafted out to meet them when he ushered her inside. "You didn't answer me. Are you happy?"

"Define 'happy.'" She grinned.

"Does living here bring you joy?"

"Yes, it does," she answered. "And so does the smell of burgers."

"I guess that puts me in my place about making you happy," he said.

"You are buying me what I love, so that says a lot."

"Well, well, well!" Bernie said from a nearby booth. "What is going on here?"

"Is she everywhere?" Willa Rose whispered.

"It's date night," Tripp answered and tipped his hat toward the ladies. "Evening, Gladys and Vera. What are y'all out doing this evening? Lights or last-minute shopping?"

"Yep to both," Bernie answered. "But first we are having supper. Y'all beat me to the punch by sneaking your first date in on me."

"Were you about to set us up on a date together?" Willa Rose asked.

Bernie cut her eyes around at her. "Busted. I was going to play a trick on y'all and set you up on a blind date together after Christmas. You would have been so shocked to see that you were meeting each other for dessert and coffee, and with my blessing."

Willa Rose raised both dark eyebrows. "Oh, really? Did you just now dream that up?"

"No, she's been telling us about her plans since that fiasco with those terrible kids and you decided to stay in town," Vera vouched for her.

Bernie removed a bill from her purse and handed it to Tripp. "That's the last of the bets paid in full."

Tripp slipped the hundred in his pocket. "How much did you lose?"

"If I told you, that would be breaking bookie/client confidentiality," Bernie told him.

"I'm not sure that exists," Tripp argued.

"It does if I say it does, and I always had confidence in you, even if you almost became my first failure." Bernie chuckled. "Now, go on and put your order in. Unless you are stalking me."

"I am not," Tripp said.

"Before you go..." Vera focused on Willa Rose. "I want to

compliment you on that great Christmas program. Having it in the barn was a stroke of genius."

"Thank you, but it was a team effort between the folks at the Paradise and the carnival folks," Willa Rose said.

"Where's the baby?" Gladys asked. "Are you bringing him to services on Sunday? Vera and I will be watching the nursery. Mary Jane is letting us use the living room in the Paradise to keep the littles in."

"Ivy is watching him for us tonight," Tripp answered.

"Mary Jane is a good woman to take that girl into the Paradise. I hear that Ivy is fitting right into the family," Vera said.

"Mary Jane has a heart of gold, and Ivy has been helping me organize the antique store, too," Willa Rose said. "But Bernie, I have a question before we put in our order. When did you change your mind about me and Tripp?"

Bernie took a long drink of her sweet tea. "I figure if you can't fight 'em, join 'em. I put up a good fight, and y'all have jumped every obstacle I've thrown at you."

"Are you taking credit for me and Willa Rose?" Tripp asked.

"Yes, I am. I do not fail in my missions. And if you don't believe me about fixing y'all up together, just ask Ivy. I asked her to save the Friday after Christmas to babysit Nicky, and I was even planning to pay her for y'all."

"I'm still not so sure I believe you, Aunt Bernie," Tripp said.

"I don't give a damn whether you do or not." She grinned.

"I led you both on a merry chase and loved every minute of it. Now get on with your date night. I've just got one more thing to say to you, Tripp…"

"I'll believe that when I don't hear you bossing me around," he told her, "but go on."

"I think you are trying to buffalo me right now. You wouldn't be taking any woman, much less Willa Rose, on a first date to a fast-food joint, no matter how good the burgers are."

"I'm a cheap date," Willa Rose argued. "And a bacon cheeseburger is on the list of my favorite foods."

"I don't admit it when I'm wrong, so I'll just say, *we'll see*," Bernie said with a grin.

"Y'all enjoy the lights," Willa Rose said as she tugged on Tripp's hand and led him up to the counter to order.

"Oh, we will," Vera called out and then whispered something to Bernie that set all three women off in giggles.

"What are they laughing about?" Willa Rose whispered. "They couldn't have planned to be here at the same time we are, could they? We didn't even know this was what we were going to do until we were on the road."

Tripp pictured the mistletoe lying on his nightstand and then visualized Bernie doing some kind of secret ritual over it before she hung it on his porch. There was no way that little sprig could pack such good luck without a little extra juju attached to it.

"I wouldn't put anything past Aunt Bernie," he replied. "She will do anything to be able to claim that her matchmaking skills got us together."

"We could have a big, public, fake argument about that hundred-dollar bill in your pocket. I could yell at you and say that our relationship is based on a bet, and none of it is real. Then I could storm out and demand you take me home," Willa Rose suggested. "That should teach her a lesson."

"No, ma'am. I'm so excited to be able to spend time with you that I'll let her have the win. I wouldn't want to waste a single minute of it on a pretend fight. And don't you believe for a minute that the feelings I have for you are not real."

"That may be the most romantic thing you've ever said," she whispered.

"It shouldn't be, and I promise to do better in the future," Tripp said.

"What does that mean?" Willa Rose asked.

"I should have told you before now that you look gorgeous tonight, but I was more than a little thunderstruck when you came out of the guest room."

Before Willa Rose could reply to that, a middle-aged lady rushed up from the other end of the place to the counter and said, "Sorry about that. I was delivering an order to some friends and didn't see you up here. What can I get y'all?"

Tripp gave her the order and turned to Willa Rose. "Anything else?"

She shook her head, but the teasing and flirting light in her eyes had gone out.

"That will be all," Tripp answered the woman and ushered Willa Rose to the side room and seated her in a back booth. "Are you alright?"

"I'm fine, and thank you for the compliment."

He had heard that same tone from his mother when she and his dad disagreed. He sat down and played the events of the whole evening in his mind. From the time they left the house until the moment he told her that she looked beautiful, things had gone great.

He reached across the table and took her hands in his. "Tell me what's wrong, because it's very evident that you are not fine."

"I want to go home. I feel like there's a rock in my chest. I shouldn't have left Nicky."

"Why?"

"I need to see him, to be sure he's alright."

"FaceTime with Ivy. She can let you look at him as often as you need to all evening." Tripp brought one of her hands to his lips and kissed her knuckles. "It's normal for any parent who leaves a child with a sitter the first time. I bet your mama felt the same way the first time she left you or Erica. My dad said that when he and my mother had a date night after Brodie was born and after Knox and I were adopted, she called the sitter every fifteen minutes. Go ahead and call Ivy. We've got plenty of time before our food arrives."

She jerked her hand back and shook her head. "I was raised in a different world than you were. I never had a babysitter. Mama took me everywhere with her, and when Daddy was home, we went as a family—even to the grocery store. Please, take me home."

"Okay," Tripp said. "But you need to get over this, Willa Rose. If there is going to be an *us*, we will need time together as a couple. It will get easier each time we go out, I promise."

"I'm going home even if I have to hitch a ride with Bernie," she declared.

"I will take you back to Spanish Fort. I'll go tell the lady to make our order to-go."

"Don't talk to me in that tone. I'll be waiting in the truck." She stormed out of the Dairy Queen.

The lady behind the counter whipped out a paper bag. "I assume you've changed your mind and want this to go."

"Yes, ma'am," he said with a forced smile.

"Problems?" Bernie called out.

"We decided to eat in the truck," he answered and hurried outside before she could ask another question.

He handed off the bag to Willa Rose, set the two milkshakes in the cupholders on the console and started the engine. "You can go ahead and eat on the way."

"I'll wait," she said and stared out the side window the whole way to Spanish Fort.

When he pulled into the driveway to his house, Willa Rose got out of the truck and was on the porch before he could even open his door. He picked up the bag with the burgers and the now cold fries, and had one milkshake in his left hand and the second now in his right one. He closed the door with his boot, took two steps toward the house, and dropped the bag and chocolate shake on the ground.

The food survived. One of the milk shakes did not. Chocolate splattered across both the legs of his jeans and his freshly shined boots. So much for a romantic first date.

You aren't getting any sympathy from me. Brodie's voice was so clear in his head that he whipped around to see if he had come home from his honeymoon early.

Ivy seemed to appear out of nowhere and picked up the bag of food. "Willa Rose said for you to take me home. What happened? I wasn't expecting y'all back until ten o'clock."

"Willa Rose happened," he answered. "I'll take that bag and this shake inside and come right back."

Ivy reached out and took the cup from him. "I think y'all need to take a few minutes to slow your roll. I'll take this into the house and be right back."

Tripp grabbed a couple of paper napkins from the glove box and wiped away as much of the mess from his jeans and boots as possible before he got in behind the steering wheel.

"The first fight is a wonderful thing. It's good that you got it over with early in your relationship," Ivy said as she got inside the warm truck.

"Why would you say that?"

"Because now you can kiss and make up," she grinned. "Romance books teach all of us that you cannot sit down on a blanket under a shade tree and fall in love. If life gave you nothing but rainbows, butterflies, and unicorn farts, how would you know if your relationship would survive something catastrophic? Divorce lawyers make millions on people who never have an argument and can't survive the relationship when they do. You need to have your disagreements, make up, and go on with life."

"How do you know that?"

"I have a notebook full of stuff from what I read and all the online self-help programs I see and the podcasts I listen to so I can learn how people react in different situations. I have to know what makes them tick if I'm ever going to be a famous romance writer like Mary Jane."

"Have you ever considered being a psychologist instead of a novelist?" Tripp asked.

"Nope. My heart is set on writing books, and I can't wait to go to public school for the social experience to help me understand that age group. I plan to start out with young adult romance books and have several ideas already."

He parked in front of the house. "Think you will ever change your mind?"

Ivy shook her head and got out of the truck. "No way. Thanks for the ride home. Willa Rose already paid me. I told her that she didn't have to give me anything, but she insisted. Call me if you need me again."

"Sure thing," he said and watched her until she was in the house.

But don't hold your breath, he thought as he put the truck in reverse.

Chapter 27

WILLA ROSE SCOOTED THE cradle from the living room into the guest bedroom with Nicky sleeping soundly in it. Then she went back, got the bag with burgers and fries and the melting milkshake, took it into the room with her, and closed the door. When she was upset or angry—and she was both that evening—she tried to ease all the emotions with food. So, she ate both burgers, all the fries, and finished it all off with what had turned into nothing more than chocolate milk.

She had just finished the last bite when she heard the front door open. When Tripp's familiar footsteps were about halfway down the hallway, her phone rang. She jerked it out of the pocket of her flowing skirt and said, "Hello, I'm still mad, so I'm not talking right now."

"I guess this means you and Tripp haven't made up yet?" Hank asked.

"Daddy?" Her tone softened.

"Yes, my daughter?"

"Who told you that we were upset with each other? Did he come whining to you?"

"No, Tripp did not," Hank declared. "Ivy called me. She

didn't know what y'all disagreed about, but she wondered if I might need to come over there. She said you were too angry to talk to her, but that you might need to visit with someone."

"I'm fine!" she barked. "Tripp was raised different from me, so this relationship isn't going to work. I'm ready to take all my things and go back to Poetry. Nicky can be raised in the same house I was brought up in."

"Tell me exactly what happened," Hank said.

"Nothing to tell," she replied.

"Then I'm coming over there and talking to Tripp face-to-face," Hank said. "I bet he'll tell me what *you* are so angry about."

"Okay, okay," she said with a long sigh, then told him the details.

"Your mother and I argued over the same thing—more than once when you girls were little. Don't get me wrong. I loved you and Erica, but I really wanted to have had some time with Vada—just the two of us with no kids around to take up all our attention."

"Why didn't you?" Willa Rose asked.

"When Erica was born, your mother had to work to support the family since her husband's temper kept him from holding down a job. He refused to keep Erica, so Vada had to leave her with a sitter. When we married and you came along, she vowed she would never leave you, and she stood her ground. She always blamed herself for Erica's behavior—said that if she could have been with her all the time, she wouldn't have turned out the way she did."

"Are you taking Tripp's side?"

"No, I'm saying that I know how he feels," Hank said. "Don't make the same mistakes your mama and I did. When you went away to college and we finally had date nights, she regretted her choices. There were times in the past—years and years—that we couldn't recover, so we tried to make the best of what we had left, and we seldom missed our date nights when I was home."

Was that the biggest underlying reason that Erica had always resented her? She'd had to stay with a sitter, and Willa Rose was treated like a princess that the queen would never let out of her sight.

"Are you still there?" Hank asked.

"Yes, Daddy, I am," she answered. "Why do relationships have to be so hard?"

"Anything worth having is worth fighting for," he answered. "Please don't take my grandson away from me and raise him in Poetry."

"I was just mad. I'm not leaving," she assured him.

"Well, if you get that crazy notion again, you should remember that your savings and what little your mother left you in that trust fund will play out in a few months. You will have to go back to teaching, and the last time I checked, they don't let teachers bring their babies into the classroom. You can take him to work at the antique store, and you have a wonderful support system here from people who love you. But if you go anywhere else, you will have to put Nicky in daycare."

"I'm staying right here," she said with a heavy sigh.

"Are you upset with your sister for not loving the baby enough to keep him?" Hank asked.

"We were raised by the same mother, so being left at a sitter shouldn't give her the right to act the way she did and does. I'm glad she didn't terminate the pregnancy, and I love this baby more than I ever thought I could. But what gives Erica the right to disrupt my life? Why wouldn't she at least give me some forewarning so I could prepare for Nicky to come into my life?"

"Maybe it's payback time for all the blame she heaped on you for thinking that you ruined her life as an only child. Just when she had Vada all to herself, except when I was home for weekends, you came along and ended what she had with her mother," Hank answered.

"It's going to take a long time for me to forgive her for the way she went about things. Good God, Daddy! She all but left him on my doorstep in a basket with a note attached to it."

"I've got one bit of advice and then I'm going to hang up and we can talk more after you've slept. Everything looks better in the light of day."

"And that is?" Willa Rose asked.

"Don't take your anger or your worry about Nicky out on Tripp. Good night," Hank said and the screen went dark.

Nicky whimpered and began to chew on his fist. Everything she needed to fix a bottle for him was in the kitchen, but she didn't want to leave the room and take a chance on running into Tripp. The lyrics from an old song from years ago ran through her head—she would love him tomorrow, but tonight she wanted to be mad for a little while longer, or something like that.

Nicky really began to fuss, so she picked him up and whispered, "I'm here, sweetheart, and I will never leave you—at least not for very long. It's just me and you against the world."

She told herself that didn't have to worry about Tripp being in the kitchen. She had heard him go into his bedroom, so he was probably in there pouting. Men didn't talk out their problems like women did. If he was anything like her ex, by morning he would expect her to act like nothing happened and everything was normal. Her mother had read a book when she was just a little girl about men being from Mars and women being from Venus. She remembered playing at Vada's feet and seeing her nod as she read and wondering if somehow her mother heard music as well as saw words.

If he is pouting, then it's nothing more than what you were doing. Vada's voice was as loud and clear as it had been before she passed away.

"I am not," she protested as she picked up the baby, opened the door, and peeked out into the hall. No one was there, so she crossed the living area and went to the kitchen.

Remember the last words I said to you? Vada was back.

"You said that you loved me and to listen to my dad," Willa Rose muttered. "I'm trying, Mama."

When she reached the open-space living area, the lights

were on and Tripp was sitting at the bar with a bowl of cereal in front of him. He looked up but didn't say a word. He had changed from jeans and boots to a pair of buffalo-plaid pajama pants, a muscle shirt that hugged his body, and a pair of socks.

Why did he have to look so damn sexy? And why couldn't he at least acknowledge her presence with a nod, if nothing more? Sure, she wasn't through holding on to anger, but he was a man. They didn't think or feel things as deeply as a woman did.

"You are insufferable just like all men," she said but got no response from him. "If I had a place to go, I would leave right now."

Still nothing.

She raised her voice. "Are you listening to me?"

He put another bite into his mouth and ignored her.

"I'm talking to you," she yelled so loud that it startled Nicky.

"What?" Tripp pulled wireless earphones from his ears and laid them on the table. "Did you say something? I was listening to music."

Willa Rose rolled her eyes toward the ceiling. Listening to music, instead of apologizing to her? Or, if he didn't care how she was feeling, why didn't he ask about the baby?

"Do you want to fix Nicky a bottle or hold him while I take care of it? Or maybe you would rather I find another place to stay until the plumber comes and fixes my house?"

"I can eat and hold the baby at the same time. According

to my mother, Oprah calls it 'multitasking.' And you will do whatever you want no matter what I say anyway, so why should I answer your questions?"

"You are more exasperating than my ex," she snapped.

"That was a low blow," Tripp said.

"Forget helping me with the baby. I can hold him and fix a bottle at the same time too. I was just trying to give you a chance to be a father, but maybe you don't want that either?"

"Another low blow." He pushed his chair back and stood up. "Are we going to talk like adults about what happened tonight, or are you going to keep throwing mud balls at me?"

"I'm sorry," she said. "I don't like to be wrong, and apparently, I was about a lot of things. Can we start over?"

He fixed a bottle and handed it to her. "I'm willing if you are."

"Are we roommates, friends, or what?"

"You tell me." Tripp sat down in his chair across from her. "*I* thought we were a couple in a relationship."

"I'm sorry I ruined our date," she said. "I was and still am mad at Erica. She doesn't even know that I can't get pregnant, and she sent me Nicky because a baby doesn't fit into her lifestyle. I want to be like my own mama, but I've been basically told that being obsessively overprotective isn't a good thing. That I will regret not spending time alone with you if we are really a couple."

"I hope we are still a couple, but that's up to you. After all, you are staying in another room, and my body aches for you to be beside me," he said.

"We have been too tired for sex ever since Nicky arrived," she reminded him.

"At least you were there beside me in the bed. Sex is great, but when we are sleep-deprived and worn out, having you beside me reminds me what love really is. Did Ivy fuss at you?"

"No, my dad, and I'm willing to put this behind us if you are," she answered. Did he say *love*? "I miss you being beside me, too, but there's no room on either side of your big bed for the cradle."

"We have a monitor with a camera so we can see him any time and hear him if he whimpers," he reminded her. "I'm not pressuring you, darlin'. You decide if you need to sleep so close to the baby that you can reach down and touch him, or not."

"I guess I can't expect him to sleep beside me until he goes off to college," she whispered.

"I hope not. He'll never survive in the real world if you protect him to that extent." Tripp chuckled. "Good night. I'm going to bed now. I'm glad that we talked. I didn't want us to go to bed angry with each other. If you need me, just holler. I'll leave my door open."

He was almost across the living area when Willa Rose called out, "I ate both burgers and all the fries. What happened to the second milkshake?"

"I dropped it, and it splattered all over my jeans and boots," he answered. "I figured you tossed the food since it had to be cold."

"I ate all of what was in the bag. Some folks can't eat when they are nervous or angry or sad. That is *not* me. I'm like a ravenous wolf at any of those times, and when I'm all three, it's even worse."

"I'll remember not to upset you just before we go out to eat next time."

"Is there going be a next time?" she asked.

"I hope so. Go ahead and eat the rest of the cereal if you need it to get over whatever you're still fighting with yourself about. We can make a grocery run tomorrow," he teased.

"Too soon," she growled.

"I'm just stating facts. Good night to you again," he said.

Chapter 28

Footsteps in the hallway brought Tripp fully awake out of a light sleep. The time on his phone said that it was a few minutes past eleven, which meant he had barely begun to doze. "Damn it, Knox. I thought you were going to help Bo and Maverick out until the bar closed," he muttered as he got out of bed. "Willa Rose is in the guest room with the baby, so stay away from there. If she screams, she will wake the baby."

"Who are you talking to?" Willa Rose met him in the hallway.

"I thought Knox was coming in…" He rubbed sleep from his eyes with his fist. "Is everything alright?"

She held up the monitor from the baby monitor and camera. "I couldn't sleep after his ten o'clock feeding, so let's see if this works. If we can leave both bedroom doors open a little, it will ease my mind."

He slipped her small hand into his and led her into his room. "No problem there."

She set the monitor on the nightstand and quickly crawled beneath the covers. Tripp got in beside her and drew her close to his side. "This feels so right."

"Yes, it does." She propped up on an elbow. "Kiss me."

"Gladly, but…"

"We are both emotionally drained, but you have to kiss me for us to make up, don't you?" she asked.

"I never figured that you were a girl who let a guy kiss you on a first date."

"You figured wrong." She met him halfway and the kiss sent desire shooting through her whole body even if she was too tired for anything else. "I want more, but I need sleep."

"We can wake up early for that *more* business tomorrow morning?"

"My thoughts exactly." She laid her head back on his chest and in minutes they were both asleep.

"So, did you and Tripp make up or are you still mad?" Ivy asked on Saturday morning when she came into the antique shop.

"We are good." Willa Rose blushed at the vision that popped into her head of just how well they had made up before Nicky woke for his six o'clock bottle.

"Was the fight about Aunt Bernie's bets?"

Nosy little teenager, aren't you? Willa Rose thought.

"No, I got nervous about leaving Nicky alone," she answered honestly. "It's nothing to do with your babysitting ability, Ivy, and all to do with the fact that my mother never left me with anyone."

Ivy removed her coat and tossed it over a rocking chair.

"No offense taken. The only person my folks ever left me with was my grandpa or a few times with Yasmin. I didn't think I would miss her so much, but I do. I made the right decision, but she was part of my life for years. I don't know why Finn doesn't propose to her. They love each other and have been together since I was a little girl."

"What happened to your folks? Or is that too personal?" Willa Rose asked.

"A carnival accident with the Ferris wheel killed both, and Grandpa took me to raise. He never needed a sitter since we were on the road nine months out of the year, but when he did have a doctor's visit or something that I couldn't go along to, Yasmin was there for me. Are you worried about leaving him in the nursery tomorrow?"

"A little," Willa Rose admitted.

"Then let's make a deal right now. I will take over Nicky's care when you bring him in. I won't let anyone kiss him on the face. He doesn't need to be exposed to anything. And I will text you every ten minutes for the whole hour with a picture of him."

"I like that idea and am willing to work with it."

"Okay then," Ivy said. "I see that you've got him settled into the crib in the bedroom area, so let's get busy putting this place in order. I doubt that we will get much done after today until after Christmas. Tomorrow is Sunday. Monday is Christmas Eve, and I've still got presents to wrap. And it's a good thing you aren't opening the shop until February because Nicky is going to need that crib until then."

"What if it's the first thing someone buys?"

"I expect you will be going to antique auctions to replenish the store, right?" Ivy asked.

"Probably, and they are usually on weekends, so I might need to hire you to mind the store on Saturdays some of the time," Willa Rose said.

"Anytime," Ivy said. "You look worried about something. Has it got to do with Tripp?"

Willa Rose shook her head. "Everything is good there. You mentioned wrapping presents and that got me thinking about Christmas morning at the Paradise. I'm not sure what to expect."

"Evidently lots of presents since everyone exchanges small gifts with each other, but Mary Jane says this is the last year we're doing that. Once all the kids are married with their own families, we will just share with her and Joe Clay on Christmas Eve and have the big family gathering with food and fun on Christmas Day," Ivy said. "The sisters don't like the idea, but Mary Jane told them if they want to have a little party among themselves, they can do that at one of their houses. Do you realize how many presents there are going to be?"

"More than twenty from me, plus something a little bigger for each of the kids," Willa Rose answered. "That's after I have presents with my dad, Tripp, and Nicky at home. Thank goodness for online shopping and gift cards or I would never have gotten it all together. And I still don't have all the wrapping done."

"We both got a late start," Ivy said. "But like you, I did most of mine online. I found a cute mug for Bernie that says *Matchmaking Queen* on the side. No one will know if she's drinking tea or whiskey from it."

Willa Rose chuckled. "You got that right."

Business was steady at the leather shop all morning with customers arriving to pick up their orders or to look through the ready-to-buy merchandise for last-minute gifts. At noon, things finally slowed down enough that Tripp and Hank could take a break and have a sandwich for lunch.

"Did you and Willa Rose straighten out your problem?" Hank asked.

"Yes, sir, we did," Tripp answered. "It might be a while before we can have another date night, though."

"Don't wait too long, or the years will get away from you like they did me."

"Got any advice about when I should ask her again?" Tripp asked.

Hank opened a bag of chips and dumped a few onto his paper plate. "As the old saying goes, 'Y'all need to get back on the horse as soon as possible.' Maybe right after the holidays. Which reminds me… We are closed on Sunday, but what's our schedule for the rest of the week?"

"Let's stay open until noon on Christmas Eve," Tripp said. "That way the last-minute shoppers can have a little time. Then we'll close on Tuesday, take Wednesday off, and reopen on Thursday. And since you are here to help me now, I'm voting that we close on weekends from now on. What do you think of that?"

"Sounds good to me," Hank said with a nod. "That will give me time to help Willa Rose get her shop in order after the New Year, and maybe watch over it on Saturdays when she needs to go to estate sales to replenish the store. She and Vada did a lot of that kind of thing on weekends."

"Hey, what's going on in here?" Knox asked as he came inside.

"We're having lunch." Hank waved over the food. "Hang up your coat and make yourself a sandwich."

"Don't mind if I do," Knox said and took a seat on the other side of the table. "I've got great news. Jack Devlin, a developer I know, has bought some land between Holliday and Lakeside City. He's going to build spec homes on one-acre lots for folks who don't want to live in Wichita Falls. It's a short commute from the city, and he's hoping to have things ready by the middle of March for me to move my trailer down there and start framing up houses. The place is only an hour from here, so I can come home on weekends."

"You left behind your crew when we moved up here, didn't you?" Tripp asked.

"Yes, but Jack says that a crackerjack carpenter named Charlie—I didn't catch the last name—has been with him for years and specializes in framing out houses can work with me," Knox answered. "And there are three other guys who will make up a team of five to do that job."

"What about rebuilding the church?" Hank asked. "Do you think you can get that finished by March?"

"Without a doubt," Knox replied. "We are starting on Thursday."

"Count me in when I'm not working here," Hank said. "I'm not much good with carpentry, but I'm a good fetcher."

"You said you could come home on weekends?" Tripp asked. "Bernie is going to be so sad, both that you are leaving, and that she can't hook you up with a local woman. She will probably make you sign a document in blood saying you won't find a woman in that area."

"Not to worry about that. This is a big project. I'll be working from dawn to sundown and sleeping in between. There will be no time for women in my life until we get those houses framed out and the finish carpentry done. I'll be busy until the end of summer."

"Poor Bernie will have to work double—no triple time—to get you a wife by next Christmas," Hank teased.

"I'm not a bit worried until Tripp gets serious about asking your daughter to marry him," Knox said. "I'm free as a bird until then. I think I can outrun Aunt Bernie when I'm home for two days. I guess I can stay at the Paradise or at your house, Tripp."

"You know you are welcome at either place," Tripp answered.

"Thanks," Knox said. "Jack is planning to have the rec center built by the time I get there, and it will have a bathroom with showers and a place to hang out for breaks or meals. Bernie won't have anything to worry about. I'll be working with a team of guys five days a week."

Tripp held a knife out toward his twin. "You want to go ahead and stick your finger now, so you will be able to sign your name in blood when Bernie hears about this? After all, you *are* next in line."

Knox punched him on the arm. "No, I do not. Like I said, Aunt Bernie is too busy trying to fix you up with anyone but Willa Rose to pay much attention to me."

"Not anymore," Tripp said. "Her words last night were, 'If you can't beat 'em, join 'em.' Sorry, little brother, she's already gunning for you, and her shotgun is loaded."

"Hey, are you still open?" Brodie called out from the front door.

"We are and welcome back," Tripp said. "When did you get home?"

Brodie sat down in the fourth chair and set about making himself a sandwich. "I need a little snack. Audrey is at the Paradise showing Bernie and Mary Jane all the honeymoon pictures. I'm supposed to pick her up in thirty minutes to go do some final Christmas shopping in Nocona. I just wanted to stop by here and see my brothers first. What's happened since the wedding? We decided to stay off the phone except for emergencies…"

"How did you know if a call was something serious?" Hank asked.

"We talked to Joe Clay and made a deal. He would only call us if there was it was a serious thing," Brodie said.

"Evidently, he didn't think any drama that went on was enough to bring us home."

"I'm going to leave in March for a new job, but I'll be back on weekends," Knox blurted out and filled him in on the details. "And Willa Rose and Tripp have a baby."

"As in a new puppy or baby potbellied pig?" Brodie asked.

"As in a little baby boy named Nicholas," Hank said and went on to explain the situation.

"Then the water pipes froze and burst under the old parsonage, so she's staying with me until that gets fixed," Tripp added. "I thought about your experience with cutting of the water supply when I was out there in the cold cussing because I had to lie on my belly to get the crescent wrench down into the frozen hole."

Brodie shook his head in disbelief. "There really was a good deal of drama going on, but I'm still glad that Joe Clay didn't call. Being free from everything was good for the soul. But I better not leave again if all this is what happens when I'm gone. And at least you had clothes on when you had to take care of water spewing everywhere."

"And you didn't?" Hank asked.

"Let me tell the story," Knox said. "It was like this. The tornado blew away all our house except one wall and the bathroom. Not long afterward, Pansy showed up. We figured the storm picked her up somewhere and dropped her close to the farm. Anyway, Brodie felt sorry for her and decided to keep her."

"A big mistake, but now I'm attached to the critter." Brodie chuckled.

"My trailer was parked out at the farm in those days," Knox went on. "Audrey and Brodie were enemies during that time. She wanted to buy his farm to put her family's two places back together, but my brother was not selling it. To make a long story short, Pansy got loose one day and was over at Audrey's farm playing chase through the cornfield. It took some doing and some rolling around in the mud, before Brodie finally chased her back onto his property. Brodie looked like he had been doused with chocolate by the time he got back to the trailer." He stopped and took a bite of the sandwich.

"Since the water was still hooked up in what was left of the house, I decided to take a shower," Brodie went on with the story. "I had just took all my clothes off and stepped into the tub when the damned thing fell through the floor and sent me into a sprawl. Part of me was still in the tub. Part was hanging outside on what was left of the floor. Water was going everywhere. I was sure the meter was spinning around like a top and running up a colossal bill, so I found my footing, grabbed the tool that cuts off the water at the main line from my truck, and ran down to the road where the thing was located."

"In the pouring-down rain," Tripp added.

Hank chuckled, then he laughed aloud. "I'm picturing all of that. Were you really naked?"

"That's right," Brodie said, "and that rain really was icy

cold. Then to top everything off, my two thoughtful brothers hadn't left anything but very colorful swimming trunks in the trailer for me to wear the next day. So, I was doubly humiliated the next day when I ran into Audrey and her sassy aunt Hettie at the feed store where I went to buy food for Pansy. End of story, and now it's time for me to go pick up Audrey. Thanks for the sandwich. I might survive until I get to the Dairy Queen in Nocona. And I will look forward to seeing the new baby tomorrow after church."

"I beat you to fatherhood," Tripp teased.

Brodie stood up and patted his brother on the back. "Not if you don't get on the ball and get married soon, because Audrey tossed her birth control pills in the trash this morning."

Chapter 29

AT TWENTY-EIGHT YEARS OLD, Willa Rose still felt like a little girl when she opened her eyes on Christmas morning. Excitement crackled in the early morning air. The smell of cinnamon and bacon wafted through the house, and that meant Hank was making his special French toast for breakfast. She rolled over toward Tripp and laid her head on his chest.

"Merry Christmas," she whispered softly.

"Merry Christmas to you, darlin'. I love you."

She was speechless, but finally said, "I love you too."

"Santa must have heard me loud and clear, because I got what I asked for."

"And that was?"

He kissed her on the forehead. "To wake up with you in my arms and to hear those words."

"So did I."

"Then we are a couple of lucky people, aren't we?" Tripp buried his face in her hair.

"Double lucky, because Daddy is in our kitchen making his famous holiday breakfast for us, and Nicky slept through his two o'clock feeding. So, Merry Christmas to us as a couple."

"I like those words, *as a couple.*"

The monitor screen showed Nicky fully awake and puckering up to cry, so they both hurried out of bed, pulled on some clothes, and headed down the hall just in time to see Hank coming out of the spare bedroom with the baby in his arms.

"I figured y'all could sleep a little longer if I gave him his bottle this morning," he said. "But now that you are awake, breakfast is on the stove, and Merry Christmas."

He said the words, and I said them, and life is going on like neither of us uttered them, Willa Rose thought. But there was a certain confidence and peace in her heart that had not been there in a very long time.

"Y'all go on and eat, and I will convince Nicky that what's in his bottle is French toast, oven omelet, and biscuits and gravy."

Willa Rose gave her father a sideways hug and then slipped her hand into Tripp's. "This has always been one of my favorite things about Christmas. We always ate together and then had presents. Tell me about your holiday while we eat."

"Mama made a big breakfast, not too much different than this one, and then we had presents. After that, us boys had time to play with our new toys, bikes, or whatever we got when we were young. Sometime in the middle of the afternoon, we had the huge Christmas dinner. The next day was always kind of sad for me because the excitement was over," he answered as he got two plates down from the cabinet. "But thinking ahead for today, I'm not sure what's going to happen at the Paradise."

"I'm sure it will be loud and crazy with lots of laughter and torn paper to clean up after we all open presents, but I can't begin to imagine so much chaos with a family this huge," Willa Rose answered. "And Tripp, I felt the same way the day after. Let's start a new tradition and do something special tomorrow so we don't have to deal with that letdown."

"I'd like that very much." He stopped and gave her a long kiss. "Have I told you today that I love you?"

She wrapped her arms around his neck, looked up into his eyes and said, "Yes, but I can hear it however many times you want to say it."

Willa Rose sat right next to Tripp with a mountain of destroyed Christmas paper surrounding the two of them. She smiled and he read her mind. Did this happen to everyone who fell in love or was it a special thing between them—or did it have something to do with the dried-up mistletoe now in the shoebox of keepsakes on his closet shelf?

He leaned over and kissed her on the cheek. "You were right. Lots of noise and ripped-up paper."

Hank rocked Nicky with several presents scattered around his feet that Heather and Daisy had *helped* the baby open. Tears welled up behind Tripp's eyes when he realized that his mother would have been so excited to be in Hank's place and rock Nicky. In that very moment, Tripp knew exactly what he wanted to do the next day. All it would take was a phone call and a little preparation if Willa Rose was willing.

She nudged him on the shoulder. "What are you thinking about?"

"Tomorrow. I would like to take you to Bandera to see my parents, and I'd like to go to Poetry and visit your mother," he answered.

"Tripp, you are talking about a day's drive there and another one back," she frowned. "We couldn't possibly do that with a three-week-old baby."

"Who said anything about driving?"

"Have you got a jet hiding in the back room of the leather shop?" she asked.

He slipped an arm around her and gave her a sideways hug. "No, but I have a little six-seater airplane in Bandera."

"You fly?" she gasped.

"Yes, ma'am. Pretty often as CEO of the oil company. I almost always had to be in two places at once, so I got my pilot's license. I've meant to put the plane on the market, but I'm thinking now that I might want to keep it. Lester, the guy that owns the private airport, is a good friend who will probably be glad to get the plane out of one of his hangars. If he's not busy, he can bring it up to Bowie and fly us back down to Bandera. Then I'll fly us home and make arrangements to house it in Bowie," he told her.

"How many more surprises do you have up your sleeve?" she asked.

"You've got a lifetime to figure them all out. Are you in or out?"

"I'm in," Willa Rose answered. "I'd like to tell Mama all about Nicky. I know that seems silly but…"

Tripp gave her shoulder a gentle squeeze. "It's not even a little bit silly. Nicky is my mother's first grandchild, and she would have been so happy to see him. We could make this our special day-after-Christmas tradition."

She scooted over even closer to him. "I would love that."

Chapter 30

As Tripp was loading Nicky in the truck the next morning, Hank walked across the yard and gave Willa Rose a hug. "Tell your mama hello for me. She knows I'm happy here because I visit with her every morning before I even get out of bed."

"I wish you were coming with us," Willa Rose said.

"I hate flying," Hank said. "When we put the houses up for sale, we will drive down there to sign the papers."

"I'm not selling my house," she said. "I'm giving it to the church to use for a parsonage. Later if they build a newer one, then they can use the place for a clothes closet and food bank for needy folks."

"Have you told the folks at the church?" Hank asked.

"Not until next Thanksgiving when our year is up, but I don't think I'll change my mind."

"Well, y'all have a good time. Even if it is cold, at least you've got clear skies," Hank said as he walked away. "Tripp, you be careful. You are carrying precious cargo."

"Yes, sir, and I agree. I'll be back to help tomorrow and Saturday."

Hank waved over his shoulder. "See you then."

She understood her father's wanting to spend time with her mother better on the drive out of town. Like her mother had most likely done when Willa Rose was a baby, she sat in the back seat beside Nicky. Had it been difficult for Vada when she had to drive and leave Willa Rose in the back seat? Willa Rose wanted to pat herself on the back for that accomplishment, but then realized that she hadn't had a choice. If she needed to go somewhere, there was no other option.

"I miss having you beside me," Tripp said.

She reached up and touched his shoulder. "I was thinking the same thing, and now I understand better why we need time alone."

He laid a hand over hers and gave it a squeeze. "I love you."

"Right back at you." She slipped her hand from his and sat up straight. "How long does it take to drive to Bowie?"

"About forty-five minutes, and then it's an hour flight to Bandera," he answered.

"Thank you for doing this for us."

"You are more than welcome. I'm glad that we will have a plane parked at Bowie from now on, so anytime you get homesick, we can fly south," Tripp told her.

"Why didn't you offer to take Audrey and Brodie to Florida?"

"I wasn't interested in going on their honeymoon with them." He chuckled. "Plus, they liked the idea of a road trip. They planned to do a two-day road trip down there, then have a few days on the beach. Audrey said that she would be glad to have Brodie to herself all day long on the drives down and back, plus their time on the beach."

Home!

That word stuck in her mind. Was she going home to Poetry, or leaving home behind in Spanish Fort? Which one would she get homesick for if she was away very long?

———

Tripp parked his truck in the empty hangar at the small airport in Bowie where his plane would be at home after that day. He got out expecting to see his training instructor, Lester, coming toward him. But a tall, lanky man with gray in his temples came out from the men's room and waved.

He crossed the room and stuck out his hand. "Hey, Tripp. Don't know if you remember me, but I'm Marcus, Lester's nephew. He has a stomach bug, and he sent me in his place."

Tripp shook with him and then introduced him to Willa Rose and Nicky. "Yes, I remember you. Good to see you again."

"Likewise," Marcus said and dropped his hand. "I promise I'll take good care of you. I have always liked the look of your plane and even more so after this morning. It drives like a Cadillac, one of those old ones that had some get up and go, not one of the newer ones that looks like everything else on the road. Anytime you want to sell that sweet little lady parked out there, I'll be glad to buy her."

Tripp glanced over at Willa Rose to see her shaking her head. "Miz Willa Rose has spoken, so I guess selling her is out of the question."

"Well, just in case she changes your mind, would you please remember that I'm first in line? Uncle Lester said to tell you that all the arrangements have been made." He turned toward Willa Rose. "Good-lookin' baby you got there. Can I help with any bags you have?"

Tripp opened the truck door. "If you'll take those, I'll carry the baby."

"No problem." Marcus handed Tripp a folder and picked up the two bags. "Travelin' light today."

"It's just a day trip," Tripp told him as they walked out to the plane.

Marcus was a talker, and never stopped for the duration of the flight to Bandera. When they finally were on the ground, Marcus handed Tripp the keys.

"Great visitin' with you. If you ever need a pilot, holler at me," he said.

"Tell Lester thanks for everything, and that I hope he feels better soon," Tripp said.

"I'll do it, and I'll help you with the bags before I leave."

"What now?" Willa Rose asked.

Tripp opened the folder. "See that SUV sitting over there in the empty hangar? That's our vehicle for the day."

"How did you…"

"I told Lester what I needed, and he took care of it for me, including calling the manager of the Bowie airfield," Tripp explained. "We'll stop by the flower shop, go to the cemetery, and then have lunch wherever you want."

"Not bad for a second date," Willa Rose said.

"Well, thank you, ma'am. I do what I can for being just a basic boring, introverted and shy guy."

"You might fool some of the people with that line, but not me," she told him.

When they were on the ground and beside the SUV, she got into the front seat of the SUV with Tripp. "Nicky is getting so independent that he rides in the back by himself when I go from place to place in Spanish Fort. He seems to think he's big enough to go a few miles without me right beside him."

Tripp wasn't about to argue with that or to say a single word about it. He simply leaned over the console and kissed her on the cheek. "Glad to have a copilot. First stop is to show you the house where I grew up."

"And then a tour of the town?"

"You got it, darlin'," he said and drove a couple of miles to a big farmhouse on the outskirts of town. "That's my old stomping grounds."

"Who lives here now?" Willa Rose asked.

"The company that we sold the oil company to bought it along with the business. There's a lot of good memories and bad ones in that house. My parents brought me home to this place when I was born. I broke my arm when I bet Knox that I could jump off the roof and land in a kids' swimming pool. My mother died in one of the upstairs bedrooms."

Willa Rose reached over and laid a hand on his. "Do you want to get out and go look around the place?"

"No, I'd hate to end up in jail for trespassing," he said. "I just wanted to look at it again."

"I feel the same way about the house where I grew up in Poetry. Lots of memories there, but even more to be made in the future in Spanish Fort, right?"

"Absolutely!"

The next stop was a flower shop with a Closed sign in the window.

"I'll be right back," he said.

"But, Tripp, they aren't open."

"Miz Maudie told Lester that she would have a couple of bouquets ready for me at"—he checked the time on his phone—"eleven o'clock. Wait right here. This won't take long."

The door swung open and an elderly lady who looked like Bernie motioned him inside, and in just a few minutes he carried two bunches of fresh flowers in a multitude of colors out to the vehicle. "I hope these are all right. I didn't know what your mama liked, but my dad used to tease my mother about hanging on to her hippie days. She loved all colors and the brighter the better."

"They are perfect," Willa Rose said around the lump in her throat.

He drove another few minutes and slowed down to make a turn under an archway with Bandera Cemetery across the top, and straight back to a well-kept grave with a tombstone reading Callahan across the top. Willa Rose wasn't sure what to expect until he opened the back door and helped her out.

"Would you be comfortable if we leave Nicky in the truck with the door open?"

"We won't be but a few yards away, so we can hear him if he cries," she answered.

He took one bunch of flowers from the passenger seat and laced her fingers into his. Together they walked the short distance to the tombstone.

"Mama, I've found the woman of my dreams, and you would love her. It's been a long time since I came to see you, but I hear your voice in my head several times a day. I brought Willa Rose to meet you and Dad. We haven't exactly done things the traditional way as in meeting, dating, and all that, but I knew I loved her even before she admitted that she loved me." He removed two daisies from the bouquet and handed them to Willa Rose.

"What's this for?"

"Pretend that our parents are meeting each other for the first time. One stem is from my mama to show that she approves of you. The other is from yours to tell you that she doesn't want to shoot me. I know that nothing about us has been the way other folks do things," he said. "I wanted to bring you here to a cemetery for a reason. My parents meant the world to me, and I wanted to have their blessing on our relationship and commitment. Daisies represent rebirth, new beginnings, and hope. That's what you have brought into my life, Willa Rose."

"You've done the same for me." She held the two flowers close to her chest and planned to press them as soon as they were back home.

Tripp dropped down on one knee and pulled a red velvet box from his pocket. "I've been carrying this around with me for more than a week, but a man doesn't ask a question before he's pretty sure of the answer. Willa Rose Thomas, love of my life and soul, will you marry me?"

A whole week. That is pretty sure of yourself.

The thought vanished when she said, "Yes!"

He slipped the ring on her finger and stood up. She took a couple of steps forward and wrapped her arms around his neck.

He looked deeply into her brown eyes and said, "I'm the luckiest man on earth." Then he brought his lips down to hers to seal their future together.

Epilogue

On the second Saturday in March, Willa Rose was having trouble standing still for Yasmin to arrange sprigs of baby's breath in the long, loose braid falling down her back. "Is Nicky alright? How about Tripp? Is he nervous?"

"Nicky is fine. Mary Jane is taking care of him," Endora said.

"According to Brodie, Tripp is pacing the floor in Parker's office," Audrey answered. "Evidently, he's about as nervous as you are. If you aren't sure, we have time to run. I've got my pickup truck right outside, and we can be on a plane headed for sandy beaches in less than two hours."

"No, I'm sure about being married," Willa Rose said and smiled at Yasmin. "I have no regrets about my choices. What's got me all antsy is the ceremony itself. What if I forget my vows? Or worse yet, what if Nicky cries while I'm saying them?"

"We've got everything under control," Endora assured her. "You won't forget your vows, and if you do, just speak from your heart. That's all that matters anyway."

Hank peeked inside the room and then came inside. "You look beautiful, my child. I'm glad you are wearing your mother's pearls." He reached inside his pocket and brought out a faded red velvet box. "This is something blue from Vada. That last week when she knew that the time was drawing near, she gave this to me and said I was supposed to give it to you on your wedding day."

Willa Rose opened the box to find a lovely sapphire ring that Hank had given Vada on the day that Willa Rose was born. "Daddy, you are going to make me cry."

He gave her a sideways hug. "Don't do that. You'll ruin your makeup, and you don't have time to redo it. The music that's playing now tells me that the groom and his brothers are already going to the front of the church. Where are your bridesmaids?"

"You are my only one." She smiled at her father.

"There's too many of us sisters for her to choose just one or two," Endora answered.

He crooked his arm. "I'm honored to be your Daddy of Honor."

She looped her arm in his, and Yasmin handed her the bouquet of white daisies and baby's breath. "I'm glad that Finn and I went to the courthouse last week, and I don't have to remember vows. I could barely get out the 'I do' when the judge asked me if I promised to love him forever."

"Okay, all of you, go take a seat. It's about time for me and my Daddy of Honor to walk down the aisle. I'm so glad that Knox and the whole community have finished the church in time for the ceremony and reception. Everything looks amazing."

Endora gave her a kiss on the cheek. "Yes, it does, and you are the first one to be married in the new, remodeled church. Welcome to the family, Sister."

"Please welcome the new Callahan family, Mr. and Mrs. Tripp Callahan and their son, Nicholas Thomas Callahan," Bo said into the microphone when they entered the fellowship hall. "We are going to watch them cut the cake, and then Tripp and Willa Rose will have their first dance as a married couple. Right after that she will throw the bouquet, so while they are dancing, all you single ladies gather up over by the door. We are skipping a reception line and going right to the potluck buffet."

Tripp handed Nicky off to Hank.

Willa Rose cut a small slice of cake and fed him a bite. "Bring back memories?"

"Lots of them," he whispered as he put a small bite in her mouth. "Shall we have dessert first?"

"Not here in front of all these people!"

"You will keep me on my toes forever, won't you?"

"Darlin', you can count on it," she promised.

He led her out into the center of the fellowship hall and took her in his arms. Bo hit a button and Elvis began to sing, "Can't Help Falling in Love."

"Perfect," Willa Rose whispered.

After the dance was over, she took a couple of steps back and tossed her bouquet over her shoulder. Even though she didn't know the blond-haired woman who caught it, she crossed the room to have her picture taken with her.

"I'm sorry, but I don't think we've met," she said, "but then I've only lived here a while and I don't know everyone yet."

"I'm here with Bernie, and I'm not so sure I even want this bouquet. Do you want to toss it again?"

Knox came up and hugged Willa Rose. "Welcome to the family. If Tripp don't treat you right, you come to me, and I'll straighten him out."

"Thank you, Brother," she said with a grin and then turned back to the short blond holding the bouquet. "I still didn't catch your name."

Bo picked up the microphone and said, "The buffet line is open now. Y'all all help yourselves."

"I'm a friend of Bernie's from back in the days when she had the bar at Ratliff City. I had my first legal drink there when I was twenty-one," she said.

"Let me make introductions," Bernie said. "This is Knox Callahan, and this bride is his new sister-in-law, Willa Rose. And this"—she turned toward the lady beside her—"is Charlotte Johnston."

Knox smiled. "Like the girl in the song, 'Swingin'.'"

"Nope, that was Johnson. My name is Johnston, with a T. I'm on my way down south of Wichita Falls right after this wedding. Starting Monday morning, I'll be working with you, Knox. I'm your new partner and we'll be framing houses together. My friends all call me Charlie."

"Small world, ain't it, Knox?" Bernie beamed.

Read on for more festive, swoony,
Texas-to-the-core Christmas romance in

Paradise for
Christmas

Chapter 1

"Holy…" Ursula was struck so speechless that she couldn't remember what to say next, but she was sure it had to be one of those four-letter words and had nothing to do with angels.

There was great-aunt Bernie, sitting on the porch with a cup of coffee in one hand and the leash to her yappy little Chihuahua dog, Pepper, in the other.

"What," Ursula muttered, "the…"

There was no mistaking her elderly aunt with all that curly hair the color of a fire engine. Even just sitting there, she seemed to exude sass and opinions. Ursula was frozen in the driver's seat, and her hands seemed to be glued to the steering wheel. Bernie was supposed to be in Ratliff City, Oklahoma, minding her own little dive bar. She only closed it on Christmas and Easter—never on Thanksgiving—so what was she doing in Spanish Fort, Texas, at the Paradise?

Aunt Bernie waved at her, and Pepper started barking. Ursula raised her hand and waved back, then opened the vehicle door. The Thanksgiving holiday had just taken a hard left turn. The old gal did not have a filter on her mouth, and she was always, always ready to give advice—whether Ursula or any of her six sisters wanted it or not.

"It's about dang time you got here. I been sittin' out here on this porch all morning waitin' on you," Bernie yelled as she pushed herself up from one of a half-dozen rocking chairs lined up across the front porch.

"Dang?" Ursula asked and managed a weak smile.

"Mary Jane says if I'm going to live here, I have to give up swearing, smoking cigars, and drinking bourbon before breakfast," Bernie said with a sigh. "But I figure it's a small price to pay. I eat chocolates instead of smokin' my Swisher Sweets, and I have a little kick of Jameson in my coffee in the afternoon."

She was barely five feet tall with bright red hair and blue eyes set in a bed of wrinkles. Ursula could still smell a faint whiff of Swisher Sweets cigars on her jacket, which meant she hadn't been in Spanish Fort for long. *Bernie's Place*, the name of her bar, was embroidered on her T-shirt, and her cowboy boots looked like they'd spent a good many years drawing up beer and pouring double shots of whiskey behind the bar.

"Live here!" Ursula muttered.

Bernie looped the end of Pepper's leash on the back of the rocking chair, and with her arms open, she met Ursula at the bottom of the steps leading up to the porch that wrapped around three sides of the house.

"Don't go getting your panties in a twist," Bernie said as Ursula walked into her arms and bent down to hug her. "I didn't take your room away from you, and I'm glad you have come home. It's time for you to get married and have some grandbabies for your mother."

Thoughts were running through Ursula's mind like screaming kids on a merry-go-round. Did that mean Bernie had moved into one of the other sisters' rooms and Ursula would have to share her bedroom with one of them? Why did Bernie decide to move to Spanish Fort? And the biggest one was why did Ursula's mother, Mary Jane, consent to such a crazy idea?

"Speak up, girl!" Bernie demanded. "You are more like me than any of your other sisters, and we speak our minds. Turn them squirrels loose that's runnin' around in your head right now."

Ursula chuckled. "Whose room did you take, and why are you living here?"

Before Bernie could answer, Ursula's stepfather, Joe Clay, and their longtime neighbor Remy Baxter came from around the house, each with a couple of boxes in their hands. Neither of them could wave, but Joe Clay's bright smile told Ursula that he was welcoming her home. Her heart skipped a beat and then raced ahead. Ursula had heard that Remy had come back to Spanish Fort to live on the small ranch next door to the Paradise, but she hadn't seen him in years.

Joe Clay wrapped her up in a fierce hug. "Glad you made it home and that you don't have to leave again. I hope the rest of your sisters do the same thing before long." He was looking sixty right in the eye, but he was still strong as an ox, as the old adage went. His dark hair had a few gray streaks and was a little longer than it had been when he first came around to remodel the Paradise, the old brothel, but back then, he'd just gotten out of the service.

She looked up into his blue eyes and smiled. "Me too, Daddy."

"Ursula, you remember Remy Baxter, don't you?" Joe Clay smiled at them both. "He and Shane O'Toole have agreed to help me with the decorations this year. Remy was our next-door neighbor until he went off to college in Gainesville and then got himself a job at his college. Smart boy here. Shane has taken over his grandparents' fishing business down on the river."

"Remy and I graduated together," she said and then glanced over at Remy. "I remember you, very well." She felt a bit of heat traveling from her neck to her cheeks. Evidently, the crush she had had on Remy when she was in high school was still there. Surely, though, he was married by now or at the very least had a girlfriend.

When she shifted her gaze over to Bernie, the woman was smiling like a Cheshire cat. Her eyes were all aglitter, and it didn't take a psychic to know what had her mind spinning, not after that crack about babies that she'd just come off with.

"I remember you too," Remy said.

"So how have you been?" she asked as she looked up at his face again.

"I'm doing great. I've moved back into the house next door, and I love being back over here. I didn't realize how much I'd missed it. Living in a walk-up apartment just isn't the same as living in the country," Remy answered.

In high school, he had been handsome, but he was also shy and a little awkward—maybe because he was so tall. He had measured more than six feet when they were freshmen and didn't top out until they were seniors when he reached six feet four inches. Since those days, he had muscled up and he seemed very comfortable in his body.

"That's great. It's right nice to have a sexy guy living right next door." Bernie grinned and nudged Ursula. "Y'all can get reacquainted now that you are home for good, Ursula, but for now, Joe Clay, you and Remy here can take all Ursula's stuff upstairs and put it in her room."

Remy nodded. "Yes, ma'am. I'm more than glad to help."

"Another of my baby girls is home for good!" Mary Jane yelled as she came through the door. "Come on up here and give your mama a hug."

Ursula's arm brushed against Remy's when she headed toward the porch. The touch was brief, and they were both wearing jackets, but the feeling was the same as when their hands had touched back in high school. They had been assigned lockers right next to each other their senior year—back in the days when he would barely even look her in the eyes. A few times when they had been closing their locker doors, their hands had touched, and sparks had danced up and down the halls like tiny little bursts of brilliant light.

Ursula jogged up to the porch and hugged her mother. Sassy, the big orange cat, came from around the house and began to rub around Ursula's legs and purr loudly. "She's glad to see me," Ursula said. "I thought maybe she would have forgotten me."

Pepper had crawled back under the rocking chair, lain down on his belly, and was growling at Sassy. The cat acted like Pepper was nothing more than a peasant and she was the reigning queen of Sheba.

"That evil critter ain't glad to see anyone," Bernie said. "She torments my poor Pepper. He just wants to be friends, and she spits and hisses at him like a demon. I think the madam of this place put her spirit in Sassy."

Mary Jane picked the cat up and carried her toward the door. "She's almost as independent as you are, Ursula, but not as much as that first cat we had right after we moved here. Miz Raven was the boss here at the Paradise. Sometimes I thought that the madam of this place left her spirit behind in that cat for sure." Mary Jane opened the door, set the cat down, and then held the door for Ursula and Bernie to go in ahead of her.

Ursula remembered the day that Joe Clay had brought the first cat into the house after they had all moved to Spanish Fort and into the old brothel known as the Paradise. She and all her sisters were elated to finally have a mama cat and a litter of kittens. Their biological father would never allow them to have so much as a goldfish or a hamster, but Joe Clay had toted a laundry basket full of babies into the house. That was probably the day that Ursula had decided Joe Clay was daddy material.

The smell of cinnamon and freshly baked bread met them

when she stepped inside the foyer. The aroma overpowered the whiff of cigar smoke that Ursula had gotten when Bernie hugged her earlier. Ursula wouldn't be a bit surprised if that half-full coffee mug out there on the porch really did have a splash of Jameson in it, even though it wasn't five o'clock anywhere in Texas.

"I'm damn"—Bernie slapped a hand over her mouth—"dang sure glad you are here. The cinnamon rolls are ready and Mary Jane wouldn't let us touch them until you got home."

"I'm happy that you decided to follow your heart and give yourself a year to write," Mary Jane said as she sat down at the table. "We've missed having you girls in and out all the time. I even thought about fostering some kids, but Joe Clay keeps telling me to give it some time."

"Time for what?" Ursula asked.

"Time for you to come home, fall in love with the boy next door, and make a bunch of babies so Mary Jane can have children rompin' and playin' in this big old house," Bernie said as she removed her jacket. "Maybe they'll even slide down that banister over there"—she pointed to her right—"and laughter will fill this place up."

"Bernie!" Ursula scolded and hoped that Remy didn't hear what she had said.

"Joe Clay swears that you'll *all* get tired of living so far away and that someday, you'll realize where your roots are and come home. You're the third one to fly back to the nest," Mary Jane answered as she led them into the kitchen. "I hated what Endora had to go through, what with the breakup with her fiancé and all. I was so glad when she and Luna both came home and took jobs at the Prairie Valley school."

"And that's why I bought a travel trailer just big enough for me and Pepper to live in," Bernie said. "We dragged it up here behind my truck, and Joe Clay got us hooked up for water and all that stuff so we're right comfortable out there in the backyard. I'm going to go finish off my coffee and put Pepper in my house." Bernie spun around, put her jacket back on, and started back through the foyer.

"What have you done, Mama?" Ursula whispered as soon as she heard the front door close. "Why didn't you tell me you'd let Bernie move here?"

"She's a handful for sure." Mary Jane chuckled as she set plates out on the table for the cinnamon rolls. "Assisted living places wouldn't allow pets, especially not Pepper, and she was my support system when your father left us. She called every day and cussed him with all kinds of words that I won't repeat. At the time, I needed her, and now she needs me." She stopped long enough to make a pot of coffee. "You can get down the mugs and put the milk on the table. I don't know which one Joe Clay will want. And the reason I didn't tell you she was here is because I was afraid that if you knew, you wouldn't quit your job and come on home where you belong. If you are going to be a writer, then you need peace and quiet, and you can't get that in a noisy apartment in a city."

"And I'm going to find it in a house with a whiny sister

named Endora who still believes Fate hates her and her twin, Luna, who is walking on eggshells because she doesn't want to hurt Endora's feelings," Ursula said with a sigh, "and then add Bernie to that! I can't imagine her letting me have hours and hours to write a novel without popping in with Pepper to visit with me." Ursula set mugs and glasses both on the counter. "Has she straightened Endora out yet?"

"She's working on it," Mary Jane answered. "Joe Clay loves her sass and banter. Endora doesn't roll her eyes as much as she did a week ago when Bernie arrived, so I think we're making progress. It takes a while to get over a breakup like she had, and I'm speaking from experience. To have all the excitement of being engaged and starting to plan a wedding, only to find out that her fiancé was sleeping with her best friend, was devastating."

"Yep, but it's time for my youngest sister to pull herself up out of the mud and move on," Ursula declared.

"Spoken just like Bernie," Mary Jane said with a nod. "As long as you are alive, that woman will never be dead. She didn't have kids, but she sure passed her genes right on down to you."

Acknowledgments

Many thanks are due to all the folks who have supported my career for all these many years. First, to my readers. Without all y'all, I'd be at the top of the endangered species list. I would much rather be at the top of the bestseller list, and you are the ones who have made that happen.

Then to Deb Werksman and all the folks at Sourcebooks who gave me the opportunity to write more stories about the Paradise. My gratitude to Folio Management for representing me, and to my agent, Erin Niumata, who has been on this journey with me for more than twenty-five years. Thanks to my family for understanding the crazy life of a writer. Every one of y'all has made me the author I am today, and I'm sending out virtual hugs to every one of you.

About the Author

Carolyn Brown is a *New York Times, USA Today, Wall Street Journal, Publishers Weekly,* and #1 Amazon and #1 *Washington Post* bestselling author. She is the author of more than one hundred novels and several novellas. She's a recipient of the Bookseller's Best Award and Montlake Romance's prestigious Montlake Diamond Award and a three-time recipient of the National Reader's Choice Award. Brown has been published for more than twenty-five years. Her books have been translated into twenty-one languages and have sold more than ten million copies worldwide.

When she's not writing, she likes to take road trips with her family, and she plots out new stories as they travel.

Website: carolynbrownbooks.com
Facebook: CarolynBrownBooks
Instagram: @carolynbrownbooks